PRAISE FOR A FASCINATING NEW THRILLER

DEAD GROUND

"Kerrigan tells his tale with extraordinary skill."
Robert Elegant,
The New York Times Book Review

"Thoroughly satisfying...a feeling for craft and invention, a sense of place and character"
The New Yorker

"Tension, fierce action...echoes of...Jack Higgins and other suspense-men"
Kirkus Reviews

"Readers will resent interruptions while they're immersed in this gripping novel!"
Publishers Weekly

DEAD GROUND

PHILIP KERRIGAN

AVON
PUBLISHERS OF BARD, CAMELOT, DISCUS AND FLARE BOOKS

For P. and P.

AVON BOOKS
A division of
The Hearst Corporation
1790 Broadway
New York, New York 10019

Copyright © 1985 by Philip Kerrigan
Published by arrangement with St. Martin's Press
Library of Congress Catalog Card Number: 85-25156
ISBN: 0-380-70285-1

The St. Martin's Press edition contains the following Library of Congress Catalog-
ing in Publication Data:

Kerrigan, Philip.
  Dead ground.

  1. Title.
PR6061.E794D4   1986   823'.914   85-25156

First Avon Printing: March 1987

Printed in the U.S.A.

K-R   10   9   8   7   6   5   4   3   2   1

In the world today, no one is innocent,
no one is neutral.
Everybody is a soldier.

Carlos

PART ONE

An Act of Terrorism

1

The man who was to plant the bomb at Waterloo railway station caught the 12:40 train from Portsmouth. He bought a second-class single ticket – he was not expecting to return.

He got aboard the train. He was a small man, black haired and running to fat, wearing a grey-blue suit, a Burton's overcoat and scuffed black shoes. He carried a cheap, leather-look briefcase. He looked like a low-powered and not very successful business-man, but inside the briefcase was a bomb. A simple mechanism – plastic explosive wired to an inexpensive alarm clock and a nine-volt battery. If the train ran on schedule, it would reach Waterloo by two-thirty. The bomb was set to explode at three o'clock precisely.

The man with the briefcase walked along the train, looking for an empty seat. The train was almost full. It was December the twenty-third, and the Christmas crowds were travelling. That was the reason for the bomb. Any businessman knows that Christmas is a profitable time. But these profits would not be counted in cash. Only in lives taken, injuries inflicted, political points gained.

He settled for a window seat near the front of the train. An old woman opposite was filling in the *Daily Telegraph* crossword. She stared at him disapprovingly and drew her feet back to let him sit down. He put the case carefully on the seat next to his. He was not very nervous, but neither was this something he did every day.

He looked out of the window, wiping the steamed-over glass with his sleeve. People were still running up the platform to get on the train. He checked his watch against one of the station clocks. Both said 12:38.

He stuck a finger under his collar and tried to ease the grazed

3

skin on his neck. Not usually a collar-and-tie man. Even though the weather was seasonal – needle-edged sleet and the threat of snow for the yuletide – he felt trapped in a suit. He tried to relax, watching the seconds tick through to 12:40, stroking his moustache with the back of his thumb. He wanted a cigarette, but had just noticed the carriage was a non-smoker. He swore quietly as the clock went through the first minute after 12:40.

The old woman with the *Telegraph* crossword filled in a particularly difficult two-word anagram. The man with the briefcase watched the clock, worrying and trying not to worry. Across the aisle, two children were settling noisily down for the journey. He wished he had travelled first class, just for the peace.

12:43. He sat up uneasily. A porter on the platform was still letting people on the train. What was he playing at?

12:44. He thought of the journey to Waterloo, all the stops along the line. He glanced at his watch again, then at the case. The old woman tapped a pencil against her front teeth, concentrating hard on the crossword. He had a copy of the *New Musical Express* in his jacket. In the left inside pocket there were four five-pound notes, and in another, a packet of cigarettes and some matches. Apart from these, he carried nothing. No cheque book or bank card, no wallet, no keys. Only the case that held the bomb. Bombs are anonymous. So are those who plant them.

He wanted to smoke, he also wanted to pee, and the train still had not moved. 12:45 and counting. He thought about the case and what was inside it, and it made his insides roll gently over and over like a ferris wheel. He wondered about the timing device. To him it was a joke. An alarm clock, made in Russia. You could buy one in Woolworths just like it. No one had told him how accurate the clock was, or how well made. Maybe a single jolt would move the alarm hand, and then he could say bye-bye. It was so easy, he kept thinking – all it took was the explosive and a detonator, and any kid with an elementary knowledge of electronics could do it.

A voice came over the station Tannoy system. He listened, waiting for an explanation of the delay. The voice announced another train's arrival. He searched the platform for the guard and saw the old idiot helping some woman with a pushchair to get on. 12:47.

4

The woman with the crossword mumbled to herself:

'Fluently mastered, thanks to the Irishman?' She said it as if hearing the clue would make the answer plain.

He looked at her, irrationally thinking that she might be onto him. But it was a clue in the crossword, nothing more. She gazed at a point six inches above his head, rattling the pencil against her teeth.

A little girl from the family across the way toddled towards him.

'I'm going to sit *here*,' she said, trying to climb up on the seat next to him. He reached for the case.

'Rebecca, leave the man alone,' the mother said. She smiled at him. He grinned back, trying to look personable. He wanted to kick the girl away before something happened. Not that it should happen; the case was securely locked. Still, he worried.

'Oi!' the father said. The girl stopped where she was and stared back. 'Over here – now.'

She went back, climbed meekly into her mother's lap. The father shrugged at him. 'Bloody Christmas,' he said.

The man with the briefcase nodded understandingly. He was starting to get angry. The clock on the platform said 12:50.

Just then, the whistle blew. The train groaned forward, the platform slid gently away. As if they had been waiting for noise to cover their conversation, people began to talk. They were mostly families or couples, going up to London for last-minute Christmas shopping. They talked about where they could go for a really unusual gift, about Harrods and roast chestnuts from a cart in Tottenham Court Road, how much booze they were getting in this year, and wasn't it expensive? He folded his hands in his lap, smiling to himself over the idle talk. The old lady opposite muttered, 'Denizen of shadows we do not see?' and the pencil flickered rhythmically to the train's increasing speed.

Then a voice said: 'Excuse me?'

He froze for a second, with every bad possibility going through his head. Nothing, however, showed on the surface. His face was impassive as he opened his eyes.

A kid, some kind of art student by appearance, stood over him. 'Excuse me, is anyone sitting here?' he asked.

'Oh . . . no, no. Help yourself,' the man with the briefcase said.

5

He took the briefcase reluctantly off the seat and slid it behind his knees. That way, it would not fall over if there was a sudden halt. The student heaved a grubby green rucksack off his shoulder and swung it up on the rack. He sat down, stretching his long legs under the opposite seat. He was fair-haired with a red beard. He looked as if his Christmas celebrations had commenced early, and he smelled of stale beer. He took out a copy of *The World According to Garp* and began to read. The woman with the crossword glared at him sourly. After that, she repeated the clues in her head.

And the man with the briefcase watched the tracks below the window shimmering by.

The journey was uneventful, the train on time when it reached Godalming. A couple of boys in army uniform shared cans of lager and played cards sleepily. The kids dozed off, the old woman filled in all but two clues in the crossword, then got stuck. The student read his book and broke squares off a bar of Cadbury's chocolate. The man with the briefcase looked at the album reviews in his *NME*, choosing the records his wife might give him for Christmas. Not that he would be home for the day. It was to be a quiet holiday away from home, that was for sure.

At the last stop before London, he checked his watch. It took about thirty-five minutes from Woking to Waterloo, so he was all right for time. He would be at the station no later than 2:35.

The train whipped past Sandown Park race course. The course was empty and locked tight in the cold. The soldiers started bawling 'Rudolph the Red-Nosed Reindeer'. They raised their cans to toast the carriage, and winked at the ladies. Because it was Christmas, people smiled instead of getting annoyed. After a couple of choruses, the soldiers gave up.

He saw Wimbledon go by, wondering where the tennis courts were. Then he knew he was in London as the buildings closed in. The first thing he recognised was Battersea power station. It had been on the cover of a Pink Floyd album years ago. When he reached Waterloo, he would know exactly where he was going; he had been to the station, studied ground plans over and over, but he had never travelled the route before. Going from Portsmouth was not important – it could have been any station.

6

The train rolled slowly through Vauxhall, and he caught sight of Big Ben. The clock face showed 2:27. The sky was a hard grey over the city, and snatches of the river between office buildings were sludgy brown.

Several of the passengers got ready to go. The old woman, who had given up on the last two clues, stopped reading and folded the newspaper into her bag. The mother and father woke their children. The student looked up from his book. He folded the corner of a page on which could be seen the words 'The First Assassin'. The man with the briefcase felt another stab of paranoia. He slipped the *NME* back in his pocket and checked that he still had the money and cigarettes. He rose, taking the case, and went to the toilet at the end of the carriage.

Inside, he put the case on the closed toilet seat. He sprang the catches and took out the bomb. It had been constructed to fit in a thin box twelve inches long, because it had to be planted in a particular place. It was with a couple of cheese sandwiches wrapped in cling-film, inside a Sainsbury's shopping bag. Delicately, he lifted the carrier bag out of the case. He re-locked the case and took it in his left hand. The carrier bag was in his right. He raised it, breathing shallowly. Finally the long box swung free inside the carrier. It was heavier than he would have liked, considering it was disguised as a box of chocolates.

He made sure no one was watching from his carriage when he stepped out of the toilet. He changed the carrier bag to his left hand, resting its weight against the case. He leaned against the door, staring through the smutty glass at a sign spelled out in a row of office windows. '26,000 SQ FT TO LET.' Then there was the white building with a sign saying 'Waterloo', and the station's high roof closed over the train. He swallowed hard. He felt powerful and scared. The student came out of the carriage and stood behind him. He had returned to chapter sixteen of *Garp*.

The platform smoothed up beside the train. The man with the briefcase fiddled with the door, pushing the window down and twisting the handle outside. The door yawned. He watched the concrete slowing, waiting to step down. The student sighed at the delay. He would have jumped.

The train stopped. He got off, being careful not to knock the carrier bag. He was like a man carrying eggs. But the student was

7

in a hurry. He leaped out too quickly, jostling the man with the briefcase.

He stumbled, almost turning his ankle. The next moment played through in slow motion. He tried to save himself, realised he could not, and watched the bag as it swung. It slammed solidly against the door, and he thought: That's it.

But the bomb did not go off.

He breathed again. In the same second, he wanted to kill the student, but told himself to keep calm. No harm had been done. At least, he hoped not. There was no way to check now, because time was running out. What if the clock had been stopped by the impact, or a connection sprung loose? There was no way to know. He stood still for a while, stopped the trembling in his knees, and went on.

Doors all along the train were banging. He was twenty yards from the red door to the main station. He moved towards it, slipping his ticket out of a back trouser pocket. People were already queueing for the return trip. A thin, stubble-chinned West Indian checked the tickets. He hardly looked as the man with the briefcase passed through.

The man came off platform nine. The refreshment stall was in front of him, the large W. H. Smith's stood on his left. The station was teeming. On an ordinary Tuesday at this time it was moderately busy. The worst times were mornings and evenings, particularly in summer. But in December the station handled more and more traffic. Two days before Christmas it was packed. People coming and going from London with their shopping, others who would have been there anyway, and all those who were going home for the holidays. It seemed to the man with the briefcase that there was no room to move. The queues for each platform constantly broke and re-formed as others passed through them. The inexperienced wandered along, staring at the giant information boards. Others lined up for refreshments, while the W. H. Smith's was bursting at all of its entrances.

The warmth was a surprise, but not the crowd. The crowd was the reason for doing the job now. The man with the briefcase took his bearings and turned left.

The four-faced clock in the centre of the station said 2:32.

He made his way to the timetables at the Waterloo Bridge end.

8

The uncomfortable, flip-up bench seats were full. It was impossible to move around without being crowded. He wanted to hug the briefcase and carrier bag to his chest, but knew that would look odd. He pretended to read the timetables until somebody vacated a seat, then walked quickly across and sat down. A very pretty dark girl sat next to him. She was reading a copy of *Options* and watching the clock. He gazed at her for a moment, looking at her breasts under her sweater, the high-heeled black boots she wore. Then he put the case down and rummaged in the carrier bag.

The air was warm and buttery with the smell from the 'croissanterie' to his right. On the left were the ticket offices and the Gents. People were milling around everywhere, going somewhere. Christmas carols played over the Tannoy system. Steam rose from mouths, he caught snatches of conversation from the babble of noise.

2:35.

He took out the sandwiches and, keeping the bag on his lap, unwrapped them. Cheese and pickle sandwiches. He had never felt less like eating in his life, but it was part of the plan. He took a bite from one. Acid rose in his throat. He wished he had a cup of coffee to help it down, but there was no time. Besides, the seat was perfectly placed; less than two feet away from a rubbish bin. He would hardly have to move.

He ate quickly, staring at the pages of the *NME* again. Some sickly Christmas record was number one in the singles chart – little kids in the choir and a sticky verse about families round the tree. He wondered how it would sound after today.

The crowd surged, gathered, dissipated and re-formed. Every time he glanced up, there were different faces.

2:38.

He stuffed the last crust in his mouth, chewing it while he felt in the carrier bag. The moment was coming – the one really dangerous part as far as he was concerned. He looked quickly around and up. No one was watching. The pretty girl was reading an interview with Dustin Hoffman.

He yawned, stuck the cling-film into the bag and wrapped the bag loosely around the box. He leaned forward, still without haste, and pushed the bag through the slot of the bin. It slid

9

down, fell gently on a cushion of papers, foam cups and hamburger wrappers. He leaned back, trying to keep his heartbeat steady. No one had seen him do it. No cameras were on him. It looked as if it was going to work.

He patted his pockets again, as if he were deciding to get on with the rest of his business. He picked up the briefcase and stood. The girl contemplated the thoughts of Dustin Hoffman. She was very good-looking. He hoped she would move before three o'clock.

He walked past the 'croissanterie' towards the escalators. People were spilling out of the Underground. No longer cautious for the bomb, he forced his way to the escalator and stepped on. As he went down, he took a last look at the station.

2:42.

At the bottom, he walked with the crowd past the exchange booth and a tramp playing a harmonica. He turned right and went to a ticket machine, paid for a ticket to Embankment and passed through the automatic barrier to the next escalator. He chose the Northern Line because fewer people seemed to be going that way.

Standing on the platform, edged back against the wall, he checked the time. 2:44. He read a long, jokey poster about some restaurant chain. Then the train burrowed out of the tunnel and whined to a halt. He got on and did not bother to find a seat. He watched a girl sitting by the door, and hung on the sprung black knob as the train started. The lights flickered briefly, and there was a smell of oil in the carriage.

It seemed to him that the journey was long, although it was no more than two minutes. With a few others, he stepped onto the platform at Embankment and headed for the exit. He ignored the signs for Charing Cross station. After climbing the stairs, he came to the ticket barrier. A fat black woman said, 'Merry Christmas, love,' when he gave her his ticket. He mouthed the words back at her and walked on.

There are two exits at Embankment. One lets onto Victoria Embankment itself. The other opens on Villiers Street and Embankment Place behind Charing Cross. Across the road is a fish and chip shop. The man with the briefcase sniffed the greasy air. Under Hungerford Bridge, which was directly overhead, the tramps and alcoholics huddled for warmth.

He looked round for the car, but it was not there. It was 2:48, and the car should have been there. He stopped the panic before it started – they had probably driven round again to avoid suspicion. He bought a newspaper from the stand by the station entrance and stood at the kerb. The air was hard like a blade, tiny specks of sleet fell out of the swelling grey sky. He saw a man not much older than him lying under the darkness of the bridge wrapped in newspaper, an empty bottle in his hand.

The man who had planted the bomb waited.

It was ten minutes to three.

2

'C'mon,' the young man said.

'You want to drive?' the older one answered.

'We should've stayed there.'

'You'd like some copper snooping round, would you?'

'We're late.'

'Well don't piss yourself.'

The two men in the blue Vauxhall Chevette waited at the traffic lights by Westminster Bridge Pier. The older man was called Temple. He was thirty-five, compact and fair-haired. His eyes were like camera lenses, and there was a white scar across his chin from a bottle fight. The younger was called Parker. He was twenty-one, thin and lank. Acne still patched his face. Both wore thick coats because the Chevette's heater had broken down. Parker had the radio on, tuned to Capital.

The lights changed. Temple released the handbrake and turned right out of Victoria Embankment. Parker twisted in his seat to see Big Ben.

'That's the place to do it,' he said, dreamily. 'See the headlines if Big Ben got blown halfway to France?'

'Wonderful,' Temple said. He did not like talk, and he did not like the boy, but he was George Parker's brother. He was along for the experience.

They circled Parliament Square. Even in December, there

were tourists: Japanese and Americans wrapped up against the cold, snapping pictures of Winston Churchill's statue. Temple turned the car up Whitehall. Parker saw the barriers around Downing Street and laughed quietly. Temple knew what he was going to say.

'We should do it there too. They'd know we meant business then.'

'Shut your mouth, for God's sake,' Temple said. 'What's the time?'

'Just gone ten to.'

'The exact time?'

'Nine minutes,' Parker said.

'Fine,' Temple said.

'*And* twenty seconds,' Parker said.

Temple took his eyes off the traffic for a second. 'If you think this is funny, get out and walk.'

Parker stared at him. Temple knew what the boy was thinking, but he also knew that Parker was scared of him. He shut up and turned the tuning knob on the radio.

'And put that on the police band. I want to know if anything happens.'

'Nothing's happened yet.'

'Do it,' Temple said.

The theatres wore gaudy decoration for Christmas. Trafalgar was a solid ring of traffic. Drab pigeons swung round Nelson's Column. Again, Temple waited for the lights. Waiting did not bother him. Parker found the police band and turned the volume low. He tapped his fingers on the dashboard. It sounded like a cantering horse.

The traffic moved forward. Temple circled Nelson and turned down Northumberland Avenue.

'Time?' he said.

'Eight minutes to,' Parker muttered.

Christ, Temple thought. Now he's sulking. He wondered what Parker would tell his brother when they got back. He also thought of what he would do when it was over. Crawl into bed with a good bottle and a good book, probably, and think about fishing.

'D'you think the others did all right?' Parker asked.

'We'd've heard if they hadn't,' Temple said. 'Everything's fine.' Across the city, two other railway stations had been given the same treatment as Waterloo. Three o'clock would be interesting, that was for sure.

They turned off Northumberland Avenue, under Hungerford Bridge. A train rumbled by overhead. Parker grimaced at the down-and-outs on the pavement.

'Poor bastards.'

'Never mind them.' Temple slowed down. 'Is Barlow there?'

'Wait a minute.' Parker wiped the fogged windscreen.

Temple looked for himself. He saw Barlow by the news-vendor's stand at the station entrance. He stamped on the accelerator.

A man stepped off the pavement. He was loaded with a suitcase and several parcels, trying to eat fish and chips out of the paper. He did not see the car.

'Look out!' Parker yelled.

Temple hit the brake. Parker swore under his breath as the man with the parcels jumped back, spilling fish and chips in the road.

'Why don't you watch where you're going, pal?' the man mouthed.

'Ah, fuck off,' Parker said, rolling the window down.

The man, who was a little older than Parker, threw the chip paper away. He came to the window. 'How about you trying that? With your exhaust pipe, maybe.'

Parker coloured. 'You want trouble, you fucker?'

Temple laid a hand on his arm. 'Leave it,' he warned. 'We're in a hurry.'

He glanced up. Something was bothering the man with the parcels. He was staring as if he half-recognised them.

'Sorry, Mister,' Temple said, thinking about the time. 'My fault.'

'Okay,' the man said. He was shaken, but obviously in a hurry too.

Parker rolled the window up, muttering, 'English bastard.'

The man heard it. As Temple pulled away, they heard him shout, 'And a merry Christmas to you too.'

Barlow got hastily into the back. He dumped the briefcase and

13

pulled his tie loose.

'What the hell 're you playing at, Temple?'

'Forget it,' Temple said. 'No harm done.'

'He looked as if he knew you.'

'No chance. If anyone's a public face, it's young Danny here.'

'You'd better hope so.'

'Time?' Temple grunted.

'Six minutes to three,' Parker said.

'All right then.' Temple nodded. He gunned the engine and headed for the Strand.

Six minutes to three.

3

The man with the parcels did not stop to watch the Chevette drive away. He was annoyed because his fish and chips were all over the road, and because he could have been knocked flat, but he didn't have time to worry about it.

He walked into the station and found his sister.

'Hi,' he said, 'been here long?'

'Only half an hour,' she said, scowling at him from under her fringe. 'I know this is the season of brotherly love, but you push it too far.'

. 'You can either give us a kiss or take a few parcels,' he said. 'The Irish community's just tried to rub me out. I'm beginning to think we should drive down. This lot's killing me.'

She kissed him on the cheek. 'Come on,' she said, picking up her own case and a couple of his parcels. 'Laura must be fuming by now.'

'She's probably only just got to the station,' he said. 'She wouldn't have escaped from the office party till two.'

They bought tickets and rushed down the escalator. They jumped aboard a train as the doors hissed shut.

Four minutes to three.

'Talking of work,' she said, as they sat down. 'How's yours going?'

'The usual,' he said. 'Make a million here, lose a million there.'

'For somebody else's benefit.'

'Ah, I'm practising with the boss's cash. When I get it right all the time, I'll use my own.'

'Seriously, how's things?'

He thought. 'Seen the new jeans advert?'

'The one with the laser beams?'

He nodded. 'All mine.'

'I thought it was posey,' she sneered.

'My concept,' he continued, undeterred. 'My layout. I even roughed out the copy for the magazine tie-in.'

'You bloated bourgeois,' she said. 'Fancy giving up your life to fool the gullible public.'

'Listen you. When you finally leave the LSO —'

'LSE.'

'Same difference. When you leave it, and get into practicalities instead of theories, you'll realise that the only way to get out of the rat race is getting rich enough to buy a cat.'

'The thoughts of Chairman Mike,' she grinned.

They got off at Waterloo and raced the crowd to reach the escalators. Michael watched her leaping up the steps. She was nineteen, and the older she grew, the more he liked her.

They surrendered their tickets. He said:

'Isn't your boyfriend coming down?'

'Why should he?' she asked, sweet-faced.

'Well, you spent the last fortnight with him, didn't you?'

'Mother's been writing to you.'

'Phone calls, to be exact. She thinks because we're both in London, I've got some kind of older-brother influence on you.'

'Devious woman.'

'You *are* her only daughter.'

'She's my only mother, but do I tell Dad to keep tabs on her for me?'

They were behind a clot of people at the main escalator. 'Come on,' she said. 'Let's go up the steps.'

'You're kidding,' he said. But she was already bounding up the first flight. He took a grip on his parcels and followed. 'My first heart attack's down to you.'

'Get on. You're the exercise freak.'

At the top, they peered across the length of the station. A pigeon settled on the ground at Jilly's feet. The big clock said one minute to three.

'See Laura anywhere?' he asked.

They wandered through the crowd until Jilly grasped his arm.

'She's over there, by the timetables.'

They moved on a little faster. Laura raised her dark head and saw them. She smiled, put down her copy of *Options* and waved.

Michael went to her, dropping his case and everything else so he could grab her as she stood up. She lifted her face and he kissed her on the mouth.

'Hello,' she said. 'Miss me?'

'Not much,' he said. She pulled him close against her and he could feel her body through her coat. It was just over seven hours since they had parted, but he still felt like a kid whenever he saw her again.

'Don't mind me,' Jilly said. She dumped her burdens and took off the bobble hat that covered her ears.

'Hello, Jill,' Laura said, letting go of him. 'All ready for Christmas?'

'Should be fun,' Jilly said. 'Having another girl in the house. I don't suppose Mike'll be his usual boring self while you're around. Mind you, you know you're in separate bedrooms, don't you?'

'At our age?' Laura smiled.

'You know how Mum is about that sort of thing. Separate beds until he makes an honest woman of you.'

Mike shook his head. 'She makes too much of Audrey's puritan streak.'

'So will you,' Jilly warned, darkly, 'when you bring a scarlet woman into the house.'

'Pardon me,' Laura swung her black hair out of her eyes. 'You're speaking of the girl he intends to marry, young lady.'

'Is she?' Michael asked. Laura hit him on the chest.

'What's the time, anyway?'

He checked the clock. 'Three p.m. precisely. We might as well catch the next train. Unless you two prefer to spend Christmas here.'

'That's not till twenty past,' Laura said, sitting down again. Jilly gathered all the luggage into a pile and sat down next to her.

'In that case,' he said, 'I'll get a paper and a couple of sandwiches. Missed lunch again.' He sorted through his pockets for money, took out two crumpled crisp packets and slipped them into the rubbish bin. 'You two want anything?'

'Two slices of British Rail coffee, please,' Jilly said, stealing Laura's copy of *Options*.

'I'll have a coffee,' Laura said. 'Need help carrying it?'

'I'll manage somehow,' he said, blowing her a kiss. He turned and left them sitting there. He was in a good mood, and beating a path through the crowd was no bother. He was taking a fortnight off work to spend Christmas with the family and the girl he loved. He jingled some change in his pocket.

Two minutes and thirteen seconds past three.

He did not know what hit him.

4

The bomb had suffered a little in its slam against the train. The mechanism of the clock jogged back slightly. Consequently, it did not go off at three o'clock. If it had, Michael would have been standing next to it at the moment of detonation. As it was, he was forty feet away from the bench seats at two minutes and thirteen seconds past the hour. Which was when the bomb finally exploded.

The rubbish bin, with its slotted sides and covered top, was a perfect container.

The explosion itself was, as always, over so fast that no one really saw it. One moment, Christmas Muzak and the jabbering echo of the station Tannoy, the smell of winter streets and thousands of people in damp overcoats, butter and burgers and coffee and newspapers, a thousand faces squinting up at the departure boards. Next, screaming chaos spreading out like a tidal wave. Nestling in the rubbish by the bench seats, the explosive charge blew the bin to fragments.

The blast sounded curiously flat in the vast spaces of the station. It blew several panes out of the glass roof overhead. A gust of hot air followed, then a rain of glass and blood. The bomb's 'extra ingredients' also took flight. Nails, screws, razor

17

blades. They travelled slightly slower than bullets, fast enough to rip clothing, tear flesh, penetrate bone.

A cloud of smoke rolled towards the roof, hung still and silent over the disaster. People began to run, not knowing where yet, only following the instinct to get away.

Those inside the blast range did not run. Packed close to the centre, they took most of the force. Nobody within ten feet when it happened survived. After the flash and the flame, the concussion and the saw-toothed storm of nails, there was not much left to survive.

The tidal wave rammed against the surrounding walls, began to surge back. All over the station, screaming broke out and people who had been running started to turn. The circle of devastation closed up. People tried to rise, limbs spasming as blood pumped out of severed arteries. Others lay on the ground making noises like animals. One man who had been spun and flattened by a terrible blow to the stomach scrabbled up in a daze, not knowing where he was or what was happening. As he got to his knees, his intestines spilled through the rags of his shirt. A woman was on her feet, blood sheeting her body as she clawed at the place where her eyes had been. In the moments that followed, people on the extremes realised their faces were damp. They wiped themselves off and found that the freckling rain was blood. Hysteria began to set in.

There was nothing left of the bin. Where it had once stood, the seats were gone, the timetables had fallen like trees.

A sour smell filled the air.

And Michael did not know about any of it.

There was no time to think. The noise and the shock came almost together. Something like a brick wall hit him hard in the back, then he was off the ground, flying. He did not understand why. Something else came up in front of him, and it was harder than the thing behind, and it did not move. It stopped him – he broke against it like a bundle of sticks. His face struck the ground, and he lay there in the cold dark, knowing nothing, until he faded out.

The emergency forces in London had a very bad time that day. On or around three o'clock, there were sizeable explosions at

Waterloo, Kings Cross and Euston stations. There had been no warnings, so there were no evacuations, no preparations of any kind. At five past three, large areas of the city were at a standstill.

At ten past three, the editors of the *Daily Telegraph*, the *Guardian*, the *Sun* and the *Mirror* received telephone calls claiming responsibility.

By that time, a lot of people were dead.

The wounded from Waterloo were taken to the nearest hospital, Saint Thomas's on the Lambeth Palace Road. The admitting consultant was buzzed from his office, and the chief nursing officer started calling in all her nursing officers. The officers got in touch with all the staff they could find. A call was made to Capital Radio. Capital put out a bulletin which warned possible patients with trivial ailments to stay clear until further notice. It was also hoped that off-duty hospital staff would hear the flash and come in.

By this time, the admitting consultant had made an estimate on how many people the hospital could deal with, once as many beds as possible had been vacated.

The accident and emergency department began to earn its title at a quarter past three, when the first of the injured started rolling in. Those who could be diagnosed with specific injuries were taken to the relevant departments. That left the undiagnosed. The doctors and nurses came from all over the hospital and went to work, dealing with the most serious first. Very soon, there were more casualties than they could handle. The ambulances kept coming until they could take no more. Some were re-directed to Guy's Hospital near London Bridge, others were sent to Queen Alexandra's Military Hospital across the river.

At Saint Thomas's, several nurses who thought they had seen everything discovered that they had not seen everything at all. Police came and went, trying to speak with anyone who was conscious. At the entrance to accident and emergency, a nurse was trying to get details of the wounded as they came in. Her badge said she was student nurse F. Kikuji, but her name was Fumiko – Foo to the other second years she was training with.

She stood there, feeling like an idiot, holding a useless clipboard while the stretchers were brought in. Most of the time she was ignored, but occasionally someone threw a bunch of personal effects at her. She collected the blood-smeared items without really seeing them.

A woman with no face was taken past, a small boy with one arm gone and three inches of a four-inch nail sticking from his cheek. She looked out of the door. The ambulances were coming and coming.

Another police car roared up. The officers who got out were carrying as much information on identities as they had been able to gather in the confusion at the railway station. One of them handed Foo several pages of scrawled notes. There was blood even on them.

'Christ,' he said. He was not much older than her. His face was grey.

'What's it like?' she asked.

He took off his cap. 'I never . . . ' he began. 'It's just a mess. A fucking mess.'

A couple of porters rolled another one through. The first porter was in too much of a hurry. He rammed the trolley against the doorway.

'Watch where you're going,' the policeman said.

'He's had it anyway,' the porter said.

Foo looked down at the man on the trolley. He seemed to be dead. There was blood all over his skull, clear fluid seeping behind his left ear. They had him on his side – shrapnel had torn up his back. In the cold air, she saw steam rising from the ragged flesh.

'Come on,' a doctor yelled, hustling them in. 'He's not done yet.'

Foo watched them go, putting the drips up, applying pressure to the minor lacerations. She turned to the policeman.

'It's very bad, isn't it?'

'Let's just say it's ruined Christmas for a lot of people,' he said.

The blue Chevette was on the M4 not far from Reading. The three men listened to news flashes on Radio Four. Parker was talking, his voice high and excited. He and Barlow were feasting on cans of McEwan's lager. Temple, his eyes narrowed by the motorway driving, said nothing unless spoken to. He was sick to death of their chatter and their relaxation. He never relaxed, not until it was finished. If you let your guard down, even for a minute, you got caught. Temple was not a man to get caught.

He listened to Parker getting more excited every time the death toll went up, and the smell of lager soured his stomach. He hated the ones who acted like kids when they were doing things no child should do. He hated the celebration. He was a professional, and amateurs annoyed him more than anything else. Particularly when they were brothers to good men.

'Will you not have a drop?' Parker said again, pushing a can under his nose.

'Get it out of my way,' Temple said.

'Ah, what's wrong?' Barlow asked. 'Didn't it go well? Didn't it go like clockwork?'

'Just let me drive,' Temple said.

'Ah, he's scared of getting caught,' Parker sniggered.

Temple's left hand slashed out. It came off the steering wheel and sliced across in one smooth, solid line. The knuckles connected with Parker's nose, snapped his head back against the seat so hard that Temple heard the click.

'You bastard,' Parker sobbed, bringing his hands up as the blood began to come from his nose. 'You've broken it, you fucker.'

'It's not broken,' Temple said, quietly. 'But it will be if you say anything like that again. Got it?'

Parker glared at him. Temple, his attention on the road, repeated the question.

'Got it?'

'Yes,' Parker said. 'Sure, I was only joking in the first place.'

'All right.' Barlow gave him a handkerchief. 'Now you just keep your jokes to yourself, right Danny?'

'Right.' Parker stuffed the handkerchief against his streaming nose. He looked down at his jacket. 'Ah, look at the blood. It'll never wash out.'

Michael was in the dark for a long time.

PART TWO

Staring into the Dark

5

As with so many injuries, Michael's looked worse at first than they were. When the blood was cleaned off, it wasn't so bad.

But it was still pretty bad.

For a while, they thought he would not come through. He was in a room with another of the bomb victims – a man of sixty-two who lost his left leg up to the thigh and died twice on the operating table while the surgeons tried to stick his chest back together. This was only for the first two days, because then the man died for the last time and nothing could bring him back again. A boy was put in the empty bed. He was nothing to do with the bombing; he had come off his motorbike on the North Circular. The room was very quiet. Michael was unconscious, the boy was in a coma.

It was not like any film he ever saw or any book he had read. There was no dream of floating in limbo, looking down at his body on the bed. He was simply out of it, like being asleep so that you don't even recall dreams. There was no sense of time passing or of pain. Total shut-down.

The first time he began to wake up, he was alone. He knew he was awake before he saw anything because of the pain. It was like a dull bar of red-hot iron going straight through his head, down the centre of his body and along the right leg. The more awake he got, the hotter the bar became, and the more space it filled inside him.

It was like coming out of sleeping pills. Everything went slowly, trying to avoid the iron bar. He phased in and out for a while, not knowing how long between the fade-outs. At some point he thought he heard someone moving around. He tried to say hello, but got nothing except the sound of his heart beating louder.

The next time, he knew he was alone. He tried opening his eyes.

Still dark.

He thought: Blind. And the pit of his stomach dropped out. The word was a knife, and someone had driven the knife into his eyes. He closed them, and the funny thing was that he could feel them – the sticky sensation of the lids sliding down over the eyeballs. He opened them again and waited.

He saw the horizontal lines first, and did not know they were a window until he realised there was a venetian blind. It was very faint. He moved his head for a better look and a thousand sparks spattered off the iron bar. He focussed, trying hard to get his mind out of the sludge. Window on the left, a small, square room around him. Blue-dark.

He thought: It's night time. I'm awake in the middle of the night. That's what it is.

He was on his side, in what they call the recovery position. He thought of his hands, tried to move them. The left rose a little, then fell. Water gleamed above him on a table. He reached for it, fumbled at the jug, and tried to sit up. The bar twisted in his guts. He lay down and started to cry.

A woman came in. She walked past him, going out of sight. He heard her breathing, the clink of glass on Formica, the rustle of bedclothes. He forced himself over on his back, grunting when his shoulder touched the bed.

The woman came out of the dim blue haze, a little star flickering in her hand. He saw only the star.

'Oh, you're finally awake,' she said. He did not recognise her voice. 'Well, it's about time. We thought you were sleeping through to the New Year.'

'What about Christmas?' he asked. His voice was tight and dry.

'Never mind that. Expect they'll keep your presents for you.'

'What time is it?'

'Half-past three.' Her hands came down. She rolled him. 'That's it, back on your side for a minute. You've got a nasty gash on your shoulder.' He felt like a length of cooked spaghetti in her hands. 'How d'you feel?'

'Great,' he said. 'Who are you?'

'I'm a night nurse,' she said.

'I'm in hospital,' he murmured. 'Shit, I'm in hospital.'

'Well, they don't have nurses at the Grosvenor Hotel.' She smiled. He still could not see her. 'You lie still for a minute. I'm going to get the doctor. You won't go away will you?'

'No chance,' he said.

He drifted out again. When the doctor came in, he was asleep. The nurse switching on a light brought him back. He blinked up at a long, tired face that looked as if its father was a horse.

'Hello, Mr Sayers. How do you feel?'

'I can smell smoke. How long have I been here?'

'Three days.'

Michael breathed.

'Is something wrong?' the doctor asked. She was checking his pulse while they talked.

'I just thought – well, you know. I thought maybe I'd been out for years or something.'

'Oh no, you haven't been in a coma or anything like that. In fact, we're not really sure why you were unconscious for so long. Skull fractures—'

'My head?'

'Do you have a skull anywhere else?'

'Alas, poor Yorick,' he said. 'What, are they children? Who maintains them? How are they escoted?' His voice was thick and sleepy, eyes glazed. Nurse Arnold stared at the doctor.

'What's "escoted" mean?'

'How should I know?' the doctor shrugged. 'I took medicine, not literature.' She leaned over him, shining another star, holding the lids of his eyes up. 'Can you see properly?' she asked.

He nodded. 'There's only one of you.'

'One's enough.' She smiled. She stepped back and picked up his chart. 'I'm Doctor Ellis, by the way. What's your name?'

'Michael,' he said. 'Michael Sayers.'

'Good, and your middle name?'

'Francis, would you believe? It was my grandfather's.'

'Fine. At least we haven't mixed you up with someone else.' She flipped a page. 'How about your mother's name?'

'Audrey. Father's called Don. Donny to annoy him.'

'What's your address?'

'Why? Are you going to write to me?'

'At the moment, I'm seeing if you can think straight.'

'That'll be the day.'

'Your address?' she said tolerantly.

'Eight Cedar Grove. Not far from Belsize Park.'

'How old are you?'

'Twenty-seven. How much more of this is there?'

'Not much.'

'My back hurts like hell. And my head, and my leg. How bad is it?'

'Not too bad. You'll play the piano again. Incidentally, do you remember what happened to you?'

He closed his eyes. The smell of smoke came back. It was so strong, he wanted to gag. 'A car hit me, didn't it?'

She watched him carefully.

'That's it. I was crossing the road by Embankment station and this maniac ran me down . . . ' He trailed off, uncertain and lost. 'I think that's it.'

'Right, I want you to rest now. If the pain's very bad, I'll get the nurse to give you something for it. We can talk some more in the morning.'

'My parents,' he said. 'My girlfriend . . . '

'Someone's phoning your family now. Don't worry, they'll be here in the morning.'

He tried to get comfortable on his side, but the iron bar jolted and ran its blistering edge down his body. He cried out. Doctor Ellis nodded to the nurse, who went to fetch medication.

For a while before the drug took effect, he was in a world of pain. He had come more or less fully awake, and with consciousness came a clear perception of the pain. He lay on his side, concentrating hard on the glimmer of the water jug, making a sobbing noise every time he breathed out. When he slept, it was uneasy and strange. He dreamed this time, but remembered none of it later.

It was still dark when they woke him. He took a look round the room. There was some kind of drip in his arm. Across in the alcove, he saw the boy. He croaked good morning, but the boy did not answer.

27

'If he does perk up and say something,' a new nurse said, 'give us a call.'

'What day is it?' Michael asked.

'Saturday,' she said. 'Twenty-seventh.' She saw his questioning look. 'Of December. You certainly like lots of sleep. Bite on this for a while, and don't swallow it.' She gave him a thermometer. She was Malaysian, but her badge said 'C. Graham'.

'How was your Christmas?' he asked.

'Wonderful.' She neatened his bedding. 'I was here the other day. Worked non-stop for thirteen hours.'

'I'm uncomfortable lying this way. Can I sit up or something?'

'Mr Jataka's coming to see you in a while. He'll look you over and say yes or no to that. I've got to clean you up a bit first. You need a shave.'

'I always let my beard grow when I'm unconscious.'

'It's too early in the morning for comedians.'

'Sorry.'

She removed the thermometer and checked it, saying nothing.

He lay quiet while a wave of pain came over him. It seemed to lie still in his body for a time, just aching badly, then rise up and take a bite out of him.

'Can you breathe properly?' she said.

He nodded. 'There's this smell though.'

'What sort of smell?'

'Smoke.'

'Smoke?'

'Smoke.'

'I'll tell Sister. Are you hungry?'

'No.'

'You're having breakfast soon. Back on solid nourishment as soon as possible.'

'I'm not hungry,' he said.

'Yes you are.'

'I'm not.'

'You will be.'

The surgeon came to see him, a man called Jataka. He consulted the notes and looked him over. Michael winced into the pillow as

28

they studied his back.

'Nice,' Jataka said. 'Needs a clean dressing, Sister.' The sister passed the message to her nurses while they turned him a little more. 'Mr Sayers, you were very lucky with this one. You could very well have lost your arm. The wound is extensive.'

'From where to where?' Michael grunted.

'Here—' a finger touched halfway up his back. 'To here.' The finger touched again near his left shoulder blade. 'Very lucky. Two inches either way, and you wouldn't be in good shape. No serious internal damage, but a great deal of mess. Very unpleasant for you, but not as bad as if it had removed your arm or punctured your lung.'

'My head . . . ?'

'We were quite worried, I will say that. There was no evidence of subdural haematoma, yet you were in something like a coma. Your skull was fractured,' Jataka said, as if it were a puzzling technical question, 'yet you seemed to be in a coma. Very interesting, I think.'

'Glad I didn't bore you,' Michael said. The smell of smoke was bothering him again. He lay still as they re-dressed the back wound. Then they turned him over and Jataka lifted the bedclothes off the cage that covered his legs.

'This is really your worst problem,' he said. 'Your leg is quite nasty, I think.'

'Why, what's wrong? I can't see through this cage.'

Jataka grinned. 'Please, stay calm, Mr Sayers. Excitement is what you do not need.'

'Have I lost it, for Christ's sake?'

'No, no. Although it was, you might say, a near run thing. A fragment of concrete the size of my fist hit your leg just below the knee. You were lucky not to lose the leg, and even luckier that the bones were not smashed beyond repair. I think I did a very good job on your leg. Of course, there will have to be more operations, and some skin grafting for your back, but you are definitely one of the fortunate ones.'

Michael blinked. 'A piece of concrete?'

'As big as my fist,' Jataka repeated. He spoke quietly with the nurse as he folded the clothes back on the cage.

After Jataka was gone, Michael stared at the wall. He was

trying to work out how he got hit by a piece of concrete in a car accident. 'One of the fortunate ones . . . '

The smell of smoke was so powerful that it burned his mouth and nose. Something was happening. Nothing in the room had any perspective, his advertisement for jeans kept recurring. He began to shudder, breathing fast as if he was racing. He looked at a row of cards on the shelf to his left. He knew they were get-well cards, but he could not read the words on them. He looked at one which, earlier on, had said 'Stop Lying Around – Get Well Soon'. The words would not sit still: they danced like butterflies.

Ten minutes later, he had the first attack.

6

Nurse Graham – her first name was Colette, she told him later – peeped in. He barely opened his eyes. She leaned back and spoke to someone in the doorway. Then he saw his mother and father beside her. He tried to sit up, but sleep had him nailed to the bed. They had put something in his arm that made him calm and sleepy.

'He's under sedation now,' Nurse Graham said to them, 'but he should be able to talk.'

'Hey,' Michael said. 'How are you?'

There was something wrong with Audrey. She was pale and old-looking. She wore dark clothes. Don had to help her walk as they came in. When he reached for a chair, she stumbled the rest of the way and sat on the bed next to Michael. She took his hand and kissed it. Even when she stopped kissing it, she held his fingers against her mouth.

'What's all the crying for?' he asked. 'I survived, didn't I?'

'How are you, son?' Don said. He was seated now, the chair drawn up close. Michael gazed at him. He had that look too, as if he had aged ten years overnight.

'Great, now they've pumped me full of whatever it is. Fully recommend it for manic depression. Maybe I could advertise it.'

'They're treating you all right?' Audrey said. She had herself under control now – at least enough to speak.

30

'Fine. The doctors tell me things. They don't keep secrets.' Or maybe they do, he thought, in the fuzzy, half-assed warmth the drug gave him. Maybe I'm going to peg out after all. That's why they're like this. He was not serious about it. Nothing seemed very serious just yet.

'They told us—' Audrey said. 'They said something about you having some sort of attack.'

'Oh, that. I just got angry.'

'What about?'

'Can't remember. They said I got angry and tried to get out of bed. That's why they drugged me up. I'm okay now.'

'Son,' Don said.

'How was Christmas? Did you save me some turkey?'

Audrey began to cry. He saw the tears start in her eyes. Then they were hot on his hand.

'Home's there,' Don said. 'As soon as you're well enough, you can come home.'

'I hope they find the idiot who put me in here.'

'What?'

'The dope who knocked me down.'

'See!' Audrey grabbed at Don's overcoat as if he were falling away from her. 'He doesn't remember. They were right.'

He wondered why she was wearing that stupid coat. Black wasn't her colour at all. 'Remember what?' he asked, trying to pull free of her.

Don rubbed his mouth. He was in slow motion. 'Tell me what you remember, son.'

'A car. A car hit me, yes? That's what happened. What's all the fuss about?'

'That's not what happened. Nobody knocked you down.'

'But I remember the car,' he protested. He sank back, exhausted. 'Let me sleep.'

'You were hurt in an explosion,' Don said. 'That's why you're here.'

'No,' Audrey began, but his father's voice continued.

'Someone planted a bomb at Waterloo station.'

He wanted to say that he never got there, that a car knocked him down outside the tube station. He couldn't say it. A door opened in his head. There was a dark room beyond it.

31

'You were walking away from it when it went off,' Don said, his face tight and sick. 'You took a big lump of concrete in your leg and a three-inch bolt in the back. The blast was so powerful it picked you off your feet. You hit a wall – that's how your head got hurt. It broke some ribs too.'

'Jesus.' Michael tried to shake his head to clear it. He seemed to remember some of it, but there was more.

'They blew up Waterloo. Other places as well. It was terrible. Forty-four people died.'

Michael stared at his mother. She did not speak. Her lips were on his hand. Her breath burned him.

'Waterloo . . . ' he whispered. 'I was meeting Jilly. We went there together.'

Don turned his head. He was skin and old flesh, and someone had put the fire out. 'Jilly's dead, son.'

Audrey convulsed. Michael put his hand on her hair. 'Oh, Mum . . . ' He glanced at his father. There was nothing to say. The thought dropped down in him like a stone. He was deep under the drugs, but the stone finally hit. Black water closed over.

'She didn't suffer,' Don said. The words comforted him somehow. 'It was all too quick. She was right on top of it, they reckon. She didn't suffer.' He had identified his daughter. He repeated it softly: 'She didn't suffer.'

Michael felt it all slow down again. He recalled Jilly running ahead of him up the escalator, pausing for breath at the top, looking around . . . looking around . . .

'Laura was with Jilly,' he said. His voice was two million miles away with his father's face, his mother's tears.

Don said no more. He and his son watched each other over the two million miles. Rain began to speck at the window. Footsteps echoed in the corridor, further and further away.

Michael shut his eyes.

7

It was a big house with plenty of rooms where you could be alone. That was all Temple wanted just now. He sat in the unlit, unheated west wing of the old place in a little attic on the second floor. There was one wing-backed chair, covered in a dust sheet. The walls and ceiling were white, the floorboards bare. The window let in dazzling light – it snowed the day after Christmas. Sitting in the chair, dressed in outdoor clothes, Temple gazed out over the fields to the village rooftops. The sky was hard, pearl-coloured. His hands, gloveless, were numb with cold. He had a bottle of Johnny Walker and a large glass. Every thirty seconds or so, he took a sip of the whisky, enough to burn his tongue and fill his mouth with the flavour.

He was content. The only sounds were birds outside, and the chimes of the church clock. He thought it was around half-past eleven, but was not sure. Nothing reached him from the rest of the house. Not the endless blare of the television, pausing now and then to ruin the Christmas programming with news reports on the search for the 'Christmas Bombers'. Not Parker's idiotic chatter about girls he had had and men he had killed. None of it reached him. He was at peace.

A book lay on his lap. Something he took from their host's library (their host, of course, was not in the house – or the country). Temple liked to read when there was time – when it was necessary to stay quiet and still. He was not an ignorant man. The book was volume one of *The Man Without Qualities* by Robert Musil. Reading the first few pages, he had thought it would be too trivial for him. He preferred the hard, financial edge of Balzac's novels, which showed people as they were; bad. Persevering, he got into the book. He began to enjoy its cock-eyed view of the world. Nothing that happened in the book seemed real. He smiled over it while he drank his whisky. He turned a page and finished chapter fourteen. Outside, a blustering wind bumped against the window. It brought some drops of rain. He stood up, stretched, walked slowly to the window. If rain came, the snow would disappear, then nightfall would freeze it over. He leaned on the windowsill, looking down at the house's wide, white lawn.

And saw the footprints.

8

In the afternoon, while he was talking to his mother, Michael had another attack.

They were alone, not counting the boy in a coma. Don was at Michael's flat, collecting a few things he needed. Michael lay propped up as far as was comfortable, and held Audrey's hand while she talked. She was not usually a talkative woman. She balanced Don's volatile energy with an easy-going calm. All through his childhood, he thought his father was a giant; fun but sometimes frightening. It was his mother who did the loving. When you were hurt or miserable, you went to her. She comforted you without words.

Now, she was broken open. She had two children: one was dead and the other had nearly died. She wanted to talk, and she could not stop.

He did not mind. He did not care about anything, so it did not bother him. It was like being disconnected, the lines were down. He listened and tried to be what he was before. His words sounded like an act.

'. . . And I went out that morning to buy some more decorations for the tree,' she said, looking not at him but into her memory. 'I thought it looked a bit sparse, even after everything was on it. It was too big really. I told your father, but he said, "The family's home, we're having a tree suitable to the occasion," and he brought home this incredible thing. Even out in the hall, it touched the ceiling. Two sets of fairy lights and every bauble and shred of tinsel I could find in the cellar, and it still looked empty. So I went into town and bought some more things. Glass balls, and those little chocolate bells. You used to eat every one of them by Christmas Eve when you were small.'

He did not remember.

'I carted it all home – and I was in the A & N, and I saw these lovely bottles of perfume, and I thought one of them would be perfect for Laura. Not as a present exactly, just as a sort of welcoming gift, to make her feel at home. After all, I remembered you saying her parents were divorced, and how she never felt as if she had a real family, and it was the first Christmas she ever spent with us. So I got one of those, and then I went down to the delicatessen. Worst day's work I ever did, having a cheque card. I ended up with masses more stuff, as if we didn't have enough already to feed an entire army of wise men.'

He winced. The sound of her voice was getting louder. It seemed that way at first, but it wasn't so much louder as harder. Her words started to hit at him. Each syllable was like a blow. He reached for the water glass and drank slowly. He was annoyed because his leg was aching and he could smell smoke.

'Anyway, I went to see your grandmother. You know she made the pudding back in September, put about half a bottle of brandy in it. She even found some old threepenny bits to put in it. She kept talking about how she was looking forward to us all being together again. We went home, and I got busy with all the rest of the decorations. We thought you'd be home about five o'clock, so we were making a big meal. Mother kept saying, "They never eat properly up there." She still thinks London's a foreign country. Your father said he was going to finish work early to be home by six. It was going to be so wonderful.'

Michael breathed deeply. His mood was getting worse every minute. Everything Audrey said was striking at a nerve inside him. He was irritated by her red eyes and tight-clenching hand.

She said: 'Then I was listening to the radio, and they started talking about bombs going off, and they mentioned Waterloo. I remembered you said you wouldn't drive down because Christmas is hell on the roads, so I knew you'd be coming from there – you and Jilly and Laura. I waited for a bit, I didn't want to upset Mother. Then I phoned your place, but you weren't there, so I tried your office and got your friend Ralph. He was drunk as a lord. He said you'd gone off to do some shopping and get away early.' She paused, shaking her head.

He thought: Shut up, will you.

'And for a long time, I didn't phone the hospitals or the police, even though they gave out a number. I thought, I'll just wait until five, then the taxi will come up the drive, and they'll all get out, laden down with parcels and bags, and we'll go in and get warm in front of the fire. It wasn't till your father came home that we tried to find out . . . ' She trailed away, beginning to break up again.

He stared at her, trembling. He wanted to hit her, to push his hand in her face.

She breathed shallowly, trying to get herself under control. 'I re-decorated your room,' she said. 'So it'd be nice for Laura . . . Jilly . . . Jilly was going to have that guitar she asked for. It took me ages to wrap it up.'

'Oh, fuck off!' he yelled, and his hands did go out. He pushed her away feebly, enough to overbalance her chair. She fell sprawling on the floor.

Nurse Graham came in. She saw what was happening and knelt to help Audrey up. 'Go and get Doctor Ellis,' she told the pupil who was with her.

Doctor Ellis looked at him. 'You are a bad boy.'

Michael was sedated again. He watched his parents dreamily.

'What is it?' Don asked. 'I mean, why is it happening?'

'Probably to do with the head injury,' Ellis said. 'The thing about smelling smoke beforehand is a clue.' She was speaking to Michael too. She did not like keeping things from her patients. 'Our neurologist, Dr Cross, ran tests, the brain scan was fine by the time he did it. Quite often, victims of head injuries can act strangely – even violently.'

'I'm sorry,' Michael said.

Audrey smiled without much spirit. 'It's not your fault, love.'

'Well, what happens?' Don said. 'Is it permanent, does it go away? What happens?'

'Until I know the exact nature of the problem, it's difficult to say. There are cases, in severe incidents, where people become subject to fits.'

'You mean epileptic?' Michael said. The last word came out rubbery.

'No, that's another matter entirely. I should guess that these attacks are temporary. Partially to do with delayed shock. You've been through an awful lot, Mr Sayers.'

Audrey reached for Don's hand. 'Are you sure he's being looked after properly?'

Ellis frowned. 'He's my patient, Mrs Sayers. I'm not in the habit of inducing fits in my patients for the sake of it.'

'Well you say you don't know this and can't say that. Don't you know what's wrong with him? I mean, it's your job—'

'That's enough, Audrey,' Don said quietly.

Ellis took off her glasses. Her long face was open and appealing without them. 'I'm sorry. The last few days . . .'

'They've been a strain on everyone,' Don said.

Ellis glanced at Michael, who was drifting into sleep. She ushered them out of the room. 'Your son's going to need all the help we can give him. I imagine at the moment he doesn't even feel glad to be alive. He's been badly hurt, he was lucky to come away from that mess at all, and now he has to come to terms with losing two people he loved. Even without that, it would be difficult.'

Audrey looked at Michael through the doorway.

'He didn't cry,' she said. 'When we told him. It was as if he stopped listening.'

'Shock,' Ellis said. 'It'll take time.'

Audrey thought of her daughter. She last saw Jilly in October. It seemed like years. And her son was not the same. It was like losing both of them.

'The animals that did this . . . ' she said. 'If they were in front of me now, I'd kill them.'

9

Temple went down to the lawn. The footprints were fading fast as the bitter rain increased. He followed them: they went from a side entrance – an old servants' door – round the front of the house, over the lawn, and disappeared into the tall poplars that surrounded the gardens. He walked in their track, sweeping the branches aside and feeling a thin shower of ice crystals flower on his face. Under the trees, it became more difficult. The footprints petered out until he could not see them any more. He looked ahead. The poplars gave way to a loose wood of beeches and oaks, then the high wall that circled the estate. He walked up to it, still searching for prints. The rain pattered on his jacket.

He paused under the wall, thinking.

Back at the house, Parker and Barlow played draughts. The sitting room was expansive, tastefully decorated. Parker lounged on the settee while Barlow walked nervously about. The television was on, volume down, playing *The Great Escape*. James Garner was about to find out that Donald Pleasance was blind without his spectacles. The games table was inlaid teak, the draughtsmen were shot glasses. Parker's men contained Bacardi, Barlow's were filled with cherry brandy. Every time one of them took a man, he had to drink the contents of the glass. They had been playing for two minutes, so neither was drunk.

'What I say,' Danny yawned, 'is we should've got out right away. Stuff all this lying around. I'm bored to death.'

Barlow stooped over the board. He took one of Danny's men. He downed the Bacardi. 'I'm going to get some coke for this stuff. It's lousy neat.' He wandered out to the kitchen while Parker went on:

'I mean, the longer we sit on our arses here, the more chance they'll get a lead on us. Besides,' he grinned, 'we missed all the Christmas piss-ups. Would've been great this year. But we have to bugger about here.'

'Ah, it's not so bad.' Barlow came in with a litre of Coca Cola under his arm. 'Pretty cushy, if you ask me. We could've been hiding out in some rat-infested barn, but this is what I call a safe house.'

'There's nothing to do,' Parker groaned. He eyed the television. Donald Pleasance tripped over Garner's foot. It was pretty clear who would not get away. 'And that bastard Temple – he really pushes it, you know. I have to take it 'cause he's a friend of Georgie's, but I tell you, he gives me one more bad word, he'll be sticking his toothbrush up his arse to brush his teeth.'

Barlow sat down heavily. 'He's not so bad.'

'He thinks he's a big man because he's been around. Big killer. He's nothing special. I'm not scared of him.'

'That's good,' Temple said, behind them. 'Maybe you'll teach me a lesson some day.'

Barlow waved at him. 'You want a drink?'

Temple came in. Danny watched him like a fox, waiting for the first sign. He expected Temple to hit him.

'Where've you been?' Barlow asked.

'Outside, for a walk.' Temple leaned with both hands against the long mantelpiece above the fireplace. In the mirror there, he could see both of them. It gave him the edge.

'Someone else has been out. Is that right?'

'Out where?' Barlow said.

Temple noticed that Danny stared sullenly at the television. Danny's handgun, a Ruger revolver, was on the coffee table. He always carried it around. 'On the lawn, in the woods. Round there by the wall.'

'It was me,' Danny said.

'Pardon?'

'It was me.'

'What were you doing out there?'

'Taking a walk. Being cooped up in here gets on my nerves, you know.'

'It's safer round the back.'

'What's the difference? The wall's so high, no one can see in. Nothing goes down that road anyway. It's safe.'

'So you were just taking a walk?' Temple said. 'In the grounds?'

'What d'you think? I go up and down the road, waving my gun around and shouting, "I'm the Waterloo bomber!" 'Course I was in the grounds.'

'Okay.' Temple turned. He went over the game of draughts. After a moment, he picked up one of Barlow's men. He took two of Danny's in a zig-zag. He downed both. 'Try it with chess,' he said. 'Makes it more interesting.'

10

The next day.

'What's that you're reading?' Doctor Ellis said.

He threw the book aside. 'The new Stephen King. Dad got it for me yesterday.'

'You like those horror stories?'

'Mmm.'

'I always think they're silly. Like the films. I'm never frightened when someone gets an axe in the skull because I'm busy wondering how they do it.'

'Mmm.'

She scribbled something on his notes, frowning. 'I'm afraid the police want to see you.'

'Police? What for?'

'They're going round talking to everyone who's in a condition to speak. It's just routine, trying to get more information.'

'I don't want to see them.'

'If you saw something, if you identified one of the people who did it—'

'Since when do bombers hang around to watch their handiwork go off?'

'All the same, you'd better see them.'

'I can't.'

'Not even on the offchance you might help them bring in the people who murdered your sister and your girlfriend?'

'It won't do any good.'

'I'll put it another way, then. If you don't talk to them, they'll probably put you down as a possible suspect.'

'Oh, come on . . .'

'I'm just telling you.' She touched her forehead, smiling crookedly. 'My lord, I thought I was a plain doctor. Here I am, turning into your solicitor too. If you were a private patient, I'd charge you extra.'

He closed his eyes. 'Okay, let's see them and get it over with.'

She polished her glasses with the edge of her coat. 'The world's not going to go away, you know. It'll be like this as long as you try to ignore it. It keeps knocking on your door.'

He said nothing. She got up, left him in the silence.

The policemen came in. Two of them. Neither was in uniform, and at first he thought they were visitors who had lost their way. The taller one showed Michael his badge.

'I thought that only happened in American cop shows,' Michael said.

40

'I'm Detective Inspector Wolfe. This is Sergeant Dawes. I expect you know why we want to see you.'

'A parking ticket?' Michael said, then shut up because it wasn't funny.

The policemen drew up chairs and the sergeant put a slim briefcase on his lap. Wolfe was a pasty, overweight man in his late thirties. Dawes had almost white blond hair cut close over his healthy pink face. They looked like before and after adverts for yoghurt or a health farm.

'Okay then, Mr Sayers, we'll try to make it short. You've been through a lot. We just want to get your version of what happened on the day of the explosion.'

'I don't know anything. I was unconscious.'

Wolfe reached for a pack of cigarettes and shook one out. 'Do you mind?'

Michael shook his head.

Wolfe lit up and inhaled. 'It would help us if you could remember anything. How about before the bomb went off?'

'We – my sister and I got to the station about two minutes before it happened. There wasn't time to see anything.' He stopped. Dawes was taking down his words in shorthand. Big, meaty hands with a Papermate Rollerball like a toothpick between his fingers. 'We went across from the escalator to . . . where my girlfriend was sitting. We dumped the bags, then I went to buy a sandwich and a cup of coffee.'

'The ladies didn't go with you?'

'They'd be here now if they had.'

Wolfe pulled at the corner of his eye, as if he had grit in it. 'What did you have in the bags exactly?'

'What?'

'In the bags. You said you put them down by the seats.'

'What is this?'

'Just a question.'

'Just a question, yeah. Like "How many pounds of explosive did you have in your suitcase?"'

Dawes stopped writing and looked up. So far, he was silent.

'Mr Sayers,' Wolfe continued. 'We're not trying to nail anything on you. There was a lot of debris to be identified after the explosion.'

Michael took a drink of water. 'One suitcase of mine, a week's worth of clothes for the Christmas holiday. Several parcels with Christmas presents inside. You know about Christmas presents? Maybe my sister was carrying twenty-five pounds of gelignite. She was a student, you know, pretty radical. That bottle of Chanel Number Nine was probably nitro-glycerine.'

Dawes wrote it all down while Wolfe smoked a cigarette. He studied the boy in the other bed.

'Now then,' he said. 'Try to remember everything from the time you arrived at Waterloo until it happened, would you?'

'Why?'

'Because you may have seen something.'

'Nothing.'

'You can't know that,' Wolfe said. He was annoyed. 'You may have witnessed something, seen someone, and at the time it didn't seem important. So far, we've got nothing on this except who's responsible for the campaign. Waterloo's a dead end, but the more of you people we can interview, the more chance there is we'll come up with something. What you tell us could mean bringing these bastards to book. You do want that, don't you?'

He could not tell them the truth. He nodded.

'Okay then. From the beginning.'

Michael told them. His face became in-looking, words coming slowly as he re-traced the path. He started with getting off the tube at Waterloo. Wolfe lit another cigarette, listening carefully, and Dawes took it all down. Now and then Wolfe interrupted to go into more detail. He wanted a description of the tramp playing the harmonica by the exchange booth, a list of any faces in the crowd that looked unusual or familiar. He asked for a description of what Laura and Jilly were wearing. Michael could not remember that. Telling it all, though, hearing himself speak it in a dull, flat voice, he was surprised to find how much he knew. The words cleared pictures and sounds that were vague before. Under Wolfe's pushing, he even recollected something that came after the bomb. A moment of waking, not knowing where he was, but hearing screams and footsteps all around; his face on cold concrete; the misted vision of a dirty corner of white brick, a toffee wrapper; the smell of smoke. It should have made it more real to him, but it was as if it had happened to someone else, like a film

42

he had seen.

None of it was much help to Wolfe. He listened just the same. Finally, he said: 'Any more?'

'Not until here.'

'That's fine,' Wolfe said. 'Thank you, Mr Sayers.' He started to get up.

Michael said: 'Where do you think they are?'

He sat again. Dawes closed his notebook and opened the case.

'It probably wasn't any of the ones who live in this country. We keep tabs on them. They've been in for questioning, of course, but alibis are alibis, much as it pains me to say so. I reckon it was boys from across the water. See, planting bombs in places like they did, they couldn't delay the explosions too long. The devices would have been found. The one at Euston was done by remote control anyway, so they were all in the country on the day. Now the blocks were on at every airport and sea crossing by the early evening. I don't see they could've got out over Christmas. They're holed up somewhere, waiting us out.'

'Should be easy enough to find them, then?'

'Certainly. Britain's only six hundred miles long by three hundred wide. No problem.'

A nurse came in. ' 'Scuse me, Constable, no smoking in here, if you please.'

Wolfe stubbed the cigarette. The nurse put it in the bin. 'These men bothering you, love?'

'Throw 'em out, Nurse.'

'I would too. Goin' round disturbing everyone.'

Wolfe grinned at her. 'You're going on my list of suspects, Nurse Davey.'

'Me? Only thing I ever blew up over Christmas was balloons.' She glanced at Michael, wondering if the joke was in good taste. He didn't seem to be listening.

'We'd like you to take a look at these.' Wolfe took a black plastic folder from Dawes and handed it to Michael. Michael did not notice. He was staring out of the window.

'They're photographs,' Wolfe explained, setting the folder on Michael's lap. 'Pictures of every known face who's likely to have been involved in what happened last Tuesday. If you could look through them, see if there's anyone you recognise. Anyone at all.'

43

Michael hummed soft and low. 'Mr Sayers?'

'Mmm?'

'Would you take a look at the pictures for us? We'd be obliged.'
The nurse stepped in. 'You don't have to if you feel bad.'

Michael snapped out of it a little. 'It's okay. Might as well do it
now. Get it finished with.' He lifted the folder and turned to the
first page of photographs.

Wolfe and Dawes left. The boy in the coma groaned twice as if
he were dreaming a bad dream.

11

Temple rolled over and woke up. It was half-past five by his
watch. The curtains of his room were drawn and it was dark
outside. He felt empty and aching from the afternoon doze. He
got off the bed, picked up an empty glass and went through to the
bathroom. His mouth was congealed and stale. He drank some
water and washed his face. Then he went downstairs to get some
food.

Barlow sat in front of the television. He had a Walther PPK in
pieces on the table before him. The parts were clean and oiled.
He was putting it back together.

'What's the news?' Temple asked, from the kitchen.

'Same stuff. Except for the outrage,' Barlow said. 'After this
long, the outrage wears a bit thin.'

Temple reached in the fridge. He took out some Ardennes pâté,
a block of Cheddar, half an onion. He sliced a chunk off the
cheese. 'Any leads?'

'They're nowhere,' Barlow smiled, fitting the gun together.
'They'd need magnifying glasses to find their pricks.'

Temple cut two hunks of bread off a loaf, yanked two bottles of
Lowenbrau from the cooler. He carried the beer and food into the
sitting room.

'This place is a mess. Why don't you keep it clean?'

Barlow shrugged. 'It's Danny's mess. He can clean up.'

Temple ripped the bread in half and began to chew. 'Where is he, anyhow?'

'Around.'

'Around?'

'Likely he's in his room.' Barlow put his gun on the table. Temple saw the change in his eyes.

'He's not up there,' he said. 'I passed his room just now.'

'Maybe he's taking a walk, then.'

Temple put the beer down.

'Where is he?'

'Around, I told you.' Barlow was sweating.

'Where is he?'

'I'm not his keeper, am I?'

'Where is he?' Like a recording.

Barlow got up. He made for the door.

Temple was known for being fast. But the thing that gave his reputation a bite, a touch of the mysterious that made kids like Danny Parker talk about him like God, was the fact that he never seemed to be moving fast at all. There was no sudden explosion from his chair. Barlow was looking for it, but it never came. Temple rose and flowed – that was the word for it. Like in the car, when he punched Danny. Temple was fluid. He smoothed gently past, and turned to ice when he stopped.

He picked Barlow off the floor and threw him across the room. Barlow struck the back of the settee and took it slewing over with him. He turned on his back and Temple was already standing over him.

'Where is he?'

'All right, all right. He's over the wall.' Temple's expression called for more. 'He's phoning his girl. We're not allowed to use the phones here. He's phoning his girl.'

'You want us all picked up?' Temple asked quietly. 'You want that?'

'I couldn't stop him.'

'Why not? It's your neck he's risking.'

'I told him you'd kill him, but he wouldn't listen.' Barlow struggled onto his elbows, still scared that Temple was going to kick his head off. 'Christ, man, I just plant the bombs. I don't get into fights with Parker's kid brother.'

Temple pushed him back on the carpet with his foot.

'Stay here,' he said.

Black-water night. Temple thrust his hands deep in his pockets and crossed the lawn. No need to guess the direction; the footprints in the snow were fresh in his memory. He walked into the woods, the house dark and silent behind him.

When he reached the wall, he debated whether to wait. Anger worked at him. He took a run-up, reached, clasped the wet moss on top of the wall and vaulted over it. He landed silent and low in the undergrowth on the other side. Keeping to the cover of the verge, he headed down the road towards the village. Two hundred yards on, he saw the telephone box; a stack of yellow squares against the starless night. It stood at the crossroads by the village sign. Three cottages huddled by the village road some distance away. It was quiet, there were no cars in sight.

He crouched in the shadows opposite the box. He saw Danny, back to him, leaning against the door. He checked the roads and crossed over.

Danny was saying, ' . . . Of course I do, what d'you think?' when the door was opened, tipping him out on the grass. He spun and lunged. Temple caught him like a baby, dumped him on the ground in one swift move. Danny sat down hard, scrabbling in his jacket pocket.

Stow it,' Temple warned.

'You, you daft fucker. I almost shot you.'

'That'll be the day. On your feet, and get back to the house.'

'I'm talking to my girl.'

'Get back to the house.'

'You'll be in the shit when we get home. You know that?'

'Yeah,' Temple said. 'You run to Georgie if you like.' He stepped into the box and replaced the receiver.

'Excuse me. Are you two finished now?'

He turned. A young woman in a raincoat and headscarf stood there, looking at Danny. She looked impatient, not frightened or surprised.

'Certainly, Missus,' he said, standing so she could not see him except as a silhouette. 'It's all yours.'

'Thanks a lot.' She stepped round him to the box.

Temple took Danny's arm and hustled him across the road. They walked back in the dark. Temple shoved him over the wall. They trudged through the woods, several feet apart. Temple did not speak. Danny watched for the first sign of violence, but it did not come. They crossed the lawn, Temple going ahead. At the back, he tapped lightly on the french windows of the sitting room. Barlow appeared through the heavy curtains and let them in.

'What happened?'

Temple picked up his plate. 'Danny boy probably just got us all caught,' he said, warming himself at the heater.

Barlow waved his gun in Danny's face. 'You stupid young bastard. You said it was never used.'

'Ah, shut your mouth.' Danny threw himself into a chair. 'She never recognised me. Too dark. She won't remember.'

'You better hope so,' Barlow said. 'Ah, sweet Jesus, we had it sweet here.'

'We still have. There'd not be a thing to worry about if he hadn't come after me.'

Temple ate in silence. He did not watch them.

'Ah, shit,' Barlow muttered. He went over and turned the television up.

Temple finished his meal. He got up with the second bottle of beer and left the room.

As far as he was concerned, war had already been declared.

12

'Christ!' Michael said. The folder dropped out of his fingers and clattered on the floor.

Nurse Davey came in. 'What's the trouble?'

'Shit,' Michael said.

Wolfe and Dawes crowded past her. Dawes picked up the folder. 'What is it, Mr Sayers?'

Michael touched the bandages on his head. 'Oh, shit.'

'Which one, Mr Sayers?'

He fumbled the folder open again. Dawes held it while he turned the pages, hands trembling.

'I'm not sure,' he kept saying. 'I'm not sure.' He stopped. His finger pointed at a picture in the centre of the page.

Wolfe snatched it up and checked the name.

'Danny Parker,' he said. 'Right, Dawes, get the lads to put this one out. Mr Sayers, can you tell me when and where?'

Michael stared at his hands seeing the minor cuts and grazes on them as if they were new. Wolfe did not understand the next thing he said.

'They did run me down,' he said. 'They just didn't use a car.'

Don came to see him later.

'You recognised one of them?'

'Maybe.' The shock had passed. He was listless again.

'What did they tell you?'

'Not much. If it is the guy I identified, he's pretty important. His brother's a big wheel. Organises the campaigns.'

'Bastard,' Don said.

'They're pretty pleased. Finally got something to follow up.'

Don's eyes narrowed. 'How about you?'

'Me?'

'You look as if you couldn't give a damn.'

'It won't bring anyone back.'

Don snorted. 'I want to see them dead. Preferably slowly. It's the only answer. You have to stamp them out.'

'And the revenge makes you feel better?' Michael shrugged. 'It doesn't. I thought about it. It doesn't make any difference. The bad thing's been done.'

'You're not well,' Don said. 'Don't try to think about it now.'

'I wish I could walk out of here.'

'Have they had you out of bed yet? Don't they try to get you moving around as soon as possible?'

'It's difficult with one leg hanging on by the tendons. They let me spin around in a wheelchair this afternoon, but where the hell do you go? Watch TV? Sit in the lounge, looking at all the others? There're people here selling their stories to the Sunday papers: "How I survived Waterloo." Some of them want to talk about it all the time. They ask you where you were when it happened, how many wounds you got. It's the most exciting thing that ever happened to them.'

'People react to things in different ways,' Don said.

'Some people reacted by dying. Everyone else makes a big deal out of it. Papers get headlines, politicians get an axe to grind. And next month they've forgotten it.'

'That doesn't matter,' Don said. 'These bastards have to be caught.'

'What for? They'll go to gaol, serve half their sentences, and come out in a few years to start it all over again. Besides, if they get put away, we have "retaliatory strikes", or some junk like that. First, it's people like us – I was an ad man, Laura was a personnel manager, Jilly was a student. Really good soldiers, right? We really oppressed the people. Then, if the ones who got us go away for a year or two, it'll be some milkman who's a part-time defence officer, or his wife and kids. We're an army all right – except no one tells us we've been conscripted until the shooting starts.' He shook his head. 'I don't want it any more.'

Don was angry. He was a man who had learnt that unless you trample on the bad guys they will walk all over you at the end of the day. 'You can't walk away from it,' he said.

Michael was not listening.

That night, he had another attack. It was milder than before, but still bad. Next day, they did more tests on him.

Meanwhile, the picture of Danny Parker was going all over the country.

13

'Shut up, will you.' Jane clipped her daughter round the ear. The child gulped back her complaint, face colouring over bright red, and began to bawl. Once Helen started, it was impossible to shut her up without a bribe. Jane hung her shopping bag on the back of the pushchair and started for the village post office. She had to get a move on or Jeffrey, her husband, would be home with no lunch on the table. She went into the post office, bought her stamps, and a bar of nougat to keep Helen quiet.

The day was bright and hard. It was a relief after all the snow and ice over Christmas. She trundled shopping and baby home to the cottage, kicked off her slush-soaked boots and made a coffee while she warmed up in front of the fire. She had time for a sit down before starting lunch. She got her cigarettes, put Helen in her playpen in the corner and switched the telly on. It was news, all about some coup in South America. She frowned: not a week since Christmas, and they were fighting again. She picked up the newspaper and read her horoscope. She was Aries.

'Domestic affairs get on top of you today,' she read aloud. 'Don't let routine stop you from pursuing your main objectives.' She screeched suddenly and leapt across the room to the playpen. Helen was trying to plait half-chewed nougat into her hair. 'My main objective,' Jane muttered ruefully, picking the pink and white goo off her daughter's head.

While she was busy, the television flashed up a picture of Danny Parker. The man she had seen outside the telephone box last night.

Temple dismantled his gun. A Heckler & Koch 9 mm sub-machine gun. He cleaned it thoroughly, oiled it, re-assembled it. He was in the empty white room. The only difference from before was that the chair now faced the door. He took a clip out of the arm pocket of his parka and shoved it in.

When Barlow opened the door, Temple's gun levelled on his belly.

'You seen it?' Barlow asked. 'On the TV?'

Temple flicked the gun out of sight. 'Yes.'

'That woman from the village. You said—'

'It wasn't her. If it was, the place would be crawling with coppers by now.'

Barlow stood at the window, scanning the trees. 'Who says they're not out there?'

'They're not. I checked.'

'Shit, Temple. What'll we do?'

'Wait.'

'Until they come and get us?'

'We've got a schedule. As things stand, we're not moving. There's nowhere to go anyway.'

'That woman recognised him.'

'No. It was someone in London.'

Barlow raised an eyebrow. 'You mean someone gave us away? They wouldn't dare.'

'No. If it was that way, they'd have all of us on the box. Someone saw him, remembered his face.'

'He wasn't at the station,' Barlow said. He leaned against the window, cold glass on his forehead. Then he straightened. 'Hold on though . . . '

Temple counted the clips in his pocket.

'What about . . . You remember the guy outside the tube station, the one you nearly ran down? Him?'

'Could be.'

'You don't sound worried.'

'I'm not. It doesn't matter who told them, only that somebody did.'

'So what're we going to do?'

'Wait it out.' He turned the chair back to the window and took out his book. 'Chances are that girl won't remember the other night. Any other chance is no chance if we run.'

'You're so fucking cool,' Barlow said.

'Better than sweating it like you,' Temple said. He settled in the chair. He had a perfect view of the lawn, the drive and the woods. He opened *The Man Without Qualities* to chapter thirty-one, 'Whose Side are You On?'

Barlow snorted and slammed the door when he left.

Then Temple stood. He climbed onto the chair, bumped the attic trap door out of its frame. Reaching, he grasped the frame and lifted himself through. There was another entrance to the attic – stairs in the north wing – but this one the other two did not know about. He stepped carefully between the moulding bric-à-brac that crammed what were once servants' rooms. Light came from muck-streaked windows. Last night, he had spent an hour scraping years of old paint off one window to unstick the frame. It opened stiffly. He snaked through the tiny gap, came out on the roof of the house. He crept over the tiles to the flat, leaded area at the centre. From there, he had three hundred and sixty degrees clear. From the lawns, paths and woods around the house, to the hills beyond the river and the village. The gateway to the road was in clear view through a gap in the trees.

He sat down to study.
He was a man who took his life very seriously.

Michael was tired. They had been working him all day. Tests, questions, exercises, attempts to make him 'part of the ward'.

He said to Doctor Ellis when she came in: 'When do I get out of here?'

'Well,' she said, 'I'd discharge you now just to get rid of you, but my colleagues wouldn't like it. And I daresay you'd soon complain if you had to go around with your leg and back in that state.'

He turned his wheelchair in a circle, following her as she looked at the boy in the coma. She was carrying copies of *The Times* and the *Guardian*.

'Would you like to see them? There's a nationwide hunt on for the one you identified.'

He made no move to take them.

'They say he's still in the country, unless he got carried out in a handbag,' Ellis said. 'There's a good chance they'll catch him. And he'll lead on to the others.'

Michael picked up the Stephen King. He was managing only about thirty pages a day because reading brought on headaches.

'As soon as we're sure about this business with your attacks,' she went on, 'I expect they'll talk to you about the operations you'll need to get properly mobile again.'

'Sounds fun.'

'It won't be. But you'll need them if you want to get around.'

'I don't want to be anybody's problem.'

'At the moment, you're my problem,' she said. 'I wish you'd try not to be.'

He tried a smile. 'You're the nicest doctor I ever met.'

She almost blushed. 'You're having a visitor soon, you know.'

'The police again?'

'Friend of yours, apparently.'

He started reading.

Temple explored the roof.

'Afternoon. Got any spare nurses you're not using?'

Michael glanced up, saw Ralph standing in the doorway.

52

'Come in,' he said.

Ralph put a bottle of Southern Comfort on the bedside table. He hoisted a carrier bag onto the bed.

'Didn't know what sort of reading matter you'd feel up to,' he said, taking out one paperback after another, 'so I brought a selection. Everything from *War and Peace* to the new illustrated edition of *Fanny Hill*.' He drew up a chair. 'How's things with you?'

Michael pointed at the cage. 'Fighting fit.'

'That's what I told them. You know, the office is in an uproar. Half the girls are wearing black for you, the rest want to become nurses. Terrible.' He rummaged in the bag a little more. 'They sort of elected me to buy you a present, so I went out and snouted round town. Finally got you one of these doo-dahs.' He took out a brand-new Mitchell reel. 'I know you're not exactly in fishing form now, but perhaps it'll encourage you to get your arse out of here.'

Michael took the reel out of its box. It gleamed in the light. 'It's beautiful,' he said. 'You bastard, it's expensive too.'

'Well, no point in getting you something that falls apart the first time you hook a stickleback. Anyway, that's from the whole department, self included.' He yawned. 'You know, they've off-loaded all your work on me. That bloody jewellery thing.'

'We were both on that anyway. Did you scrap my drafts and start again?'

'No chance. I borrowed your sketches and outlines. The lads in the copy room are beginning to hate me and you. We're putting them out of business. I put your name on the stuff, of course.'

'That means I'll get the credit.'

'Call it a Christmas present. How are you to know I didn't cock the whole thing up anyway?'

Michael paused. 'It feels like all that stuff's a million years ago.'

'Try telling that to Dixon. He wants you back behind the drawing board within the month.'

'Done any fishing over Christmas?'

'You're joking. Went up to Suffolk for the family celebrations. Whole bloody tribe there. Every relative I ever saw, plus a few I *never* saw before in my life, *plus* guests. Most of the time it was like the party scenes from *The Great Gatsby*. Couldn't move for empty

53

bottles and retired MPs discussing their share prices.'

'Same boring old routine, right?'

'Naturally. The old man must be down to the last penny in the coffers by now. I tell you, you and Laura should've come up with me—' He broke off, pursing his lips. 'Sorry.'

'It's okay.'

'Look, I'm not going to talk about it any more. You know how I loved Laura – and you for that matter. If there's anything I can do . . . '

'Let's keep off that,' Michael said.

Ralph took out his cigarettes, lit one up. 'I know it's a non-smoker, but hospitals give me the jitters, and that always makes me long for a weed.' He puffed on it with relief. 'Let's toast the New Year before they come and confiscate the liquor.'

He took a bottle of soda water from the bag. Two glasses from the sink in the corner. He filled up with Comfort and soda. 'Wonder if they've got any ice . . . Well, perhaps not. Here's to you being back on your hind legs and chasing accounts with the rest of the rats.'

They drank.

'Talking to the nurses before I came in, making sure they hadn't mixed you up with some case of typhoid or other. They said you've had some trouble with attacks.'

'They're fading,' Michael said. 'The doctor thinks they're a result of the head injury and shock. More emotional than physical, she says.'

'And they're going to chop bits of you off to cover other bits up, is that right?'

'More or less. I should be out of here soon, though they want me back for more work on the leg.'

'What're you going to do?'

'Do?'

'When you leave.'

'Dad wants me to go home for a while. He thinks Mum could do with us being around.'

'Probably right. Besides, good fishing down in Surrey. Even this time of year, something should be stirring. We haven't done any in a dog's age. If you fancy trying out the reel and freezing to death on a river bank, I'm game.'

'Maybe,' Michael said.

Ralph tipped his glass. 'Here's to getting those animals behind bars.'

Michael did not accept the toast.

14

Jane had the morning to herself. She left Helen with her mother, told Jeff to have lunch at work, and took the bus to town with her friend from up the road. They visited the new shopping centre, choosing all the things they would buy if they had the money, then went to their favourite pub for lunch.

Afterwards, they wandered along the high street and paused in front of an electrical shop. The friend said how much she would like one of those hi-fis that played records vertically. Jane said they would soon need a new telly because the contrast was going on the old one. She looked at a twenty-six inch colour set with stereo speakers. One like that would do, she said, with a video. She was looking at a picture of Danny Parker.

She had seen it maybe five times since the police issued their bleary snapshot to the media. It had been on every television news she had seen since Monday. This morning, it stared at her from the front page of the *Sun*. In the photograph, Danny was more boyish than when she saw him, with long hair. But it was the same man. Up until now, she had not made a connection.

Up until now.

She blinked, leaning towards the television.

'What's up?' The friend nudged her. 'Think you've seen him, do you?'

Jane rubbed her nose slowly with her forefinger. She always did this when perplexed. The picture switched to scenes of important policemen talking to the press. The thought hung on for a second, then she shook it off. Like everyone else, she thought, No, it couldn't happen to me.

The people at Waterloo station probably thought the same thing.

Temple took an Adidas holdall from the wardrobe in his room. He unzipped the bag, and began to dismantle his Heckler &

Koch 9 mm sub-machine gun again. He cleaned the parts, humming along to Elgar's Cello Concerto on Radio Three.

Michael received a phone call from Laura's mother. They talked for half an hour, but said nothing. He had met her twice before and both times had been uneasy. The only thing they had in common was loving the same person, and that was not something they could talk about.

She promised to write to him after the funeral, which he could not attend. He did not think she would.

Another day passed.

Wednesday: over a week since the bombings. The last day of the year. In London, people were still a little nervous about going out. But it was time to celebrate and they would go out eventually.

Michael laboured through another chapter of Stephen King, Doctor Ellis bothered him about the news, and his parents came to see him. For them he pretended some kind of feeling. Inside he was numb, the only pain was in his wounds.

He read about terrible things happening to people in the King book, and it was strange, because things like that did not happen. People did not get torn apart by bogey men or vampires or ghosts. They got hurt by other people. Other people were the monsters.

The baby was asleep upstairs, Jeff had trotted down to the turf accountant's to place some bets on the afternoon racing, and Jane was in the garden shed.

She was certain she had not thrown away the newspapers. Jeff liked a stack of them in the shed to use in his DIY projects. She sorted through a pile under a layer of sacking in the corner.

The idea had been growing in her mind all yesterday. She was still convinced it could not be the same man, but the picture kept flipping in her memory. She just wanted to take a good look, see that it wasn't the same man, and stop worrying about it.

She turned over a grubby copy of *Mayfair* and found it. She unfolded it and took it out of the shed. She studied the photograph in clear daylight. Her heart began to beat a little faster.

For about ten minutes, she stood in the little back garden while sparrows pecked at toast crumbs under the kitchen window. Then she went indoors. She put on her coat, slipped the paper into her pocket because it gave a number to call if you had any information. She wondered about the baby, but she would be gone only five minutes. She closed the front door behind her and walked up the road to the telephone box.

The following day, Danny was watching *Rio Bravo* in the lounge, when the telephone rang.

15

He jerked as if a current had passed through him. The phone was on the floor under the coffee table.

Upstairs, Temple heard the extension next door chirp into life.

Barlow came running from the cellar, where he was sampling vintages. He burst into the sitting room, face dough-coloured and sick.

'Don't touch it!'

'For Christ's sake,' Danny sneered. 'What d'you take me for?' He was badly frightened. He remained seated, but his body was tense, the cords strung out tight in his neck.

'Shit,' Barlow said, as the phone rang on. 'Everyone's supposed to know the place is empty.'

'It's a wrong number,' Danny said. He stared at the phone as if flex, receiver, all were alive.

'Could be one of ours.' Temple strolled in. 'Did you think of that?'

'They wouldn't,' Barlow said. 'Strictly no contact. That's the rules.'

'Certainly,' Temple said. He had the second volume of *The Man Without Qualities* in his hand. 'But what if it was an emergency? A real emergency. How else would they get to us?'

Barlow looked from him to the phone and back again. The new

doubt worked on him.

'They still wouldn't,' Danny interrupted, getting up. 'It's a wrong number, that's what it is.'

'Or it's the cops, seeing if we're here.' Temple almost grinned.

The phone kept ringing.

Barlow shifted from foot to foot, rubbing his chin. 'Let's pick it up then. Cut the noise.'

'Leave it,' Danny said. 'Stop shitting yourself.'

'You watch your mouth.'

The two of them stood over the telephone, drawn tight. Temple gazed at the television screen.

Then the telephone stopped.

Temple looked round at their relieved faces. He began to laugh.

Later, he went up on the roof. He sat on the south side of the house, watching the gates. He had the book with him. He read, glancing up whenever there was movement. When a helicopter flew over at less than two thousand feet, he scrambled inside again. He watched it pass. It could have been anybody – there were no distinguishing marks. It did not pause over the house. It swept by, the whipping blades loud in the still air, and disappeared towards the hills.

He slipped out again, sat near a chimney stack and went on with the watch. At half-past two, he saw the police car. It was not much even then. It passed the gates, doing about thirty miles an hour. It never slowed or turned. He saw the white and orange; that was all.

He waited, listened. Now and then, faintly, the sound of lorries and heavy machinery. Any other time it could have been tractors in the fields or tankers on the main road not far away. But not today. He shifted position, went at a crouch across the roof.

In doing so, he realised he was in good condition. The exercise he had been taking every day in the west wing had kept him efficient. His system was clean. He had stopped drinking the moment Parker made the first stupid slip. He felt cold sunlight on his face. It was good. He was ready.

He knelt by the chimney on the west side. Last night he had

been certain the house was being watched. He saw nothing, but he was certain. He waited, patient and still. Someone always made some kind of mistake; it was in the rules of the game. He saw the sudden flash under the trees and was not surprised. It might have been a drop of water catching the sun as the trees swayed, or a piece of broken glass. But not today.

He remained on the roof for half an hour, watching, then he went down again. He looked at *The Man Without Qualities* sadly. He was enjoying volume two – it was a pity he would not have time to read volume three.

Ralph brought Diane and Linda from the department to see Michael. The visit was not a success.

'He seemed all right at first,' Diane said, when they left. 'But later on . . . I don't know.'

'You must remember, old dear,' Ralph said, 'he's been through a lot.'

'His girlfriend,' Linda said. 'I never met her. What was she like?'

'Nice. No . . . fascinating. I introduced them, you know. She was very talented. Youngest PM her company ever had. They'd probably have asked her out to one of their European branches next year.'

'They were going to get married, weren't they?'

'Only slightly. God, he was potty about her. Never thought he had romance in his soul until she came along. It was her who got him moving at work too. She gave him direction, I suppose.'

'And now it's gone,' Diane said.

'Ah, he'll be all right,' Ralph said. 'Give him a pencil and a good account to work on, he'll be fine.'

'I hope so,' Diane said. 'I don't like to see him like that.'

Danny had the television on, but neither he nor Barlow was pretending to watch it. Barlow was in the kitchen, frying eggs and bacon. The radio was also on. Radio One's music mixed in with the warm smell of bacon. It was an ordinary scene, except for Barlow's gun on the table. Danny whistled low, making a tuneless drone through his teeth.

'Christ,' he said. 'I'll be glad to get out of this dump.'

Barlow chewed some bread and shifted the bacon in the pan.

'Another week, we'll be out of here and home,' Danny continued. He checked his nostrils with the long nail of his little finger. 'What'll you do when you get back?'

Barlow said, with mouth half-full: 'Live a nice quiet life for a while.'

'I'm going to catch up on all the things I've been missing. Haven't had a woman for three weeks, you know that?'

'Christ, you should take holy orders.'

'Three weeks is a long time when you're my age.'

'You're not much younger than me.'

'Ah, but some fellers are more virile than others.'

'Shit.'

'I've got a lot more to give the world,' Danny grinned. 'And when I get home, I'll be giving it to every woman who wants some.'

'You're all talk. What about that girl of yours?'

'She can wait her turn.'

Barlow came in with the plate of bacon and eggs. 'Now when I was a kid, I could—'

The doorbell chimed.

'This is getting ridiculous,' Barlow said, a forkful of egg and bacon poised midway between plate and mouth. Yellow yolk dripped on his trousers. 'First the phone. Now this. It's likely Temple, playing us about.'

Danny turned the television sound down. He took out his gun, stood quivering in the centre of the room.

The doorbell chimed again. The owner's joke: Big Ben.

'Get to the window and see who it is,' Danny said.

Barlow picked up his gun. He crept through the ground floor, looking for a vantage point. In the hall, he stared at the door as if staring hard enough would make the man behind it visible. He thought, If we stay quiet, we're okay. Nobody knows we're here. He climbed the stairs as the chimes went again. From a landing window, he could see the visitor. A Ford Granada stood in the drive, and down on the steps a young man in a suit was leaning on the button. He carried a briefcase. He looked like an estate agent or a solicitor's clerk. He did not appear to be armed. He seemed more bored and irritated than anything else. A man who had come out to do some business with the owner and found the house empty. He turned away.

A crash from below. Barlow sprang back to the top of the stairs and saw Danny scrambling to pick up the pieces of a vase he had knocked on the floor. Cursing the kid, he dashed back to the window in time to see the young businessman moving back. He was dropping the case, reaching under his jacket, squaring off. Barlow recognised the moves. Not many businessmen in England are in the habit of wearing a shoulder holster.

He knocked a pane out of the window, levelled his gun and put a bullet into the businessman's chest. The businessman's suit grew a flower of blood; the impact smacked him off the steps, spun him into the drive. He fell against the car.

Danny clattered up the stairs. 'Shit. What was that for?'

'He's a copper,' Barlow said. He looked at the businessman. There was no movement now. 'Get upstairs and find Temple. I'll get the bastard inside and hide the car.'

Danny went. Barlow steadied himself. The gun felt ice cold in his hand.

He was halfway down the stairs when he heard Danny's yell. In a second, the kid was tumbling down to him, his eyes wild.

'I can't find him.'

'What?'

'He's not here. He's gone.'

Barlow covered his face. He fell back against the wall, automatically pointing his gun at the door.

'What're we going to do?' Danny screamed, shaking him. 'What do we do?'

Maybe Barlow would have come up with the words of wisdom. He had always thought himself good enough to lead. Maybe he would have told Danny exactly what they were going to do, given precise plans on the defence of the house, or the routes of escape. Maybe he would have proven himself equal to the hour. But he never had the chance to try.

Half a second later, all hell broke loose.

16

Michael did not hear about it until late that evening. Nurse Arnold came in as he was lying in the dark trying not to think. He had taken to this without any decision. It seemed much easier to stay in the dark.

'Are you awake?' she said, popping her head round the door.

He snapped the lamp on. 'What is it?'

'I thought you'd like to know. I heard it just before I came on duty. They've caught one.'

'Forget it,' he said. 'I don't want to hear it.'

'Some big house down in the West Country,' she said. 'There was a gun battle.'

He switched the light out again.

'Two of them,' she said. 'One got killed.'

'Thank you,' Michael said. 'Goodnight.'

There was no way to avoid it. In the morning, a woman who had lost an eye in the bombing, and was in a wheelchair, rolled in. She waved a copy of the *Daily Mirror* at him.

'Look at it! Look at it! They've got one of 'em. Caught one of the bleeders.'

Michael pressed the button for a nurse to come. The old woman wheeled up right beside him.

'How about that? Police finally started doing their job. 'Bout bloody time, I say.' She threw the paper on his lap. There was the picture of Danny Parker again, and the banner headline:

CHRISTMAS KILLER CAPTURED.

Below it, in slightly smaller type:

TERRORIST DIES IN POLICE GUN BATTLE.

He scanned the story while the old woman ranted on, sweeping back and forth in her chair.

'Thank gawd for the SAS, I say. Bet they had a hand in it. Swinging in through windows and stuff like that. Says there they attacked the house before them buggers had a chance. Shot one of 'em dead between the eyes. Right way to treat 'em, I say. Save the cost of a trial.'

A nurse came in, saw what was happening.

'Now then, Mrs Greaves, you shouldn't be getting everyone excited like this.'

'Good news, this is,' Mrs Greaves said, stabbing a bony finger at the newspaper. 'Best news I've had since them buggers blew me up.'

'Tell you what, let's go back to the others and you can tell them all about it.'

Mrs Greaves was taken out. Michael sat looking at the paper. He tried to believe in the things the story said — terrorists holed up in some country house while the owner was away in the West Indies, armed police, SAS men brought in to advise. Guns and blood in some little Gloucestershire village that no one ever heard of.

The report said a policeman died and two others were badly injured. Parker was captured as he tried to make a getaway in a police car. According to the paper, it was a successful operation which would lead in the end to many more arrests.

He threw the paper aside. It lay face up, with Parker's arrogant grin drilling out of it. He thought about a man killing people he never met. He wondered how it felt to point a gun at someone and know you could destroy them — how it felt to *want* to. Parker was one of the monsters, or he was a psychopath with a gun, or he was a freedom fighter, carrying the war onto the streets. Depended on your viewpoint.

Michael picked up his Walkman and put *Songs in the Key of Life* on to calm his mood, but then Don and Audrey came in. He could see Audrey was brighter. She sat down and handed him a parcel.

'It's from Kim,' she said, as he unwrapped the paper from a cardboard box. 'She put a letter inside, I think.'

Michael opened the box. Don started to laugh when he saw what was inside. First, a Rubik cube, then a Viewmaster with a packet of *Supergirl – The Movie* slides, a bag of marbles, a set of ball and jacks, a one-glass bottle of *rosé*, and a little plastic travelling chess set.

There was a note. It said: 'Some things to pass the time. Love, Kim.'

'Isn't that lovely?' Audrey said. 'She came round this morning.'

Michael picked up the Viewmaster. 'I'd better write some letters to all the people who've sent me cards.'

'That's a good idea, love. Shall I bring you some paper and envelopes?'

'Please, later. How are you?'

'We're fine, aren't we?' She glanced at Don.

'I've broken off a busy morning of ulcer making,' he said. 'You'll have to get out of here soon. The board think I'm shirking responsibilities when I keep using the same excuse for having the morning off.'

'What do the doctors say today?' Audrey asked.

He told them what the doctors were saying. They talked for a while, then Don said: 'Fancy a game?' and pointed to the chess set.

'I haven't played since I was at school, probably forgotten where the pieces go.'

'No trouble. I was school champion once.'

'Well, if you two start playing that,' Audrey said, 'I'm off to get some paper.' She got her handbag.

'Will you be all right?' Don asked.

'Of course,' she said. She left them alone.

They played for a little while. Michael's memory was better than he thought. He even remembered that the usual first move was pawn to king four. Don turned out to be better than average though. In a few minutes, he had two pawns, a bishop, and both the knights.

Michael hesitated over the next move. He picked up the queen and placed it on queen's bishop four, then shifted it back uncertainly.

'Once you leave a piece,' Don said, 'you're not supposed to play about with it any more.'

'Does it matter?'

'Well, put it this way. Where you just put it, I'll have your queen and checkmate in three moves.'

Michael shrugged. 'How do you know?'

'Analysis and forward planning. That's what it's all about.'

'It's bad enough trying to remember what I just did.' He picked up the queen and replaced it in the threatened square.

'You don't have to,' Don said.

'If that's the rules, that's the rules.'

'All right.' Don took the queen with his bishop. He said, offhand: 'Hear the news this morning?'

Michael nodded. He thought about taking the bishop with his king.

'Can't do that,' Don said. 'You'll put yourself in check . . . Your mother perked up a hell of a lot when she heard it. She's not been sleeping well. I'll wake up in the middle of the night, and she's not there. She's in . . . she's in your sister's room, looking at all the junk there.'

Michael tried another move.

'Don't bring that one out,' Don said. 'That's your only protection on the left flank.' He poured himself a glass of water. 'They brought all Jilly's stuff back from the LSE the other day. A friend of her boyfriend's did it. Nice lad, not much older than her. He said he could see how we'd feel if we had to get it. Brought it in a bloody transit van. All the rubbish she accumulated between September and Christmas – you wouldn't believe it. I've told her a million times, she's got no organisational sense . . . ' He frowned at his mistake in tenses. 'She never did throw anything away. So your mother, instead of sleeping, she's been going through the rubbish. I found her playing Jilly's favourite records the other night. Half-past four in the morning. Bloody awful music too.' He blinked quickly, stopping the tears.

Michael saw that he could not take the bishop. He moved a pawn to threaten the king's knight.

'She woke me up this morning, five o'clock. She'd just heard on the news.' Don sipped the water. 'It's the first time she's looked half alive since all this started.' He moved a pawn up on the right hand side. Michael tried to work out what good it was doing him. Then Don said: 'I hope he never gets to trial.'

Michael recalled that you are supposed to castle when you get a chance. He picked up the king and reversed its position with the

65

king's rook.

'Not like that,' Don said. He demonstrated where the pieces should go. 'If the bastard gets into court,' he said, 'it'll be all over the television and the papers for months. How's your mother supposed to get over it if it's there in front of her every day? And then they'll probably get him off on a technicality, or swap him for someone we want. Or he'll turn supergrass and make more money than I've ever seen in my life, selling his story to the *Sunday People*. It's always the same.' He moved in on Michael's king. Michael was in the situation of knowing he was attacked, but not knowing how to defend. 'Maybe with a bit of luck, he'll get his head kicked in while he's in custody.'

Michael put his remaining bishop out. It was a delaying tactic, nothing more. He knew he was beaten.

'Pity they didn't finish him off when they got the other one,' Don said. His face was savage.

'What's this with Kim?' Michael asked.

'Don't know, son. I didn't see her this morning.'

'Mum was acting like . . . Christ, me and Kim, that was all over ages ago.'

'You're still friends, aren't you? You didn't expect her to ignore you now?'

Audrey came back. She put the Basildon Bond and envelopes on the table. 'There we are. Don't forget to send a thank-you letter to Kim. She's been worried about you.' She looked at the board. 'Who's winning?'

Michael took his king out of the board and tipped it over. 'I resign,' he said. 'Chess is like crosswords. Useless pastime.'

'It's the thinking man's warfare,' Don said.

'Who needs any kind?'

Doctor Ellis came in.

'Ah, Mr and Mrs Sayers. If you hold on a second, you can hear what we'll be doing with your son over the next few weeks.'

'Here we go,' Michael said, sinking down in his bed. 'Blood and gore time. Can't you do the operations without me?'

'You be quiet,' Ellis said. 'We're trying to cut expenditure, and I suggested doing your operations without anaesthetic to save money.'

'Butcher,' he said, and turned over.

17

The long process of skin grafting and repair work on Michael's leg began. A lot of people (Michael was one of them) think that skin grafting is easy, something that can be done in one go, and no trouble afterwards. The truth is much more painful. The fluid balance of the body must be restored, the wounded flesh has to recover from the trauma of extensive damage. Then, if the wound is not large, the patient's own skin can be used to patch the affected area. If, however, the wound is extensive, zenografts or homografts will be considered. Zenografts use pig skin, homografts are made with skin taken from the National Skin Bank in London. The skin comes from cadavers.

When an operation is over, the transplant site must be covered with a pressure bandage, and for three days, the new skin lives off fluids from the flesh beneath. Then the body should have put out capillaries to the new skin. Five days after the operation, the skin has its own blood supply. This is assuming all goes well. Often, the graft simply does not take, or patients who feel well move about too much.

For a small area, it is ten to fourteen days in hospital, followed by months of great care and frequent checks. Michael's wound was not a small area.

Doctor Ellis told him all this, and got the feeling he did not care about his back. He seemed only to want his leg in working order, so that he could get around. But she persuaded him that grafting was wisest. He was easy to persuade.

She mentioned it to his parents. It was her opinion that Michael might need psychiatric help to get fully over the bombing. She tried to make him see someone while he was at the hospital, but he would not talk about it. He never talked of the bombing at all. He brooded and spent hours in silence. His only pastimes were trying to read, despite the headaches that recurred, and playing chess.

It began when he got the little travelling set. For a few days, he played around with it half-heartedly, then he asked Don to get him some kind of beginners' book. Don brought Lasky's *The Adventure of Chess* and *How to be a Winner* by Reinield.

He found that chess was not just 'more complicated draughts', as Ralph called it. It was a game where you had to think, plan, use your mind coolly and clearly. In a way, it also had a relationship with the fishing and shooting he did: it was a game where you had only yourself to blame. If you missed a wing shot, it was your eyesight or reactions at fault. If you lost a fish off the hook, you were not doing it right.

He asked Ralph to get him a book with real games and problems in it. Ralph came back with *The Golden Dozen*. The game came in handy after the first grafting operation because, for three days, he was hardly allowed to move. He lay on his side, the chessboard on a table set as low as it would go, and arranged problems from the book. Then he solved the problems – how to get mate in four moves with the pieces in this or that position; he would think for hours at a time, submerged in silence. For this reason, some staff thought he was a good patient who had started the emotional recovery from his personal tragedy. But Doctor Ellis did not like it.

'He's withdrawing even more,' she said. 'Staring at that board all day.'

The people who came to see Michael – by this time, there were several – said: 'Well, he's all right with us. Getting better all the time.'

Doctor Ellis frowned and thought: But he's not. He surfaces for a few hours a day, when his visitors call, and he chats to the nurses and cleaners. But that's it. There's been no breakdown, and the rest of the time he switches off.

Doctor Ellis was a busy woman. Michael was no longer her patient and, in the end, she was not a psychiatrist. The patient's physical health was her concern, and in that respect, Michael was doing well. She had to be satisfied with healing the body.

So months were to pass. During that time, Danny Parker was remanded in custody. No more of what the popular press dubbed the 'Christmas Bombers' were picked up.

And in late January a meeting took place.

18

The room was small and dirty; the floor bare boards, the walls distempered. Through the single window, a view of sunset sky, bare ploughed fields, twisted grey trees.

In the centre of the room, an old wooden table, and on it, a sputtering oil lamp. No electricity. Four kitchen chairs around the table, a fireplace full of dead ashes, a picture on the wall; the baby Jesus. The picture edges yellow and cracking.

Cars pulling up outside. Then the crunch of boots on the doorstep. Three loud knocks sounding in the corridor. Footsteps from the next room. A key turning, old hinges grating rustily open. Low voices.

The door opened and three men came in. In the semi-dark, their faces were shadowed. An old woman followed them, wiping her hands on a tea towel.

'You'll be wanting to see him, then?' she said. She was small, crippled with arthritis. Face like a mousetrap.

'If you wouldn't mind,' said the biggest of the three men. He kicked over the ashes in the grate as the old woman left them. They heard her climbing stairs. He turned to the younger man.

'See if you can find some wood and get a fire started. This place is a morgue.'

The young one had a bad nervous twitch. It affected the left side of his acned face. To minimise it, he smiled lopsidedly most of the time. He was thin and red-haired. They called him Ticker.

'Sure,' he said, 'she'd've lit a fire if she wanted one.'

'I don't care what she wants,' said the big man. 'I'm not freezing my balls off to save her wood.'

Ticker went out to find the makings of a fire.

'Don't worry, Georgie, I brought some central heating along,' the other one said. His name was Riley. He was fortyish, with a flabby drinker's face. He took a bottle of Jameson's from his overcoat. 'We'll see if the old woman's got any glasses.' He glanced at the damp room. 'Probably still drinks out of her hands.' He sat down, breathing hard.

The big man walked around the room, as if he did not trust any room until he was certain of all its dimensions. He leaned close to the smutty window, watching. He was broad and heavy. He came back to the table and sat down. He turned the lamp up. The greasy light spread.

'No curtains on the window,' he said.

Ticker came in. He rolled up sheets of newspaper, stuck them on top of the ashes in the grate. He added some splinters of wood and got a fire going with his cigarette lighter.

They heard the old woman on the stairs. She looked in. 'He says he'll be down in a minute.'

'Hey,' Riley said. 'You got any glasses, old woman?'

'Might have,' she said. 'And my name's Bates. *Mrs* Bates to you, boy.'

'All right, Mrs Bates.' The drinker smiled, face dimpling. 'Would you be so kind as to bring us some glasses – and one for yourself, of course.'

'I'll do that.' She glared at Ticker. 'Watch you don't set the house alight, boy.'

The big man rubbed his face with one hand, holding it as if re-shaping it.

'What's he doing up there?' Riley said. 'Dressing for dinner?'

'Lend us a fag,' Ticker said.

'Certainly. Give us a light, will you.'

'They lit their cigarettes. The smoke hazed over the table. The big man did not smoke.

'Where is the bugger?' Ticker said.

'Taking a bath and shave,' Riley said.

'Maybe he's afraid to come down,' Ticker said.

'Has to face it sometime.'

'Well, I say he's got plenty of explaining to do.'

'Yes.' Riley steepled his fingers, leaning the chair back. 'Should be a pretty little story he'll tell us.'

'I don't need to hear it. I know who's to blame.'

Temple spoke. 'And who would that be, Ticker?'

None of them had heard him coming. Only the big man saw the door open. He half-smiled.

70

'You all right?'

'Fine.'

'Sit down, then.'

Temple drew a chair out. His chosen place gave him views on the door and window. He nodded silently to Riley.

'Right,' the big man said. 'We're going to talk.'

The old woman came back with the glasses. She put them on the table, not bothering with one for herself. She left again in silence. The door closed, and Ticker came to the table.

Riley poured the whiskey.

'How did you do it?' the big man asked, raising his glass.

Temple pursed his lips. 'By being quicker and cleverer then they were.'

'Details, man.'

'Okay. After the mess at the house, I holed up in the country for a while. Then, when things relaxed a little, I made it to the coast. From there, a boat took me out as one of the crew. The captain wasn't too particular, but he was expensive.'

'Start at the beginning,' Ticker said, staring hard at his impassive face. 'What about the house?'

Temple took a drink. 'Simple. We were ambushed, and I was the only one to escape.'

'Why's that?' Ticker said. 'How come it was only you?'

'Because the other two were fucking amateurs.'

'Barlow was the best bomb man—'

'He was lousy with guns. No nerve.'

Riley stabbed a finger at him. 'What about Danny? Did you not think to get him out with you?'

'If I'd tried that, we'd both be waiting to go on trial now.'

'We've had people talk to young Danny,' Riley said. 'He tells us you were gone before the first shot was fired. How about that?'

Temple did not lose his temper, or sweat. He looked at Riley with his flat grey eyes.

'Danny should've kept his mouth shut. Trying to shop me to the coppers. It's a shame they didn't plug him instead of Barlow.'

Ticker sat forward, face twitching violently.

'You hear that?' he said to the big man. 'You going to let him talk about your own brother like that?'

The big man lifted his hand. 'Calm down, Ticker. We're not

71

here to interrogate anyone, just to find out the facts.' Still, he watched Temple carefully, as if he had him pinned to a board. He said:

'Temple, tell us how it happened.'

'Simple story. Your damn brother gave us away.'

Ticker jumped up. He stalked away to stand over the smouldering fire.

'I don't believe that.'

'Danny wouldn't be such an idiot,' Riley said.

'You lying bastard,' Ticker said.

'He acted like some stupid kid all the way through,' Temple went on, undisturbed. He told them how Danny had gone out to the phone box. The big man sat, hands on the table, staring now at his glass, shaking his head. As Temple described what happened with the woman, he said: 'Stupid little bastard.'

'And then what?' Riley asked.

Temple said: 'We sat it out. I figured there was a fair chance she wouldn't recognise that picture on the box. And there was nowhere the three of us could run then – the country was swarming with coppers. We sat it out.'

'Get to the point,' Ticker said, turning back to them.

'I said steady,' the big man muttered.

'Ah, come on, Georgie, he's making it up.'

'Steady,' Parker repeated. His voice was deep and cold.

Ticker sat down again, refilling his glass. His eye fluttered with the tic.

'On the day they came for us, I'd been checking all the escape routes,' Temple continued. 'Whatever happened downstairs, the two of them messed it up. I think the coppers were watching the house for a couple of days – maybe not. Anyway, they blew some feller away on the doorstep. He was trying some kind of clever disguise bit that didn't come off. Next thing, the place was like an assault course. Couple of men came through the windows, they put tear gas into the ground floor, and Barlow tried to shoot it out with about fifteen coppers.'

'Where the hell were you?' Ticker whispered.

'Upstairs. I saw what was going on, and I knew we didn't stand a chance. But I knew I could get out on the roof. So I did it. Took out one of the uniform boys, got into his gear, came down from the roof, and mixed in with the rest of them. While things were still mixed up, I slipped off into the woods and made for the river.'

'And left Danny and Barlow behind?' Riley nodded thoughtfully, as if the subject under discussion were art, or cricket.'

'If I'd hung about,' Temple said, 'they'd have got me too. I'm not a hero, understand, and I'm not stupid. I left that to Danny.'

Parker took another drink. 'Seems to me you were bloody lucky to come out of it at all.'

'No luck involved.'

'It's a pity you couldn't get Danny out too. Would've saved us some trouble.'

'Is that it?' Ticker said. 'Is that all? He tells you that, and you believe it?'

Parker put his hand flat on the table. It seemed huge. He flexed the fingers. 'You want to shut your mouth, or would you prefer that bottle between your teeth?' He spoke quietly. He always spoke quietly.

'I've had it,' Ticker said. Trembling, he left the room. The door slammed.

'He can't help it,' Parker said. 'Danny and him . . . '

'Well now,' Riley said. The three men relaxed a little. They were of similar age.

Parker focused on Temple. He said: 'Stephen, tell me. Is what you said the truth?'

'There's no point to lying. It's true. Your brother fucked us up, but if there'd been a chance of saving him, I would've gone back. Like Ticker said, he's your brother.'

There was a silence. Parker and Temple watched each other in the smoky gloom. Then Parker said:

'All right. That's good enough.'

'The question is, what next?' Riley said, not a little relieved.

Parker unwrapped the scarf from his neck. Temple swilled whiskey round in his glass.

'What about this business with Danny?' he asked.

'How did they get him, you mean?' Riley waved a pudgy hand. 'Seems someone at the bombing saw him.'

'You found out who?'

'The police aren't exactly going to print his name and address,

73

now are they?'

'We're working on it,' Parker said.

'I think I know,' Temple said. 'I'd like to find out for sure. If it is that one, then he saw me too.'

'You've no worry.' Riley smiled. 'No record.'

'Danny started giving them plenty on me, didn't he?'

'He's been told to shut his trap about it.'

'The damage is done. The name's no matter, but if the face gets around, I'll have to change my appearance before I can go back into England.'

'No danger of that for a while,' Riley said. 'Everybody's keeping low at the moment. We took a risk coming out here tonight.'

'What happened about the house?'

'Naturally, the owner was away. He was just as surprised as everyone else to find his place was being used for a hideout.'

'You think he'll get away with it?'

'I don't know. He's staying out of the country for now, anyway.'

'But that's a safe house lost. And everything else went so well.'

'The operation was a success,' Parker said. 'The follow-through was lousy.'

'And what do we do now?'

'That depends. Danny can't tell about the rest of the operation, who was involved and so on. He only knew your part of it. So we're covered there.'

'They must know you're involved.'

Parker nodded. 'They would've guessed that anyway. But they're not catching me.'

'What's the action on Danny being in gaol?'

'We'll see how it goes. The way things are, there'll probably be some retaliatory executions. But you're out of it for now. You're to keep your head down.'

'And the eye witness?'

'We'll see about him. Bet on it.'

When they were gone, Temple climbed back to his dingy bedroom and lay down with his eyes closed. He relaxed. It had gone very well. Ticker could have been a problem, but Temple knew that George Parker trusted him. All the years behind them saw to that. He knew Georgie would believe his story.

It was not true, of course. The truth was that he had seen the raid coming, and got out of the house, out of the area while the law was still setting up.

It was reasonable. There was no way the three of them could have beaten that kind of firepower, and he saw no reason to risk his neck for fools like Danny and Barlow. They were so big on fighting for a cause, then they should be prepared to die for it. So, he escaped while the going was good. At least somebody came back.

He stared at the cracks in the ceiling, wondering how long he would have to lie up. Wondering, too, about the one who had seen his face.

19

Don stopped the car.

'Here we are,' he said. 'Hang on, here comes your mother.'

Audrey came out of the house, waving.

Don took the wheelchair out of the boot and began to unfold it. Audrey came down and opened the car door. Michael waited until they had the chair ready, then they helped him out. It was not easy; he felt the new skin on his back pulling against the rest. His leg was the worst problem. It was in plaster up past the knee. He manoeuvred onto the chair and they pulled him back slowly. Don was slotting a support under the leg when a labrador-retriever puppy bounced out of the door and skittered around them on the gravel. It yapped frantically at Michael.

'Even he's come out to meet you,' Audrey said, noticing his surprise.

'You bought a dog again?' he said. 'I thought after Boris you weren't going to.'

'He would've been put down if we hadn't taken him. Besides, I thought he might be company. His name is Pug.'

The puppy tried to climb on Michael's lap. It was light gold in colour, like straw before it turns white.

'He likes you,' Don said.

Michael pushed the puppy down gently.

They wheeled him over the drive and managed to get him up the steps to the door. He pulled off his scarf and threw it at the coathanger.

'Don't strain that skin,' Audrey said. She went to re-hang the scarf before Pug could get his teeth into it.

'Are you warm enough, son?'

'After all this time in pyjamas, it's weird wearing clothes again.' His voice sounded strange in the spaces of the hall. He looked around. Everything was in place – the old clock, the telephone table, the coatstand. Only the wallpaper was different.

'I haven't been here since last August,' he said. 'Seven months.'

'Nothing's very different,' Audrey said. She opened the door to the dining room. 'We've made your room up in here. Weren't sure if you'd be able to manage the stairs.'

'Looks as if we were right,' Don said, trying to sound light.

'Besides, we hardly ever use the dining room now.' Since Christmas; the words hung unsaid. 'I just brought down a few things for the moment. You'll have to tell me anything else you want.'

He saw the bed by the window. Most of his belongings were still at the flat in London, but there was nothing there he wanted or needed. He had not been back. There were some books on the shelf, volumes he never took away when he first left home. Also, his old radio-cassette.

'All the furniture's been scattered round the house,' Audrey said.

'So don't be surprised to find the best silverware in the bathroom,' Don added.

Michael turned his head, breathing out slowly. His face was troubled. 'Could I have the big chess set in here?'

Don said: 'I'll give you the odd game, if you like. Try to get myself back up to scratch.'

'Thank you. I think my game's improving.'

He gripped the wheels of his chair and started to push forward.

'Don't do that,' Audrey cried. 'You mustn't put any strain on your back.'

'It's okay,' he said. The wheelchair bumped across the carpet.

76

He stopped at the window, tried to lift the sash.

'Are you sure that's wise?' Don said. 'You're not supposed to catch cold either.'

'Want to get some air.' He tripped the catch on the sash. Audrey lifted it for him, making him sit back.

The garden's lawn sloped away from the window, the plane trees at the bottom were below him. Their upper branches were level with his eyes. Through their black winter branches, he saw the north-east side of Guildford. The cathedral on Stag Hill, red and ugly above the staggered university buildings, Onslow and Stoughton, and across on the opposite hill, the ruin of Saint Catherine's chapel. The sky was misted blue. The faint, rushing sounds of the city came up to him. He heard a train leaving the station. At night, in warm weather, the sky lit up like lightning as the trains struck sparks off the rails.

'Do you fancy some lunch?' Audrey asked.

'Please.'

'I'll have to rush it,' Don said. 'Supposed to be in Reading at two o'clock.'

'The perils of big business,' Audrey said. 'One day it's Paris, the next it's Reading.'

'Want a game before lunch?' he asked Michael.

Michael stared at the branches that meshed over parts of his view. He looked as if he were trying to solve a problem that was bothering him. 'Have you got a pencil?'

Audrey's smile hung by the edges. She rushed to the kitchen, rummaging out a pencil from the drawer.

'Going to do some sketching?' Don said. 'I wondered when you were going to get a pencil back in your fist.'

Michael took the pencil. His left hand fluttered up. Don found a sheet of paper on the shelf. He backed it with one of Time-Life's series 'The World's Wild Places', and handed it over. Michael sat still. He put the flat of his hand on the paper. He rolled the pencil between finger and thumb. He watched a car going up the Farnham Road, looking like a toy.

The pencil did not touch paper.

'Maybe later,' Audrey said.

'Go on.' Don's voice was low. 'Go on, son.'

Michael put the paper down. He dropped the pencil.

'Doctor Ellis said no more work for a while.'

'Sketching isn't work,' Don said.

Michael did not answer. He reached down and ruffled Pug's ears.

After lunch, Michael shut himself in the makeshift bedroom. It was the first time he had been alone for months. In hospital, he was never alone, even when he managed to forget the boy in a coma. He wished he could lock the door, but the house was old and the key long lost. He sat for a minute, eyes closed, listening to the mumble of Audrey's voice in the living room.

He pushed the chair up to the window, heaved the sash up again (she had closed it). He saw the pencil on the windowsill where Don had put it. And the paper.

There was a tiny figure up by the cathedral. Probably a student with a free hour. The cathedral was a good place to go and think. The town looked peaceful. It was no great city, but it was all right. He was thirteen when they moved there. He thought then that it was a dump. It was the kind of place where nothing ever happened.

Except for the occasional pub bombing.

He rolled back to the bookcase. There were no pictures on the walls now. Once, the dining room had been off-limits to him and Jilly. It contained most of the family pictures. They were gone. He ran his fingers over the spines of the books. They were mostly club histories or Jack Higgins and Jeffrey Archer. He thought: Maybe I'll get through *The Eagle Has Landed* this time.

He touched the battered brown spine of an older book. He slid it out.

He started to shudder.

The title was in gold on the cover: *Treasure Island*. He opened it, saw the carefully shaky letters inside:

'GILLIAN ELIZABETH SAYERS'.

Underneath, her address, and then the note: 'Stolen off my brother.'

He flipped the page and found the maps she had drawn, done up with pictures of ships, skulls and crossbones, and a treasure chest. On the facing page, a drawing of Long John Silver with a huge black beard and two peg legs.

It used to be his book, but she got a craze for it after seeing the film. He let her have the book, and for weeks she had maps on her wall, and old boxes full of plastic beads were buried all over the garden. She would have been about eight then. He was sixteen or seventeen, and she annoyed hell out of him: 'Give me the book, give me the book!' Stupid kid couldn't even see that Long John Silver had only one peg.

Something stuck out of the middle pages. He pulled it out. It was a card for Jilly's eighteenth birthday, hand-drawn by him, with embellishments by Laura. They made it together one weekend, and Laura kept thinking of one more joke to write inside, one more verse about getting old. They posted it on the Saturday afternoon, and on Sunday, they went down to the coast. They ate strawberry ice cream on the beach. She wore a light blue bikini with dashes of red and yellow on it. He looked at her signature in the card, the big, dashing loops of her name next to his, then he slipped the card back inside the book.

He held it for a minute like a fragile ornament. He wanted to throw it out of the window – further than that. Somewhere where he would never see it again. He closed it, sliding it back on the shelf with the spine to the back.

His head bowed. He thought: Maybe I'll cry. But he did not cry.

20

Back in hospital, Michael saw a girl with no face. She had lost most of it in the bombing. She was undergoing plastic surgery; they were trying to make her pretty again. He knew she was pretty because she showed him a picture.

'See,' she said. 'I used to look like that.'

He looked at her face now. All that remained was the blonde hair. Her face was a gargoyle's. Even the eyes were not the same. The things she had gone through changed them too.

'People said I should've been a model,' she said, standing next to him. 'I had lovely hands too.' Her hands were scarred across the back like his. She snatched the picture away. He tried to read the expression on her stiff mask of flesh.

'He goes to trial this week,' she said. 'Did you know?'

'I didn't,' he said.

'They didn't waste any time, did they? My father said that even the British legal system can move fast if people are outraged enough. I wanted to go to the trial, but they won't let me. I wanted him to see what he did, but they said it'd be too much of a strain for me.'

'They'll put him away for a long time.'

'Not long enough.' Her eyes gleamed under what remained of her eyelids. She could not blink properly. 'If there were a way, they should sentence him to life. Then keep him alive for as long as they could. When he wanted to die, they could keep him alive for a bit longer, like the politicians in Russia. Keep him alive until he was so old and tired that he was begging them to put him out of his misery. If he lived for a hundred years like that, it'd be almost fair.'

Michael fumbled with the wheels of his chair, trying to back out. The girl followed. He thought: I'll have to call someone. Then Ralph appeared at the end of the ward.

''Scuse me, Miss,' he said, grabbing the chair, 'I've only got half an hour to talk to my friend here.' He wheeled away to a quiet corner of the lounge and sat down.

'Thanks,' Michael said.

'Poor bitch,' Ralph said. 'With any luck, somebody outside the court's going to plug that bastard when he comes out.'

Michael stared out of the window.

'Not much chance of that, though,' Ralph said. 'Security's the watchword. I thought about going along, but it'll be packed out. They're not going to call you as a witness, are they?'

'Wolfe said they don't need me. After all, I didn't actually see the guy at the station. They're getting him on the murder of that policeman or something. Besides, they're scared someone would try to kill me.'

'So would I be. Just hope your name never gets into print.'

Michael shook his head. 'If they were going to do anything, they'd have done it by now.'

As he said the words, Angela Davey, the nurse on duty when the police first came to see him, was changing the sheets on a bed in the next ward. She chatted to the girl who was helping her, she smiled a lot. She was feeling very good, because she was seeing a terrific man just now. She met him at a party two weeks ago and had thought, There's a body I could go for. As it turned out, the feeling was mutual. By two o'clock in the morning she had him all to herself, and at half-past three, when he suggested that the party was dying, she was happy to agree. They went back to her place, and she went wild over him. He kept laughing and whispering, 'You'll wake the others,' because she shared the flat with a couple of second years, but she did not care. She moaned and thrashed, made him groan. She thought the bed would collapse because one side was held up by books. She had not enjoyed herself like that for a long time. *And* he made the coffee in the morning. The perfect gentleman.

He was a car salesman or something. He wasn't married (you could always tell the ones who were). She had seen him two or three times in the last fortnight. He did not mind the odd hours she had to work. Once, they went out to the pictures; he bought her flowers and chocolates. He was old fashioned and lovely.

He was even interesting to talk to. She liked to tell the story of her life. She made good, funny tales from most of it. And nursing, which she loved, got into the conversation a lot. He listened to her, and although she knew he was probably bored to death by all the operations and bedpan talk, he said Yes and No in the right places, even asked sensible questions.

One night, when the other girls were out, they spent a quiet evening in (it was anything but quiet by the time she finished with him). He made a joke then about knowing what they meant in hospital programmes on TV when they said, 'Nurse, go and treat that man in Marlowe Ward.' She laughed and kissed him. They fell to talking about her work again.

That was when she mentioned she had worked with the bomb victims.

He was surprised, then disgusted about the whole thing. He said whoever did it should be strung up.

She went on, telling him about the worst injuries. He listened, his face pale. 'At least someone identified one of the bastards,' he said angrily.

'Yes,' she said. 'It was one of my patients.' And she told him all about Michael, the policemen and the book of photographs.

'Well,' he said, 'it's lucky he spotted that one, isn't it?'

She tucked the bedclothes tight under the mattress and laughed at something the other nurse was saying. She thought she was seeing him again tonight, which made her day. She did not know yet that he would not turn up, not this night or any night.

21

Danny was brought in. Since he was under maximum security, they gave him separate visiting hours. The other spaces along the table were empty. His brother-in-law was the only visitor.

'Dan, boy,' he said, as Danny sat down. 'How's things?'

'Just fine,' Danny said. Some of his old swagger had come back. He looked angry now instead of frightened. He leaned close to the glass partition. 'Food here stinks,' he said. A glance at the guard by the door. 'And the company's worse.'

'You keeping busy?'

'Oh yeah, they let me out every day so I can go to work.'

'You know what I mean.'

'Maybe I'll write my memoirs. Sell 'em to the *News of the Screws*.'

'They'll make a film of it,' Fynn said. 'You're a real hero now, you know.' Fynn had been at school with Danny. He always looked up to Georgie but could never get close to him, so he settled first on Danny, and finally on their sister.

'Your ma's okay,' he said, thinking of things to say. 'Georgie sends his best, and Eileen. Everybody asks after you.'

'What's Georgie doing for me?' Danny asked. 'Have they caught—' He stopped, thinking about the guard behind him. 'Has he seen that lawyer yet? Temple?'

Fynn shook his head. He had not been told that Temple was home and in hiding. 'They couldn't get him.'

Danny swore. 'And what about Ma? Why didn't she come over? She'd have done it for Georgie.'

'Ah, you know she's sick. She wanted to come, but the doctor said she was to stay at home. All this,' he shrugged, '– it's put a strain on her, you know?'

'She'd have done it for Georgie,' Danny said. 'What does he say, anyhow?'

'They're doing everything they can.'

'Sure, they'll get me out of here, I suppose.'

'Ah, don't take on like this.'

'I feel useless sitting here. What good am I doing?'

'You might be doing a lot of good,' Fynn said.

'How's that?'

'I'll tell you next time I come. Just one thing: you believe in what you're doing don't you?'

Danny blinked. 'Me and Georgie, we've been fighting for it since we were kids. What do you think?'

'You'd do anything for the good of the cause?' Fynn persisted.

'Anything. You know that.'

Fynn paused. 'I'll tell them that. They wanted to know.'

'What for?'

'Next time,' Fynn said.

Another round of grafting was done. There was a period of complete rest. Don came in to the hospital when he could get away from work. They played chess a lot. Michael won most of the games now, but he was not enthusiastic about playing; it was something they did while they talked. Michael preferred to set up situations from Hort and Jansa's *The Best Move* on the wooden travelling set Don had bought him, and lie for hours thinking about them.

Audrey spent time with him, reading to him because the headaches were still bad. Her voice was strange, reading *Gorky Park*, but he liked it anyway. It was soothing.

Ralph came in with news of what was going on at work – who was climbing over which backs to reach the top. One day, he said:

'If you don't start thinking about getting back in the rhythm, they'll forget all about you.'

And Michael said: 'No matter.'

They let him go home again after a week. He helped Audrey to train Pug, and it was clear that the dog was growing to be more his than hers. Otherwise, he spent hours sitting by the window, watching winter fade into spring. Audrey had suggested he have

Jilly's portable television, but he said no. He would not listen to the radio either, and he never looked at the newspapers. He listened to tapes on the Walkman, sealed off with the music. He knew when there was news – it was impossible to ignore, because Audrey always clattered downstairs in the morning to pick up the paper. The trial was front page news throughout the dull month; it was on her mind and Don's all the time, but if they raised the subject with Michael, he became distracted.

Don was constantly trying to get him moving again, asking if he had done any drawing, if he had heard from work lately, whether he would have any friends round some time. He said that his firm needed some local marketing ideas, did Michael have any? Michael's silence on all these grated on him, but he pretended it did not. He loved his son, and he thought that time would bring him out of it.

One afternoon, Michael picked up the Time-Life book Don had given him as a makeshift drawing board. He opened it to slide some sheets of paper inside, and began to look through the photographs. The book was about the Great North Woods. He turned some pages to a map and saw where the woods were, then flipped back to a double-page of aspens and paper birches in the autumn. It was a picture of gold, sunlight and air. He went on a little, found one of moss and ferns over a fallen tree. He could almost smell the wet earth. Then there was one of rapids on the Granite River. Rock, water, pines and firs. A sense of open space.

The first chapter was called 'An Infinity of Trees and Water'. He thought about when he was a kid; Don taking him and Jilly on camping weekends to Dartmoor and the Pennines, fishing in lonely places and eating only what you caught and picked, shooting on early winter Saturdays. He would be with the other kids in those days, beating ahead of the guns to raise game. When he was fourteen, Don bought him a gun, and he learned to use it safely and well. The crisp snap of frost, the hard, sulphured edge of the gunpowder.

He wished he could get out of the wheelchair and take a walk to somewhere far out.

Danny thought about the trial a lot. He had borrowed some legal books from the prison library because he was certain the defence was not doing enough for him. Cross and Jones's *Introduction to Criminal Law* was the one he tried to read. His attention span, however, was short. He could not handle the long sentences and references at the bottom of the page to cases and rulings. He wanted to know what they could do for him, but the sections on proceedings before trial and trial itself gave him a headache. As he said to his counsel:

'But isn't there a law or something – about acts of political violence? I'm at war with the state, aren't I? That makes me a soldier. I can't be treated like some bastard who tops his wife for kicks. That's right, surely?'

His counsel wasted no time in telling Danny what the government, and the law, made of his idea.

So Danny brooded. The only good news was what a hero he had become back home. He saw the TV news. It was packed with stuff about him – riots, pictures of marches in his honour, people speaking in his support. A couple of part-time defence volunteers had been executed as part of the counter-strike. People were making up songs about him. Him. He was bigger even than Georgie now.

He was happy in a way. A man in his own right. When he got back, all those bastards who used to sneer when his back was turned, they would be bowing down and scraping their foreheads on the floor. When he got back, he would be a leader.

He knew he would get back. There had been deals before. After the fuss died down, things would start clicking. Oh, he would be inside for a while, sure, but he had got used to that already. He thought a few years inside would be okay, if he had to do it. All it took was staying cool and thinking about all the great things they would do in your name while you were gone, and the celebration there would be when you came back.

Near the end of the trial, Fynn came to see him again. Danny had not been sleeping. They met again in the visiting room, alone. Fluorescent tubes whined overhead. The room had no windows, but it was night.

Fynn said: 'You're bearing up well?'

'I just sit and listen,' Danny said.

'That's good. Refusing to give evidence – it shows what you think of the state.'

'If you don't recognise the state,' Danny quoted from the slogans, 'you can't recognise its laws.'

'Everybody's rooting for you, you know that?'

'Yeah, I saw on the television. That march was really something.'

'People are really worked up about it. You're the biggest boost we've had for years. People see you against the whole fucking government. Back home, there's just you, Georgie Parker's brother, against the filth, the army, and the whole government. It's showing everyone how they try to run us down when they get us on our own. Solidarity, that's what's happening. People getting back together after years of fighting among themselves. They're getting something to believe in again. They know you're fighting for them. You're a hero, Dan boy.'

Danny smiled. He thought of the television pictures; people waving his photograph over their heads, banners with his name written large. That made the demonstrations outside the court small in his mind. Out there, they were burning him in effigy, saying he should be hung. But he was sure that most people did not see it that way. The longer the trial went on, the more they could see he was a revolutionary fighting a corrupt system – one man, like Zapata or Che.

'I had an idea,' he said, excited now. 'Something I found in a law book.' He took a piece of paper from his pocket and read the scribbled note. 'It says, "If the accused does not wish to give evidence, he may make an unsworn statement from the dock on which he cannot be cross-examined."' He looked at Fynn. 'How about that? All the way through, I've refused to say a word, then all of a sudden, I stand up and say my piece. No one interrupts me, I say what I want. I can tell the real truth, why we did it, what we're fighting for. It'd get in the papers, right enough. They'd send it all over the world.' He screwed the paper up and threw it aside. 'What d'you think?'

Fynn frowned. 'I don't know about that law book stuff,' he said, thinking. 'I mean, if they let you do that kind of thing. You sure you read the book right?'

'It was in the big green book,' Danny said. 'All down on page—' He reached for the scrap of paper. '. . . Well, it was all

86

there. You think I can't read?' He raised his hand to the glass. 'Is it an idea or not?'

Fynn lit a cigarette. 'It's an idea.' He nodded after a time. 'But it's not the best idea.'

'Tell me a better one.'

'You remember last time? When I asked how far you'd go?'

'What of it?'

Fynn blew smoke out. It steamed against the glass, flattened into a haze between them. 'Sorry . . . ' He wafted it away. 'Look, they've been thinking how best to follow up on this. How to help the cause the most. See, we're on a high now – all the publicity and support. The Yanks're going crazy over it. Last week, *Time* magazine was full of it. Some group out there marched to the British embassy to hand in a petition for your release. We're giving the government a really shitty reputation abroad, because their evidence against you is so lousy.'

'So?'

'So, they thought that you could take it a step further. You know, really put it on the front page here and over there for a while longer. Work it right up.'

Danny's eyes narrowed. He had been covering his mouth. Now he took the hand away, staring at the palm. 'It's down to me, is that right?'

'You're the focus, Dan boy. You're the one everyone can see when they turn on the box or open a paper. You're the symbol.'

'What is it they want me to do?'

'Take it one step further.'

'How?'

'Hunger strike,' Fynn said.

Danny swallowed hard. He froze for a moment.

'It's the right thing to do,' Fynn said quickly. His face was sweaty and troubled. 'The next logical move. You refuse to accept their law, their sentence, their whole rotten system, like you said. You say that, and you say it from a hospital bed, people have to listen. They'll hear what you're saying like they've never heard it before. You could announce it at the trial, as the final kick to your speech.'

Danny lifted his head. 'Did Georgie give the nod for it?'

87

'He said he'd go with the majority decision.'

'And they said – he said – okay?'

'He did.'

'How far do I take it?'

'Until the point's been made, till maybe we can get you transferred to a prison back home. We're going to hammer them about that. It'll be so bad, they'll have to do it. Then we can work on getting you out. They'll have to do it, they don't want a martyr on their hands. You're the one to bring it all into focus, see. You're the symbol now.'

'I need to think on it,' Danny said. He tried for a smile. 'It's not something you do every day, right?'

Fynn dragged on his cigarette. 'You think it over. They don't want you to go ahead unless you want to. Georgie told me to tell you, he knows you're for the cause one hundred per cent, and he knows you're man enough to do it. If it goes ahead, there'll be others joining you. Maybe ten all at once this time. It'll be like Gandhi or something. A few guys here, some more back home. All of you on the strike . . . ' He paused. 'But you'll be the man, Danny. You're the one they'll listen to.'

Danny cleared his throat, wanting a drink badly. His mouth felt clogged with sand.

He said: 'Tell Georgie – tell all of them . . . I'll do whatever they say.'

Michael was looking at the Great North Woods book when Ralph knocked on the door. He slid it down the side of the armchair and tried to get up. He could not make it.

'Come in,' he said.

Ralph stuck his head round the door. 'Well, at long last. They told me you'd stopped trying to break the land speed record in that chair of yours.'

Pug got up and sniffed at his feet.

'You've got the beast well trained, haven't you?'

Michael shrugged. 'He's six months old now. Excuse me if I don't get up.'

'Oh, you're getting up all right. I haven't seen the inside of a pub for a day and a half. Either you come down with me, or I'll carry you.'

88

'I'd rather not.'

'Nonsense. Trouble with you is obvious.' Ralph picked up the pills that Michael was on. 'They forgot to prescribe your daily pint of best bitter.'

Michael protested, but Ralph was not listening. He threw the crutches at Michael, then went to the kitchen, where Audrey was doing the *Guardian* crossword.

'Hello, Mrs Sayers. Taking your boy out to get him drunk. That okay with you?'

She watched them go, Ralph cajoling as Michael struggled out on the crutches. She laughed when Ralph had trouble fitting the crutches in the car, and she waved them off from the front door. That, she thought, was more like it.

She went into the living room and switched on the television for the one o'clock news. Today they would give the verdict. She was sure they would.

They went down to the Jolly Farmer by the river. Warm sunshine glittered like coins on the water, but there was a stiff breeze, so the terrace was quiet. They ordered food and a couple of pints of bitter, and went onto the terrace. Kids in canoes came stroking up from the boathouse.

'I needed this,' Ralph said, eating quickly between gulps of his pint. 'I've been drawing for three days, solid. This is time off for good behaviour.'

'Why? What's going on?'

'They got that Manuel account. Dixon wants ideas on a follow-through campaign. I mean, how do you make plastic parts for catering equipment exciting? I've drawn the same damn part six times since Tuesday, and I still don't know what it's for.'

'Maybe you should get out,' Michael said. 'You've got enough money and contacts.'

'What? I'm just about to scramble up another step on the ladder – if I can come up with an exciting new angle on plastic parts.'

Michael watched the river. A boy and girl rowed by in a hired boat. The girl had a bottle of wine. She trailed it in the water to cool it. She was slim and dark. She was very pretty. He saw how she smiled at the boy who was rowing.

He picked at a sandwich.

'What've you been doing?' Ralph asked.

Michael said he had been doing some drawing, playing chess, watching his bank account dwindle.

'How d'you fill up the time? Don't you get bored?'

'It passes.'

'Haven't listened to the news, I suppose.'

'Some pop star pegged out, didn't he?'

'You know the jury's out, don't you? They'll probably give the verdict today.'

'You said you'd lay off that.'

'I just thought you ought to know.' Ralph stopped talking to eat.

'What's that book you're reading all the time?'

'*The Great North Woods.*'

'Good plot, is it. Ever been there?'

'No. It's good to look at the pictures.'

'Travelling by proxy, yes?'

'Seeing open space, no people, it makes me feel better.' Michael took a drink. 'I wish – I'd like to get out somewhere like that. When they're finished sellotaping me together. I want to get away.'

'You'll need a holiday.'

'No, not a holiday. I want to go and not come back. It's strange . . . being alone always bothered me before. Now I want to go away and forget about everything.'

Ralph shook his head. 'First of all you want to ignore what's going on in the world, then you're running off to the wilds to make a good job of it. Next, you'll be looking round for desert islands to buy.'

'You sound like Don.'

'Okay, but don't you realise, the longer you avoid getting back in the swing, the harder it'll be? You should come back to work for a while. Old Dixon says you could do a few hours a day at first. There's some work he reckons would be just right for you.'

'Nice of him.'

'Nothing nice about Dixon. But he knows you're bloody good. Also that you're worth any three copywriters. He knows you did the copy on that jeans thing.'

'I can't get excited about that any more.'

'Who the hell's excited about plastic machine parts? I do have other things on my mind too. But that's where the folding comes from. You can't be that rich, even with insurance. You'll soon get back into things when you come back.'

Michael said: 'I don't think I'm coming back.'

Ralph dropped his fork. It clattered on the table, fell on the grass. He looked at Michael for a moment, then, without a word, he picked the fork up. He speared a scampi and started eating again.

'You notice I'm not commenting on that statement,' he said. 'Because you're a friend.' He emptied his glass. 'Want another one?'

'They said I wasn't to drink too much. Besides, there's half this left. I don't need another one.'

'Well I do,' Ralph said. He got up and headed for the bar.

When they got home, Audrey was crying. They heard her sobbing in the kitchen.

'Oh, shit,' Michael said.

'Shouldn't we . . ?' Ralph asked.

Michael hesitated. Ralph snorted and went into the kitchen.

'Mrs Sayers, are you all right?'

She got up from the table. Her face was streaming, but she did not look sad.

'They put him away,' she said. 'For life. The judge said "life" means for good this time.'

'Thank God for that,' Ralph said.

'It means he'll never hurt anyone again,' she said.

Michael, leaning in the living-room doorway, saw the television picture change to 'News Flash'. Sue Lawley appeared, and began reading the latest report.

Audrey walked past him, listening to the news. As the words came through, she sank down on the settee. Her crying stopped.

'Hunger strike,' Ralph muttered. 'The bastard's going on hunger strike.' He turned to get Michael's reaction.

The dining-room door slammed shut.

91

22

If a man really goes on hunger strike, then it does not take long. The ones who do not mean it can pad out the process by taking a little food now and then. Or, by allowing the doctors to put essential minerals and vitamins in their liquids, they can last for months. But Danny did not do it by half-measures. Through Fynn, he passed messages back home: an all-out attack, he said, would force the issue that much faster; if he screwed around, they would know he was only bluffing and they would wait him out. Doing it right would get them scared. So he started refusing food when they brought him back from the court.

He was scared, true, but he believed in what he was doing. The bastards would have to listen when he started to fade. They would listen because the rest of the world would be watching.

He felt fine the first day, as his body burned off the food he had been eating. The second day was bad. He had a headache, his stomach groaned all the time. The warders brought him a three-course meal and left it in his cell. They smiled to each other as they closed the door on him.

He sat and stared at the tray. Roast chicken, mashed potatoes, buttered carrots and spring peas; apple pie with fresh cream; cheese and biscuits; coffee to follow. The smell of the chicken filled the cell. He lay down on his bunk, mouth watering. The rich essence of the percolated coffee wafted by. He saw steam rising from the cup.

It wouldn't matter, he thought, if I just had a little bit of that chicken. Nobody would notice. He sat up, leaning towards the table. Or maybe just a drop of coffee. I could do with a drink, that's for sure. Just a drop of that coffee wouldn't do any harm.

A blob of cream slid silently down the side of the apple pie. He could taste the sharp tang of the apple.

He thought: Just one mouthful.

The door clicked. He glanced up quickly and saw the spyhole slide shut. With one hand, he reached forward and heaved the heavy tray over. It crashed to the floor, chicken and peas flying all over, cream splattering the wall. The coffee splashed his face.

'Your cooking's lousy,' he yelled at the spyhole. 'Take this shit away.'

'Morning,' Ralph said. 'How's the leg?'

Michael turned round. 'It's not bad. Walked to Saint Martin's just now. How did you find me?'

'Your mother said you were on Pewley Down. I got directions, a compass and a couple of tracker dogs, and followed your scent up here. It's lovely.'

They sat on the hillside, looking down into a shallow valley. It was very hot, and Chantries Wood on the other side was a blaze of green, yellow and brown. Pug was hunting rabbits down by the lower pathway.

'You wouldn't know the city was over the hill behind us,' Michael said. 'Except for the people.'

'This is where you come to meditate, Maharishi?'

'And train the dog,' Michael said. 'It's quiet. You don't have to worry about who's coming up behind you, what might happen in the next five minutes. There's no TV and no radio.' He watched a tractor rolling over the fields down by South Warren Farm. A border collie ran behind it. They were so far away he could not hear them.

'Have you told your parents about the job thing?'

'Not yet. It doesn't matter anyway. They wouldn't try to stop me.'

'You're buggering up a good career, you know that, don't you? You're ten times the draughtsman I am, much as it pains me to say so. Dixon's throwing a blue fit about it.'

'He got my resignation?'

'And how. The office was like a battlefield all day. He threw out three different campaigns we worked up on the Jikara account.'

'Did he settle on anything?'

'Yes. He settled on me coming out here to persuade you not to resign,' said Ralph.

'That's over. He's got my letter. Besides, I can't think of anything about Jikara's cameras or anyone else's.'

'What are you going to do, for God's sake?'

He picked a stalk of grass and began eating the soft heart of the stem. 'Go somewhere, like in the book. Somewhere with trees and water, and no people.'

Ralph sighed. 'You want to live in dreamland.'

'Maybe I need to.'

'All right. Point taken.' He stood up. 'If you really want to go through with it, I think I can help you out.'

A touch of enthusiasm lighted Michael's eyes. It was the first Ralph recalled for months. 'How?'

'I was talking to the old man the other day, trying to get him to sub me for a new car. That bloody Jensen's costing me the earth to run. Anyway, I told him about you and your fantasy. I mentioned he owns quite a bit of land, didn't I?'

'Just a few million acres.'

'He's not James Goldsmith, but he likes property.'

They were both up now. Michael limped behind him as they went along the hillside. Pug followed them below.

'The point is, I was quizzing the old geezer, and it turns out he's got a big slab of land up in Norfolk. It's near that big forest they've got there. Mostly farmland, but there's a house. No mansion, by any means. More of a farmhouse really, with a couple of sheds. It's been disused for about ten years, falling apart at the seams, in fact. He's been thinking about selling it off when prices go up a bit. But here's the kicker: it's right off the beaten track, in the middle of woods. The nearest village is five miles away, and that's only one street and a pub. There's a river nearby, and good shooting when the season starts. If you don't mind living rough, it'd be fine.'

'That's it,' Michael said, leaning on him for support. 'A place to sleep and fresh water.'

'In that case, this is the property you've been looking for. And it's offered to you, courtesy of me and the old man, for a rent of nought pounds and nought pence. Only thing I ask is that I can come over sometime and we'll do some of that fishing we talked about. I'll be spending part of the summer at home with the folks, and it's about fifty miles from there.'

Michael stopped leaning on him. He raised his hands awkwardly. 'Thanks. I'll think about it.'

'Don't think about it, do it. At least that way, you'll be doing something.'

'You're a better friend than I deserve.'

'Don't go sentimental on me, for God's sake.'

They carried on over the hill, the sun behind them. Ralph began discussing tackle and flies for the fishing.

At the end of the second week, Danny stopped caring about food. By that time, he was in hospital and they had let his family in to see him. Ma had finally made the journey over, and his sister, and Fynn. Sometimes, he thought there was Georgie too, but this was an illusion. In his clear times, he knew Georgie was not there, because the police would have taken him. Still, he saw Georgie with Ma sometimes, and he would start talking to his brother even though Ma said: 'It's not him, Danny. It's Fynn. Can't you tell the difference?'

They had him in a room off the main ward in the prison hospital. He was the only one in there, and they kept a watch over him most of the time to see that the trusties who cleaned the rooms did not pass or take messages. When visitors came the warders listened closely to everything that was said. Danny thought that the room was bugged too, but he could not be sure about this. He had a feeling that there was more going on than they were telling him. Of course, they would not let him see the television or newspapers. They did not want him to see what effect the strike was having, so they cut him off from those.

He was allowed to read books and magazines, and after that first bad week, he found he could concentrate again. He asked for Marx's *Das Kapital*, because he had never read it and he thought the time in bed would give him the chance. At first, he found it easy. Every word seemed to stand out from the page as if it were written in light; it jumped out and burned into his head, and he thought: This is simple stuff. But then he found himself waking out of a light doze, his hand resting on, say, page three hundred and forty-one, and not remembering any of it. As fast as he read, he forgot what he had seen.

He got interested in the way his body was breaking down. It was very interesting after he stopped worrying. He realised that it was not such a bad thing after all, because he felt no different, except maybe a touch lighter. He became detached and could think about himself as if he were someone else. He looked at himself in a hand mirror and was surprised how fast his face had thinned down. His eyes looked strange too, the way they did if he went a day or two without sleep.

He was weakening fast now. He did not realise how weak he was until he tried to get out of bed to take a pee. He managed to get on his feet, but when he took the first step his whole body seemed to loop under him and he staggered against the wall.

He tried to recall everything he knew about starving to death. He was very vague about that. Didn't Bobby Sands last for thirty-seven days? He was sure it was thirty-seven. Take away how many? He was not sure how many days he had been doing it. The doctors came to see him all the time now. They whispered together over the bed. Once, he heard one of them say: 'We should force-feed the little bastard.' And that made him smile. They could not do that. All they could do was let him take a little water now and then. He agreed to that only when they told him that without water he would be dead inside a week. A week would not give them time to build up the story with the press, or to work up public support. He took water now and then, although it made his stomach hurt.

He listened to Ma. She held his hand and wept. She begged him not to do what he was doing, for it was a mortal sin, the thing he was doing. His sister cried too. Fynn sat watching him, anguished and guilty. Danny smiled at that too. After all, it was for the papers and TV. Once they had seen that the government would give in, he could stop. He would be the hero.

He lay in bed, breathing the cool air from the window that looked out on a brick wall, and he read *Das Kapital*.

'So they bring the bloody priest in to tell him not to do it,' Don ranted. A quarter past nine. Michael lay on his bed in the dark. He tried not to listen, but his father's voice was loud in the house. '"Don't do it, my son. It's a sin to take your own life. Think of all the people that love you. No one wants you to die." Jesus!'

Audrey's voice; lower, a murmur. Reasoning.

'How d'you expect me to react?' Don cried. 'They shouldn't be giving the little bastard all this coverage. That's why he's doing it. It's a publicity stunt, and the media go and play right into the trap. Everyone's forgetting what he did. You'd think he was wrongfully imprisoned or something.'

Again, Audrey's softer tones.

'Someone's got to get worked up about it. The only blessing is they haven't agreed to any of those demands. That'd be the last straw.' His voice, calmer now, sank down so the words were unclear.

Michael thought about going away, how it would be when he ran. Not that he could run: but walking pace, even crippled, slow limping, would be enough.

He reached up, turned on the light, stared at the chessboard again. He had been thinking about the best move for problem seventy-two in the Hort and Jansa. After so much practice, he was able to work out problems without seeing the board. He pictured it in his mind and went through the permutations on a mental board. In problem seventy-two, he was white and it was white to move. He thought he had a decisive advantage, despite having no queen. He thought: I should take his knight in exchange for my rook. That forces him to let me in. He picked up his rook and removed the black knight.

It was nine-twenty. In a minute or two, when the news was finished, Don would come in to see him. It was part of his routine now. He would come in, take a seat, they would play absent-mindedly while Don talked about his day. They had developed a way of chatting for hours without saying anything a long time ago. On Don's side, it had always been difficult for him to talk to his children, even to tell them he loved them. With Michael it was a remainder of childhood. Now, the situation was intensified by the shared pain. They exchanged only words, without meaning.

But there would soon be things to say. Michael knew that. Soon enough.

'What do we do, then?' Ticker said. He rammed his fist on the table. 'He's getting weaker all the time.'

They sat in a modern kitchen, pallid under the fluorescent

light. Ticker, Riley, Bryce – a thin-faced leader from the east side of the city – and Yates, the old man who had been in the business longer than anyone. They were eating fish and chips from the paper, drinking cans of Skol. A portable TV stood on the counter by the sink. A jazz programme pushed out low saxophone music.

Ticker was angry. Face twitching, he kept pouring salt on his chips, then more vinegar. The bottom of the paper was a soggy mess of vinegar and grease. The smell filled the kitchen.

'What do we do?' he said again. 'How about some suggestions round here?'

'I suggest we wait on Georgie,' Riley said.

'Agreed, sure.' Yates spoke through a mouthful of fish and crisp batter he was trying to gum. 'Forgot my teeth again. It's a hard life for a man when he takes to false dentures.'

'Get some of that glue,' Bryce muttered. He looked and talked like a knife blade.

'Glue?' Yates asked.

'You fix your teeth in with it.'

'I never knew that. I'll have to get some.'

'Jesus,' Ticker said. He opened another can of lager. It was warm and tasted of the metal.

'Ah, you've got to learn patience,' Riley said, smiling at him. 'You only get your blood pressure up worrying like that. Now look at it this way; till Georgie arrives, we can't do a thing, so we might as well relax. You can't go about humming like a dynamo all the time. Take a lesson from the old hands.' He indicated the others. 'Keep the peace.'

All the same, there was tension in the room. It was risky enough, getting together like this. Yates, who ate sloppily even for an old man, was sweating on it. Ticker knew he was a tough old sod, but even he was stirred up. Bryce, that undertaker countenance, picked over his fish as if it were rotten. He kept one eye always on the television.

'You know,' Riley said, 'I was walking down Jubilee Road this afternoon. The whole bloody street, you wouldn't believe – every window with Danny's photo in it. It made the heart glad.'

'He's a hero, all right,' Yates said, chewing hard.

'One of the best.' Bryce nodded. 'Lots of guts too. Never thought he'd decide to go on with it.'

'He wouldn't if his mind was right,' Ticker said. 'That's the problem. For God's sake, he's gone weak in the head.'

'Don't you say that,' Yates exploded, spraying shreds of fish and potato. 'A man decides to lay down his life, you don't make a joke of it . . . Weak in the head,' he repeated disgustedly.

'Danny wouldn't do it if he was in his right mind. He knows that was never the idea. You know what Fynn said: he's not making sense half the time.'

'He makes sense enough to know what he's doing,' Yates said. 'Nobody does a thing like that without knowing it.'

'Ah, shit. What do you know about it anyhow?'

Yates's yellowed eyes glittered, hard like glass.

'You young fuck. I've been through all this before. While you were still dirtying your nappies.'

'Lads, lads,' Riley said.

'You act like a big man because we let you have a gun in your pocket,' Yates went on, face turning red. 'You're an office boy, you hear me? A tea boy. You ever do a real job? If you were up to anything, you'd've been over there with young Danny, doing the real work.'

'I was a known face. They couldn't use me.'

'Ah, you're talking shit. Who brought this puppy along?'

'Lads,' Riley said. He touched Ticker's shoulder. 'Solidarity, remember?'

Ticker screwed up his chip paper and threw it away.

The jazz programme on the TV finished. A short film on Iceland replaced it. Then, as Bryce reached to switch it over, Parker walked in.

He nodded to the older men, cleared a space at the table and sat down. He pointed at the cans of lager. Ticker opened one and handed it to him. He drank half the can at a pull. He was withdrawn and tense.

'Did you see 'em?' Ticker asked.

'I saw them.'

'Well, what'd they say?'

Parker hawked a mouthful of phlegm and spat in a chip paper. 'Seems they want my fucking brother for a martyr.'

There was a disturbance round the table. Ticker recovered first. 'They don't mean it?'

'They do.'

'But, Christ, the government's not given in to a single demand. We've won nothing.'

'Which is why,' Yates said, 'if it doesn't go on to the end, it weakens us. Is that right, Georgie?'

'The general opinion is that it would suit the circumstances better.' Parker repeated words someone else had used.

'A martyr's only a martyr if he takes it all the way,' Yates said.

'Is that supposed to be funny?' Ticker said.

'Just stating a fact, boy. If Danny gives it up now, if we tell him to stop it, with no concessions made, we'll be the losers. If he takes it right to the end, though . . .'

'The end is dying,' Ticker said.

'He knows that,' Bryce spoke up. 'He's a good lad, and he knows what the cause needs most.'

'I think perhaps we're letting natural enthusiasm get the better of us here,' Riley said. He pressed his hands together as if in prayer. 'I mean, it's always easy to see another man make the supreme sacrifice. I wonder how we'd all feel if it was our brother they had locked up over there.'

'My brother, Tommy, was a hunger striker back in twenty-two,' Yates said.

'Did he die?'

'No – but he was ready to.'

'Like shit,' Ticker said.

Bryce looked at Parker. 'Georgie, it's your brother they've got. What d'you say?'

Parker hit the side of his can with his thumbnail. A persistent, pinging sound.

'It's my decision,' he said slowly, 'but I'm taking the votes on it. Nobody'll say Danny was stopped from doing what he believed in because he's my brother. No way. Like you once said, Yates, we're all foot soldiers when it comes down to it. No one's exempt.'

'Good boy,' Yates said. His smile was toothless, pink-rimmed.

'The man's delirious from starvation,' Ticker cried. 'He's not thinking straight, and you bunch of animals take the advantage. Georgie, they're going to kill your brother.'

'Shut up,' Parker said. 'The only ones who'll kill him are those that put him inside. The one who identified him, the coppers, the

100

judges – all of them. They're the ones we're fighting, and don't you forget it.'

There was a short time of quiet. The television blared pictures and sounds of Iceland. Mud pits and volcanic steam.

Then Parker said: 'So tell me what you think.' He glanced round the table at the men.

Yates, being oldest, had first say. 'Georgie, I hope to the Lord you'll forgive me, but I say yes.'

Bryce's thin lips. A single word: 'Yes.'

Ticker's eyes, one beginning to twitch wildly. 'No, no, no.'

Riley, shoulders shrugging. 'Yes.'

Parker ran a hand through his hair.

'All right, then. All right.'

Danny's worst times were the nights. He knew he was supposed to sleep, but sleep came hard. Too often, the dark was filled with dream shapes and faces. He would roll on the surface of sleep as if it was the sea and he was tied down in a boat so he could not dive in. The nights were white: not in any way that he could see, but in his head. They were white and hard and cold. They whined and spun through him. He heard waves breaking around the boat – white waves on a dark ocean of sleep – and could not reach the water.

It was at night that the pangs came. They woke him with furious gnawing in his belly. Times like those, he wanted to think of food. So he thought of it – egg and bacon with piles of bread and butter and a steaming mug of tea. The image would grow, the smell would start. He would convulse weakly and try to throw up, but nothing would come. He had not eaten for a long time (it was thirty-one days, but he did not know that).

During the day, when he was not dozing, it was less hard to do. A sense of peace came over him when there were daylight and people around. Then he remembered why he was doing it: because it was easy to do, and would be very useful; because people would love him and God would love him. The way they all loved Georgie.

He was sure that this would cause a revolution. People would not sit still and let him go unavenged. They would go on the streets back home, they would fight like they were supposed to fight. They would realise their cause again, and go out to prove it.

Sometimes, he thought he was there with them, like when he was a kid. Out on the streets, using every rock and brick and table leg as a weapon, any dustbin lid as a shield. Dodging those rubber bullets. The smell of petrol in the bottle as you lit the rag, then being scared to death that it would go off in your hand before you could throw it. And the feathery wash of fire as it hit a wall, splashing orange-yellow in the darkness with a low 'whoof' of sound. The reek of petrol.

His sense of smell was the worst. Everything was so acute. The stink of the hospital cleaning fluids, the sharp odour of sweat from some of the doctors. The musty smell of the priest's robes.

They had given him a real priest, like back home. Robes and a cross, and a black Bible in his brown, hairy hands. A face like earthenware pottery. He spoke in a soft voice, and Danny did not mind because, even when the priest repeated his attempts to stop Danny from going on with it, his voice was comforting.

He raised his hand – thought he did; it was less than a fluttering of the muscles. He asked the guard for a little water. The guard did not know if this was allowed. He told another one to go and find a doctor. The doctor, the bald one with a beard, came in. As they gave him a few sips of the water, the doctor said: 'Mr Parker, your family will be coming in soon.'

Danny blinked at him. 'Georgie?'

'Your mother and sister.'

Danny began to choke on the water. His stomach twisted in a tight knot. A little of the water dribbled from his lips. The doctor wiped it away, and Danny smiled at him.

'How long d'you reckon?' he whispered.

'You're using the king's bishop's gambit,' Don said.

'How did you know?' Michael took Don's pawn.

'Haven't forgotten everything, you know. That's pretty old stuff.'

'Still works though.'

Don thought about the next move. He took a mouthful of the whiskey and soda he always drank late in the evening. 'I think that boy's going to die.'

'Boy?'

'The one who killed your sister.'

Michael almost said, 'And Laura,' but he never spoke of those things.

'He's nearly blind, the news said. Soon be too late to change his mind.' Don moved queen to rook five. 'Good riddance, anyway.'

'How was business today?'

'You know, they picked up another one.'

'How was business today?'

'They think he had something to do with it, anyway. Didn't catch him here, though.'

'Stop it.'

'I'll stop it.'

Michael played a bad move.

'Concentration slipping?' Don said.

Michael looked at him. 'What's wrong?'

'Nothing. Oh, nothing at all. I'm just waiting for you to start saying your piece.'

The clock in the hall struck ten.

'There *is* something I have to tell you,' Michael said.

'Like you resigned from your job?' Don asked. 'Or that you gave up the lease on the flat? Which first?'

'Don't push me. I'll explain if you give me a chance.'

'It should be interesting.'

'Please . . .'

Don stood up suddenly. 'What is it I'm supposed to hear? Your mother and I, we've tried to help you through all this, even though we were hurt too. We've tried to be here when you needed us, and be some kind of support. But all the time, you've hidden yourself away and sneaked behind us as if we were too damn stupid to understand anything. You know how I found out about the job and the flat? I had lunch with Ralph and forced him to tell me.'

'You could've asked me.'

'I shouldn't have to. You're my son, aren't you? You should've told me.'

'I – I couldn't.' Michael was still cool outside. But his control was breaking down.

'You couldn't? Look, son, it's been six months and more. You've got to start coming to terms with it. People lose people all the time, but they don't crawl into a hole and hide for the rest of their lives. Not people your age. You don't even try.'

'It's not for ever,' Michael said. 'I just want time. That's why I'm going away.'

'Where to?'

Michael told him where.

'What for? What the hell are you going to do out there?'

'Live,' Michael said.

Don snorted. 'You could've been doing that here, all through this six months. You could've been learning how to pick up the threads. Even your mother's starting to do that now, and I never saw her more hurt than she was when . . . when it happened. The world isn't going to stop and wait while you bury your head in the sand. It's not like that. You can't crawl away under a stone and pretend nothing's happening.'

'I don't want it. It's—'

'You don't have to want it. You've got it. We all have. We're stuck with this whole mess. The only way to make it better is to go out kicking. Nobody who ever got sent away for murdering people got caught by the rest of us saying, "Ignore him and he'll go away." '

Shaking now. 'Would you let me—'

'You can't do it, son. Give up your job, cancel a lease, go somewhere where nothing reminds you of what you lost; it won't work. It's a dream for kids . . . only happens in films. You can't beat the bastards by pretending they don't exist. Ever since you were a kid, you wanted life to be a romance – you've never taken a hold on it. Never learned that you have to get out among the bastards and find out how to do it, then start doing it better than them. You've got to face up and fight, not lie around moping because they hurt you and killed some girl you were fond—'

'That's enough!' The rage burst out of him and splattered his father's face. Don stopped dead, shocked.

Michael drew a breath, tried to control his shaking. 'You . . . ' he began, then started again. 'You never call her "some girl". Understand? She wasn't "some girl", not ever.' He wiped tears from his face. 'I don't want to talk about this, not any of it. But there's one thing you should hear, because you don't understand at all.

'You say I'm not facing up to things. You talk about standing

104

up and fighting for myself. Well, you listen. Six months back, I was just rolling along, nice and peaceful. Money in the bank, saving to buy a house and get married to a beautiful girl who loved me, good job – something I liked doing and was good at. I never saw a violent crime, except on TV. I never even had a serious fight at school. I was brought up here, believing life was really nice, you know? Despite you being a cynic, and everyone else saying, "Life's shitty", I never really got over the suspicion that it's a pretty good thing.

'And then, somebody blew Laura and Jilly to pieces, and they put me in hospital. They killed two people I loved, and knocked my head around, and gave me a limp I'll never get rid of. They smash hundreds of people, they take away what you love – and you never did a thing to them. You just happened to be the one passing by.

'You say, face up and fight. But I don't know who they are, and they've already taken all that away from me, made the rest of it sour. They nearly killed me, and you say get out there and take some more. Well, I'll tell you something – I'm scared to death. I don't want to see them or know them . . . ' He broke off, the tears swelled in his eyes again. He shook his head, trying to get the words out. 'I'm scared . . . All right? . . . '

'Danny?'

'Ma?'

'Danny, oh Lord.' Sound of crying. The sensation of his mother's crying vibrating the bed.

He said: 'Let's have your hand.'

She was a little deaf, and his voice was like paper. 'What? What is it?'

He found her hand, clasped it weakly.

'How are you?'

She coughed, mopping tears with her handkerchief. 'I'm fine, Danny. We're all fine. Even your brother. He's well.'

'Georgie's here? About time. I've got to talk to him, see. Things he should know.'

'Don't talk,' Fynn said. 'Georgie's not here. He's away at home, but he's thinking of you all the time. They all are.'

'With pictures and flags?'

'With flags and banners and marches. Everyone's thinking of

you.'

'Shouting my name in the streets, are they?'

'Everywhere,' Fynn said.

'Georgie, you know this'll work.'

'It's Fynn, Danny.'

'You know this'll be good for the cause, right?'

'It's wonderful,' he said.

'Danny, do you feel all right?' This was his sister. She was close by him.

He smiled. 'Fine. Sort of warm all over, not cold like before. Come closer up. I can't see you.'

'I'm here.'

'I can't see so well now. That's the worst. I was reading *Das Kapital*, but now I don't read it any more. Maybe you could read it to me . . . Is Georgie coming in?'

'Maybe later,' Ma said.

'Good, there's some things he should know.'

'Don't tire yourself,' Fynn said.

'Who's tired? I just want to talk to Georgie for a while.'

He could still see a little. The room was dark, only a directional lamp turned to the wall. There were vague shapes, as if these people had turned to shadows. He did not know which was which, since their voices did not come from any particular place. They were hollow in his ears, fading in and out like a badly tuned radio. And Georgie came back and forth in the room. Sometimes, Danny knew he was not there, other times he wondered when he could come back.

He blinked. It was painful to do. He was in that house, watching Barlow firing off shots all around as men came crashing through the windows. Three men were firing as they swung in. One of them screamed, dropped, a mist of blood exploding from his thigh. Then he heard noises upstairs. He turned, cowering down, lifting the gun, yelling at Barlow. Barlow kept saying, 'Oh Jesus, oh Jesus,' fast and sharp, and the gun blasted in his hand, hitting at Danny's ears like a hammer. He looked up, heard Barlow grunt and his legs kick against the wall. Then something warm and wet dropped on his hand. He stared at it; greyish-white piece of meat, flecked and smeared with blood. Deafened by the gunfire, he turned, saw Barlow's fingers scrabbling at a ragged hole in his head. He saw the brains dripping out, and

106

Barlow's eyes turning up while his mouth foamed, opening and closing like a fish. He saw Barlow's fall, slow and loose down the stairs. Blood was everywhere.

'Danny?' Ma said. 'Danny, are you all right?'

He stirred, groaned. You had to lean close now to hear what he said.

'He's going to be proud of me, Ma.'

'Son, stop it. Stop it before it's too late.'

He heard Fynn hiss at her, saying: 'Leave it now,' but she cried:

'Please, don't do it. Don't.

Danny's hand fell away from hers. A bundle of sticks. 'He's going to be so proud of me.'

The news was given out on the radio at four o'clock on the morning of Wednesday the nineteenth of August. Danny Parker had slipped into a coma two days previously, and died at two-thirty a.m. He had taken final confession and been given the last rites. Not even a plea from the Roman Catholic Archbishop of England had stopped him. He faded into the darkness and died. It took less than thirty-five days, and afterwards there was no revolution.

Don and Audrey sat stone-faced by the radio later that morning, listening to a full report. The coffee and toast went cold on the table. Ralph saw the headline while he shaved, watching *Good Morning, Britain*. He turned to Diane and said: 'Rejoice, sweetheart. That's one less thug to worry about.' Doctor Ellis saw it on the front page of the *Standard* as she went home in the afternoon.

Michael did not hear about it for several days, when he was shopping for equipment in town, but he had known too. His mother's face told it, Ralph's voice told it on the telephone.

He passed by the television shop with its rank of sets showing the Ceefax headlines, and he thought: It's finished. All finished and done with.

But that was not true.

Parker raised his head at the opening of the door. He watched Ticker as he ushered the man in the parka across the threshold. The single forty-watt bulb cast a sick yellow light on the room.

The man's face was shadowed under the hood.

'Sit down,' Parker said. His eyes showed the strain. They were shot with blood, blue patches smudged under them. He looked older and tired.

The man sat down. Parker waved Ticker away. The door closed, and the man pulled the hood back.

'All right, Temple,' Parker said. 'You've heard what's happened?'

Temple nodded. No words of sorrow or comfort.

'It started off as a way to force their hand,' Parker said. 'Just a stunt, you know. That's what I thought, anyway. But you know Danny. You were with him back there. Maybe you didn't think much of him, maybe he was a stupid little bastard, but he had some guts.'

Temple nodded again.

'He got it into his head to go the whole way,' Parker said. 'He knew it was better for the cause that way. Maybe he was delirious at the end, I don't know, but his heart was in the right place. We could've stopped it, you know? One word to Fynn, he'd have told Ma to let the doctors at him. As it is, I think Ma'll hate me for the rest of her days for letting it go on . . . But that's beside the point.' He took out a pack of cigarettes, lit one, passed the pack to Temple. Temple shook his head.

'The point is,' Parker said, 'the rest of the committee on this thing talked it out and decided to let him go on, and I couldn't interfere. If it was another man's brother, I'd have voted for it to go on – I couldn't change that because it was Danny.'

Temple watched Parker's face working for a moment to stop emotion showing. He thought about the boys who were gathered in the next room for a meeting. Nine months back, you wouldn't have had a good word for Danny Parker from the lot of them. Now they were wearing the black armband and talking about him as if he were the next saint. In Temple's opinion, which he would never speak, the only useful thing Danny ever did was starve himself to death.

Parker straightened, coughing on the grey cigarette smoke.

'The decision was made,' he said, 'and that's all. Danny died a hero, and he won't be forgotten. They'll be marching for him like they marched for Bobby. He's safe now – he's not our business

108

any more. But the bastard who put him away, he's our business all right. He's the one we deal with.' He paused, his voice drained and cold. He reached into his pocket, took out a piece of paper torn from a notebook. 'I hoped we'd not be needing this, thought it wouldn't go this far. But this one, this one killed Danny as sure as if he'd been the copper, or the judge, or the warder.'

He put the paper on the table between them. Temple picked it up. He glanced at the name and address written there, then he screwed it up and threw it back on the table.

'What do you want?' he asked.

Parker said: 'Give him justice. He's guilty of killing Danny. Give him the justice he deserves.'

'Is this purely personal?'

'It is not.'

Like hell, Temple thought.

'He murdered one of our men. And he saw you,' Parker said. 'He might just remember that some day soon. We can't take the risk. *You* can't.'

Temple stood up. He opened the door, then Parker said:

'And Temple . . . '

'What?'

'Make it hard on him. Slow.'

Temple pulled his hood up. He watched as Parker's head sank again, then he stepped out, closing the door quietly behind him.

PART THREE

Trees and Water

23

It was five past three on a warm late-August day when Michael arrived at Oak Farm. He came limping out of the forest along an old cart track. Pug was beside him, nearly two-thirds grown now – a solid, easy-going animal, happy to be off the lead.

Michael wore an old Barbour shooting jacket which used to be Don's; brown cord trousers, pale and worn at the knees; a pair of scuffed Adidas running shoes; and his father's old fishing hat. He carried a heavy canvas rucksack, stuffed to bursting; an army-issue sleeping bag, rolled and strapped beneath with a thin roll of foam rubber; a bag with his fishing gear in it; and a BSA .22 air rifle.

He walked out of the trees and went a hundred and fifty yards along the track as it descended into a shallow depression. Coming to a turning off the main track, he eased down on the overgrown verge and took out a map.

Behind him, and to the left of the way he had come, the forest stretched over rolling country, a dense mass of firs and pines. To the right the fields rose up to an outcrop of oaks. The light breeze scudded clouds across a pale blue sky. The scent of the pines was keen. He took his hat off, wiped his face with it, then checked the map.

He and the dog had come up alone, though both Don and Ralph wanted to drive them. They had taken an early train to London, Pug whining in the guard's van, passed through Waterloo station, Michael sweating at the sight of the recon-structed bench seats. They took a taxi to Liverpool Street and boarded a train to Ely. At Ely, they changed for Norwich. They got off the rattling local train at a small stop called Borden. Then they walked the rest. Eight miles. Although he had been practising for it, Michael was exhausted when he came to sit down. His leg ached, the new skin on his back itched so that he wanted to scratch it all off. Doctor Ellis had not approved of his going away; she and the surgeons said the grafts needed more time and attention, but he told them that he could not wait any longer. He had said goodbye to his parents at breakfast that morning, knowing they did not want him to do it. But he had to do it, because nothing was worth a damn the way it was. So, he kissed them goodbye, ignoring the look in Don's eyes, and he left them. The surgeons had prescribed some pain-killers in case he needed them, but he wanted to do without drugs.

Snouting in the grass, Pug disturbed a bird. It sailed up and over Michael. He watched its flight into the forest, trying to remember what it was. Greenish breast, brown back. A crossbill, wasn't it? Once, as a kid, he knew things like that: names of birds and trees, the plants that grew in the verge beside him. He wanted to remember them again. Whatever he could eat, he would eat, and anything useful, he would use. He had a little money on him to buy supplies in the nearest village. The rest was in a post office bank account. Everything he had left when all the dust was settled.

He leaned over, wincing at the pain from his back, and picked up a stone. It was rounded, about two and a half inches across. He turned it over, brushing the dust off. It was mostly greyish-black, but a band of sandy colour ran through the centre, casting threads out into the grey. What sort of stone was it? He put it in his pocket.

The oaks were at the top of the rise half a mile away. Their leaves were olive green after the hot summer which Michael had missed. They were unusual because they had grown to a good size. In the chalky soil of East Anglia, oaks do not usually grow above forty feet. These were almost full-size. Between them and the lane was a meadow, a wide expanse of rough grass, dotted with some stunted yews and bushes. To the left, horse chestnuts and sycamores formed a wall against the rest of the countryside.

Michael looked at the map. He saw the red cross Ralph had marked for him, and knew that the farm lay within the oaks. He picked up the fishing gear and stood. He adjusted the rucksack straps over his shoulders, bent his knee several times to ease the leg, and started for the oaks. At the entrance to the meadow, he saw a rotted five-bar gate lying in the undergrowth, and beside it in a tangle of elder branches, an old letter box. In peeling red paint on a once white surface was the name, 'Oak Farm'. He picked the box up carefully and leaned it on its post against the elder. It was not a thing he would need – any letters would be care of the post office in Middlecott – but he smiled at having the box stand there. He left it, and started the walk over the fields.

He could not see the farmhouse until he was among the trees. He walked in under the heavy green shade of the oaks; then it was ahead, as if it had always been there and the trees had grown up around it. Michael knew from Ralph that it was built only in the eighteen-sixties, but not of the local chalk and flint. It was red brick, roofed with black slate; a square, ugly house, as plain as a child's drawing. Only a small porch, which was the front door, disturbed the simplicity. It stood in a wide clearing among the trees, and parts of a rusty fence remained round what was left of the garden. He paused at the gate, looking at the thicket of grass, cow parsley and blackberry bushes. The front of the house had two windows on the ground floor and two above. All were smashed. The roof overhung the windows slightly.

He walked round the house. There were outbuildings at the back, two sheds with caved-in roofs and doors hanging off the hinges. The back door was in pieces on the ground. The house never had electricity or running water. He found a well, boarded over with decaying planks. It took a few minutes to uncover it, then he leaned over the crumbling wall and stared down into the dark.

The frame of an old bicycle rested against the shed, black paint scaled with rust. Blackberry vines twined through it.

He took off the gun and rucksack, removed the shooting jacket and folded it neatly over the bicycle frame. He stretched his arms up slowly, breathing the clean air. It smelled a little of the house, a dusty brick smell.

The house was built solid. Its framework was sound, only the windows and the back door were broken in. He unbuckled a pocket of the rucksack and took out a small torch, then went into the house by the back door. The floor, tiled with red stone, was covered with earth. Tendrils of the plants outside curled over what was once the kitchen like electric cables. Rusting tin cans and brown newspapers lay in the corners. An old stone sink under the window was scattered with cigarette ends and dead leaves. A check cap, sodden and matted with age, hung over the windowsill.

He went through the door into what would have been the living room. The ceiling bulged like a storm cloud; there were shreds of some floral wallpaper still clinging here and there, and a damp patch over the fireplace where a mirror once hung. In the cold grate were the remains of several makeshift fires.

He kicked a mound of rubbish aside to open the door to the hall. This was different; he needed the keys which Ralph had given him. The hall was closed off on all three sides. The porch door was locked, as was the entrance to a smaller room which would have been 'for best'. The wallpaper was still up, there was a scrap of linoleum all but trodden into the floor. The only light came from a panel above the porch door. He shone his torch up the narrow stairway. A shaft of sunlight showed at the top. It looked undamaged, but he could not tell how strong it was. He tested the first step. It held, so he grasped the banister rail screwed into the wall and slowly went up. Several steps creaked, but none gave way. He pulled himself up to the landing.

The layout upstairs was the same as below – except it was cleaner and better repaired. Off the landing on the right was a small spare room, on the left, a larger one. He crossed it and looked into the master bedroom, which ran the width of the house at the front. Here the floor sagged dangerously. He did not try to walk through. He closed the door and checked out the second room. It had two windows, one on each outside wall. The frames were intact although the glass was gone. He undid the latches and leaned out. He was looking down on the path he had come up. Through a gap in the oaks, he saw part of the path down to the cart track, the letter box under the elder tree. Over that, further away, was the forest. It stretched miles in that direction, to the river where he intended fishing and swimming later on.

The house was built facing south. To the east, the oaks mixed with other trees and eventually merged into Forestry Commission land. The place was almost surrounded by the forest.

He walked around the room, covering each part of the

floorboards, making sure the walls and ceiling were sound. The walls had been painted plain white some time before. They were yellowed now. The floor was fairly clean. He decided this was the room he would use. It was safe, and more roomy than the one on the other side of the landing. It had a fireplace he thought he could use if the chimney was not blocked, and it had a good view of anyone coming up from the track.

He went downstairs and unlocked the porch door. There were some planks nailing the front door shut which he had to prise free with the Lynx knife he had been given on his tenth birthday. He let air into the porch. It was the only part of the house which seemed to suffer from damp, except the master bedroom. He figured on using the porch and second bedroom, the spare room for a store, and the downstairs room for keeping any game or fowl that needed hanging for flavour.

He went back to the garden and picked up the rucksack, hefted it with him to a shady spot under the trees. He sat down with his back against a curved trunk and undid the buckles on the top flap of the sack. Smelling the food, Pug bounded over and stuck his nose in. Michael delved inside and found the sandwiches Audrey had made him, also the beer.

'Food,' he said, and realised it was the first time he had spoken since getting on the train at Liverpool Street. His voice was loud in the quiet. He set down a Tupperware bowl of pig's melts for the dog and began to eat.

In a minute, he thought, tearing into the sandwiches, I'll find a note, like Linus in 'Peanuts'. He sprang the top off the beer and swigged a mouthful. It was warm but it took the dust off the back of his throat. His fingers reached inside the sack again, touched paper. He took the envelope out. It was from his mother. He opened it and read the note inside.

Michael,
Please look after yourself while you're away. After all – old cliché coming up – you're our only child now. I don't ask you to keep in touch all the time, but it would be good to know that you're safely there.

Try to understand how your father feels. All the time I've known him, he's been a fighter – it used to worry him so

114

much that you didn't seem ambitious. Now he thinks you're trying to bury your head in the sand, and he's anxious about your future. He hasn't really recovered from losing Jilly, you see – he does a very good job of seeming to so that he can support me. But, in truth, he hasn't really accepted it yet. So he puts a lot of his sadness into working hard and worrying for you.

Don't think he's angry with you. He's not. In a way, I think he still feels responsible for you, even though you're twenty-seven. He wishes you were still a child so that he could tell you what you should do and look out for you. It's been very difficult for him.

Anyway, try to call or send a card occasionally, otherwise we'll be on the phone to Ralph, sending out search parties and all that.

Look after yourself (again),
Love,
Audrey.

He closed his eyes. A hot wire burned through from his eyes to his brain. He folded the letter and put it back in the rucksack, then he took another drink of beer and settled back to sleep for a while.

24

The following day he woke at dawn, took the gun from its place in the corner and went downstairs. He limped across the dewy grass with Pug. Out on the meadow, he stood with the sun behind him. The forest below was rusty in the light, the yews and sycamores in the meadow looked bigger against the pale pink sky. He brought Pug to heel and, in quick succession, shot two of the rabbits who were swarming over the grass.

'We'll make you a gundog later,' he told Pug, as he went to pick them up.

He reckoned the meadow would give him plenty of meat, as long as he did not overdo things and frighten the rabbit population away. Then there were pigeons and other birds. He reckoned on three pigeons a day for the right protein – more to feed Pug – and it would be fun trying to get them with that gun and with his scruple about clean kills.

He took the rabbits back to the house and hung them in the small room downstairs. He drank a little water from the five-litre plastic container he had with him, then took up the rucksack – now empty and light. He went out over the meadow to the gateway, turned right along the cart track and began to walk to Middlecott.

The village was small. Houses, shops and a chapel straggled for a quarter-mile along the main street. He walked up to the war memorial outside the church as the clock struck eight. A tractor roared by on its way to work. He put Pug on the lead, tethered him to the memorial's iron railing and crossed the street to the village stores. There he bought some food and supplies to carry him through until he discovered more sources in the woods. The little woman behind the counter stared at him as she got the goods together, not hostile, but itching to ask questions. He went out, untethered Pug and walked back the way he had come. Freed again from the lead, Pug rushed ahead, investigating everything. Michael swung the choke chain in his hand, wrapping it hard around fence posts along the roadside.

When he arrived back at the house, the weather was on the change. Grey smudges of cloud gathered to the south-west. The air was still and flies swarmed. He pushed open the porch door and went inside. Pug leapt past him up to the bedroom. So the stairs were safe enough. He dropped the rucksack by the door and knelt down. The twingeing pain in his leg reminded him that it would be a good idea to rig up some kind of chair.

In a corner of the bedroom was a small built-in cupboard. He had lined it with some plastic sheeting he had brought along, and all the food and eating utensils were to go in there, along with slugs for the rifle. His only real concession to old habits was a large tin of ground coffee and a packet of dried milk. Somehow, he could not give up the morning cup. It could have been worse, he thought. What if I smoked?

He took another cupful of water from the container and sat down on his sleeping bag to think about priorities. This was also something he learned as a kid, when Don still had time for

116

weekends away. He detailed the essentials in order:

Shelter, which he already had; fuel; fire; food; water.

The fuel was all around him in the woods and forest. Fire was provided for: he would use the matches sparingly, relying on striking sparks off the lighter flints with his knife. He could make some tinder later on. Food – he already had two rabbits. Water? He planned to check the well, then look around. If all else failed, he could visit the village churchyard every couple of days and use the tap there.

He had few luxuries. *The Observer's Book of Wild Flowers*, to identify edible plants if he was in doubt; and the wooden-boxed travelling chess set. He thought that working out problems he had memorised from *The Best Move* would occupy him if he got bored. Also, when he unpacked the night before, he found one of his parents had put in a six-by-four sketch block and two Berol 1B pencils. He guessed Don had done it. He was the one who was always at him to start drawing again.

'Listen, you,' he said to Pug. 'From tomorrow, we're going to make you a gundog, right?' Pug beat his tail against the wall and waited for Michael to move. Michael put out his hand. The dog came close and began to mouth his fingers. His teeth never hurt or broke skin. 'Shall we go hunting?' Michael asked. 'For wood, that is?'

The dog looked happy either way. So they went out to collect firewood.

As the warmth of the afternoon waned, he went with Pug across the fields again. He crossed the cart track and went into the forest to the south-west. It was easy walking because most of the forest was planted in large squares with pathways running between. As he went, he found plenty of stinging nettles – he had never eaten them, but Don said they made a soup like spinach. Wild parsnip grew all over the place around the fields, also sow thistle and dandelion. The ground under the trees was layered with fallen pine cones which would burn sweetly.

After three miles or more, the forest ended. Michael was on a slight rise, looking down on an expanse of rough gold stubble. The harvests were mostly in, and, sooner or later, someone would burn off the stubble. The river was at the end of the field.

He let Pug go ahead as he strolled down. He saw that the river flowed out of the forest to the north in a wide curve, then wound off over the countryside. It was cool and green, slow-flowing in the dull afternoon light. There would be plenty of watercress in the shallows, and it looked clean and safe. He wandered along the edge until he found a sandbank where he could wade in. He would wash here in the mornings, because he did not want solitude to make him filthy. Pug went past him and splashed in with all four paws. Big drops of water glittered like shot glass. Michael noticed the deep water out in the middle, wondering what fish he could catch. He filled the container, then took off shoes and socks to cool his feet. He sat with the dripping Pug, watching the water's changing face.

Later, he reached home with pockets full of pine cones and some chickweed he had found on the way back. The early evening was so pleasant that he built his fire in the garden in front of the house. He cleared a flat space and got it going with twigs and pine cones, adding branches as it caught. He set some of the water to boil in a billycan – it would need boiling three times before he drank it. Then he fetched the rabbits and set to work skinning them. There were no signs of myxomatosis round the eyes. Both were big specimens, almost three pounds each. He cut the feet off above the knees and lay each rabbit on its back, tail towards him. Pug hovered nearby, drooling frantically. Michael grinned at him and used the knife to cut into the first rabbit's belly. He pulled the skin away from the thighs, towards the tail, turned it round, cut over the head and pulled the rest of the skin away from the body and legs. He sliced through the stomach, removed the guts, thought about saving them for fishing, then threw them to Pug. He repeated the operation on the other rabbit, then wiped his hands on the grass. He was pleased: it was years since he was taught to do that. Now they were to be cleaned and, supposedly, soaked in cold water for a couple of hours, but he was too hungry for that. He cleaned the rabbits, jointed them and got them ready for the stewpot.

The sun dropped behind the trees. He did not know what the time was, but he thought it was around seven o'clock. By the time the stew was cooked, he would be ready for sleep.

So far, there had been very little chance to think about

118

anything except food and water. That was the way he wanted it. He made a pint of coffee from the thrice-boiled water and ate an apple as he lay on the grass. Cool air fanned his face, the fire grew brighter as day faded. Pug lay nearby, sleeping off all the exercise.

It was almost like being happy.

25

The telephone rang. Don was watching a documentary on Vietnam; he did not move. Audrey put down the book she was reading and went out to the hallway. She picked up the phone and gave the number.

A low voice said: 'Can I speak to Michael, please?'

'Is that you, Ralph?'

'No,' the voice said.

Audrey frowned. She did not recognise the voice. 'What's the problem?'

'No problem,' the voice said. ' . . . I was working with Mike before he left the company.'

'Really? Which campaign was that? The Bergon thing?'

'That's it. I wanted to ask him about a couple of points.'

'Well, I'm sorry,' Audrey said. 'Michael's not home at the moment.'

'Oh well, I'll speak to him later, maybe.'

'No, you don't understand. He's gone away. Been gone for over a week now.'

There was a pause on the other end. Then the voice said: 'Could you tell me where? I really would like to get in touch with him.'

'I'm sorry. He's asked us not to tell anyone. Sounds silly, but he wants to be out of touch.'

'Could you not tell me?' the voice cajoled.

'Not even if it were a matter of national security.' Audrey smiled. 'He'd kill me. If you like, I could write to him and ask—' She stopped, stared at the phone as if it had bitten her.

'Rude little devil,' she muttered, sitting down again in the living room.

'What?' Don asked, eyes never leaving the screen.

'One of Michael's friends,' she said. 'Just slammed the phone down on me because I wouldn't give him Michael's address.'

In a telephone box at the bottom of Guildford High Street, Temple replaced the receiver and swore under his breath. He stood tapping a coin against the glass while he wondered who to call next. There was no one, not at this time of night.

He opened the door and stepped out. Seven months had changed him: some of the changes were time's, others he had engineered for the purpose of coming back to England. His hair, which had been short and blond, was now brown and several inches longer than before. He had been clean-shaven, now there was a moustache. He never wore glasses normally, but he wore them now. They made his eyes seem larger, changed his face. The scar on his chin remained. During his enforced confinement he had gained a few pounds, despite exercising every day. During the London job, he wore jeans and sweatshirts most of the time. He wore a suit now.

Even his name was different. He was not Temple; he was Lawrence Jackson, a commercial traveller selling the products of Kurthaus, a German manufacturer of household electrical appliances. It had taken the best part of six days to get passport, driving licence and other paperwork which proved this. Meanwhile, Temple had been selecting the tools for the job. He chose, among other things, a 7.62 Lee Enfield sniper rifle, as used by the British police. He took great care over the car and all the trappings of his identity, wanting nothing to be out of place with Lawrence Jackson. He obtained a year-old Renault Nine, and had the engine tuned by a firm who always did such work for him. His clothes were bought in the town of Slough, where Lawrence Jackson's passport said he lived. He had sheaves of information in the back seat of the car concerning the products of Kurthaus, and a number of their smaller appliances. He also researched the company well enough to pass if questioned. He knew how many speeds the Kurthaus Kitchen Blender was capable of; he could tell anyone who asked why the Kurthaus Four-Slice Toaster had won design awards across Europe. He

120

could have given directions around Slough too, if anyone cared to know – though it was doubtful anyone would, from what he had heard of the place.

All this preparation was necessary, because Temple was a professional. And on this job, he was not looking out for somebody's idiot younger brother. He was working alone, and he never left any of his work to chance when he was alone.

To complete the preliminaries, he took a ferry from Rosslare to Le Havre. From there he drove on down the Seine to Paris. He spent a couple of days there, being a tourist. He sat in the late summer sunshine at a bar along the Rue de Rivoli, and went to Galignani, the English bookshop, to buy the third volume of *A Man Without Qualities*. On his last night, he dined at a restaurant in the Place du Tertre. The food and wine were not bad. After Paris, he drove down to Lyons. He stayed in small, family *pensions*, travelling slowly. From Lyons he tracked back up to Orléans and Alençon, finally reaching Cherbourg on Friday the twenty-eighth of August. By Saturday he was in England. The customs never bothered him, since the equipment he had ordered was already in the country. He travelled to Bristol to collect it. On Monday he was in Guildford, watching the address Parker had given him.

After a day or so, he figured either Michael Sayers was away, or he stayed indoors all the time. That was when he decided to try a telephone call.

Now he knew the target was not there. This was a pity, because he had hoped for a quick, easy kill. Also, he was not too clear on what Sayers looked like, having seen him only for twenty seconds eight months ago.

He went back to the boarding house up by the castle and got into bed, thinking over the next move. He was a lone agent, authorised to do whatever was necessary to find and deal with Sayers. Those were Parker's orders.

He clicked off the light and turned over, thinking.

26

One afternoon, being at a loose end, Michael set up some tin cans on the wall of the well and took target practice on them.

He had been living alone at the house for more than a week, and his mind was steadier than it had been for a long time. The days went by quickly with all he had to do just to live and eat. He knew now where the plants grew, and had come upon fruit trees here and there, so he was eating unripe cooking apples that were sharp as ice on the tongue. Every morning he rose as the sun came over the forest, ate whatever was for breakfast, then walked down to the river, stripped off and washed himself. He washed his clothes there too. Then he went hunting for the day's food. Sometimes it took an hour, other times – because he would not risk a chancy shot – it would be past noon before he returned to the house. He had eaten various unlikely creatures: pigeons, the occasional blackbird, one illegal pheasant was hanging in the downstairs room, and – just once – a squirrel which he knocked off the upper branches of a pine in the forest. He had been fishing too, but nothing worth cooking had come to his hook.

The afternoons had also been busy. Using a knife and bare hands, he had dug a cesspit fifty yards from the house, and a greasepit for firelighters under the kitchen window. After a noon rest, he would explore his land, running to strengthen his leg and build his fitness; train Pug; fish; play out the chess problems he remembered. He went out with the flower book to learn the names and know the differences between species. After three days he began to sketch flowers and leaves. He had not seen another human being since that day in the village.

One night a USAF Phantom jet roared over at less than a thousand feet. It scared the dog, who ran round the garden barking his head off for five minutes after. Michael watched it disappear to the east, remembering what Ralph had told him about the country. There were air force bases and army camps all over the place, even a battle area not far away. He listened until the jet's engines echoed into the peace, then turned back to what he was doing.

He missed no one, he thought. But inside, and when he slept, he missed the one person he could not have.

He shot the cans into the well and went back to the kitchen to get some more. As he came out, he heard voices. Women talking, one of them swearing. He turned, hissed at Pug to follow and headed for the porch. In a moment he was upstairs, looking out of the bedroom window for the intruders.

He ducked. Two girls on horseback came into the clearing. One – thin, dark-haired – was still cursing furiously. He listened as they came closer.

'Must be around here,' the dark one said. 'I saw smoke. Look, there's the fire.'

Michael closed his eyes, praying they would go.

'Hey,' the girl called. 'Come on out.'

He stayed where he was.

'You, whoever you are. We know you're there.'

He did not move. Then Pug leapt up to the window, barking at the strangers. Michael stood up too. He said:

'What do you want?'

'What do we want?' the dark girl said, while her red-haired friend on the bay looked embarrassed. 'We want to know who you are, for one thing, and what you're doing on this land, for another. And then, to finish off, you can explain why the bloody hell you're taking pot shots at us.'

Michael scratched his chin. His half-grown beard gave him a disreputable appearance. 'Any more questions?'

'Just one,' she snapped back. 'How would you like a visit from the police?'

He did not lose his temper. Jilly was like this girl when she was fifteen. This one was older, but more spoilt. He said: 'You know who owns this land?'

'Of course I do. Mr Bernard Wodehouse, who happens to be a friend of my father's. He's given me permission to ride through, which is more than you can say.'

123

Michael took an envelope from his pocket and tossed it down. It fell on the grass. The red-haired girl dismounted to pick it up.

'What is it, Caro?' the dark girl asked, not taking her eyes off him.

Caro coughed softly. 'It's a letter, signed by Bernard Wodehouse. It gives Mr Michael Sayers permission to live on this land until further notice.' She glanced up at Michael. 'I think that's Mr Sayers.'

The dark girl took the letter and gave it careful study. It was headed notepaper, with the Wodehouses' Suffolk address. She also knew Bernard's signature. She gave it back to Caro.

'That still doesn't explain why you were shooting at us, *Mr* Sayers.'

'It's a .22,' Michael said. 'It might have stung your horse, for which I apologise. But I doubt a twelve-bore would penetrate your hide.'

'There's no need to be so bloody rude.'

'No, you're right. Let's give it a rest.'

The dark girl coloured. 'Now listen here, you—'

'Jo, leave it,' Caro muttered.

'I will not. You come here without a word to anyone,' she said to Michael, 'then lurk about like a tramp. Well, don't think we'll stop riding across this land.'

'Just keep out of my way,' he said, trying to look calm.

'You take any more shots at me,' she said, 'and *I'll* come back with the twelve-bore.'

'I'll remember that,' he said.

Finally, the girl let Caro, who was tugging at the reins of her horse, lead her off into the trees.

Michael sank down against the wall. He was sweating.

The girls ambled through the wood. Jo fumed in silence. Caro said nothing, because she hated upsets.

They broke out of the trees. Jo spurred her mount into a gallop over the meadow, Caro following. Caro came up fast, passing her before they reached the gate. They reined in by the letter box.

'You're still better than me,' Jo said.

'You don't take it seriously,' Caro said. 'Your dad's got those lovely stables, but you don't ride enough. Only when I come to stay.'

'It was Mother's thing, really. Dad keeps the horses because they remind him of when she was here. He can't ride to save his life.'

They went along the cart track at a gentle pace.

'You shouldn't have lost your temper,' Caro said. 'It wasn't worth it.'

'You're soft,' Jo snorted. 'You'd let people walk all over. What if he'd hit one of us? What if he was some weirdo who liked shooting people?'

'Oh, honestly, Jo.'

'I just don't like men who think the whole world belongs to them.'

'He looked quite nice.'

Jo stared at her. 'Fancy a bit of rough, do we?' She grinned. 'You've been at that school too long.'

'Just because you've made extensive studies of the male population.'

'You bitch.'

'Well, some of the men you've been out with . . . '

'We're not all training to be nuns, like you.'

'Now who's the bitch?'

'Men aren't the only ones who benefit from a little experience. Although I'd draw the line at the tramp back there.'

'Oh, never mind,' Caro said.

'You're right. He's not worth worrying about. I'll just tell Bennet to look out for him on our land. He's probably a poacher.'

The forest closed around them and left the afternoon quiet.

Michael set up the chessboard and started a game against himself. Pug, dozing on the other side of the fire, opened one eye. It was liquid brown.

'You're white,' Michael said. 'Who d'you want to be? Capablanca or Alekhine?'

The dog showed no preference. Michael let him play pawn to king four.

The woods shivered in the dark. A cool gust went by, bringing a shower of rain. He sat still by the fire, knowing it would pass in a moment. The fire sizzled as it ate raindrops. He let them trickle

125

on his face, and played a dozen moves of the game.

The rain passed. He stretched out, guessing it must be nearly ten o'clock. He thought about the visitors. The red-haired girl had been quite nice. A little overweight, but better than being thin and mean like the other one. Their horses were well groomed, so were they. He threw some cedar twigs on the fire, inhaled the fragrant smoke as they burned.

He hoped they would not come back. He hoped they came from miles away and would not bother to make the ride again.

'Well, come on,' he told the dog. 'Make a move.'

27

Temple spent the morning watching the house in Guildford. He was there when Don drove off to work at eight o'clock. He was hanging around when the old woman (Michael's grandmother) came along in her Mini Metro to visit Audrey. He saw the old lady leave, then a van drive up to the house. At ten o'clock the van left. He waited for a while, listening to a Brahms concert on Radio Three. At eleven twenty-two Audrey came out of the house carrying a shopping bag. She got into her car, backed out of the drive and made off towards town. On past viewing, this was her daily tour round shops and friends. She never arrived back before half-past one.

He grabbed a briefcase from the back seat and got out. His suit was a little creased, but it would pass. He had his Kurthaus identification card with him, a briefcase full of Kurthaus promotion material. And some other items which Kurthaus did not sell.

He crossed the road, went up the driveway to the house, up the steps to the door. He rang the bell, heard it ding-dong inside. No one came. He knocked quickly, looking for movement at the windows. There was some kind of windowed attic above. What if Sayers were hiding up there, just telling everyone he had gone away to get some peace? Maybe the Sunday newspapers were after him.

When he was sure that no one was in, he moved round the back and opened the Chubb lock on the kitchen door. He went straight to the hallway and ran upstairs. He checked the attic, which was a spare bedroom, then the lower floor. The parents' room, one full of feminine junk, and then one which looked like a student's. This was Michael's, and all his remaining belongings were there.

Temple went through it, looking for clues.

When she had parked in Sainsbury's multi-storey in town, Audrey realised she had come out without her purse, cheque book or cash card. She frowned, cursed her bad memory and got back in the car. She twisted the ignition and backed out of her space.

It was not her morning.

Temple found an appointments diary. The name in the cover was Laura Allen. He checked the addresses in the back but there was nothing about Sayers. He picked up a hardback copy of King's *Pet Sematary* and read the inscription:

> To Mike,
>   This is a hint. I want a cat.
>   Love, Laura.

A Christmas present. He threw it aside, looking for something personal.

Audrey got stuck behind a Mercedes which stalled at the mini-roundabout by the Odeon. She did not hit the horn like everyone behind her. She sat and murmured to herself about how the whole world was against her this morning. The Mercedes finally started. Audrey followed it round.

Temple did not lose his temper either. He replaced everything exactly and gave up there. He went downstairs to the hall. He opened a door and found the dining room. There were pictures on the dresser in one corner. He looked them over, found a recent one of the family. There was Sayers – he recalled him now – arm round some pretty girl, and a blonde kid next to them. Temple slipped the picture in his briefcase. He went back to the hall, picked up a telephone pad and flicked through the names and numbers. There was a London number for Sayers. He scribbled it down and looked into the living room. There was a bureau in an alcove by the window. This was where Audrey kept paper, envelopes and her address book. She never locked the bureau. Temple riffled the magazines under the television, opened the top flap of the bureau. He shook his head. He reached to pull open the drawer.

Audrey pulled in at the gate. She left the car there while she stamped up to the house. She put the key in the front door. She stepped inside.

At the first footstep outside, Temple froze. He glanced at the window, saw the car below the house. He stepped back behind the living room door, setting the briefcase down. He waited, heard the key fit the lock. He reached in his pocket and took out a length of silk cord. He wound the ends around his two hands and stood, arms raised slightly in front of his body.

Audrey threw her handbag on the telephone table, trying to think where she had left her purse. Probably in the bureau. She started for the door.
  She snapped her fingers. It was on the dressing table in her bedroom. She pounded upstairs to get it.

Temple moved. He put the cord away, picked up his briefcase, and moved. No creaking floorboards, no fumbling. He got out through the open front door and walked quickly down the drive.
  When Audrey left two minutes later, he watched to make sure she suspected nothing. Then he drove out of Guildford. He had lunch at a pub in Shere, and decided he could not try the house again. It had been risky to do it in daylight at all – twice would be pushing his luck. And a night job was out; the house was wired solid.
  Sitting in the pub garden, he memorised the phone numbers and Sayer's face in the photograph. He took a moment to study the dark girl, wondering who she was, not knowing he had helped

128

to kill her. When the face and the numbers were safe in his head, he threw them away.

It was a start.

28

Yew trees are not easy to draw, not if you want them to look alive. He had sketched the same tree four times, trying to get the life into its complicated shape. Now he was going at it again, sharpening a pencil with his knife, squinting in the sunshine, filling up the hour of his afternoon rest.

He sat under the trees on the edge of the meadow. A blustery wind swept in over the forest, putting an edge on the bitter sunlight. It was a day for thunderstorms. He watched a rabbit hopping through the scrubby grass. It did not see him. Thinking of dinner, he wished he had his gun. But it was only greed; there was more than enough for the pot.

'Well, Pugnacious,' he said to the dog. 'Looks as if they've given up now.'

He was talking about the girls on horseback. For two days after the initial row they had come through the garden as before. The red-haired girl looked nervous, the dark one purposeful. He was upstairs the first time, and watched them pass without a word. The second time he was checking the well and gave them a cursory nod.

He knew roughly what time it was by the sun, and they were late.

'She's given it up,' he told Pug. 'Made her point – she's not going to be bossed by peasants. Now she can retire from the field with honour intact – and it probably is.'

Pug did not get the joke. Michael scuffed the dog's smooth head and went on with the drawing.

The girl rode out of the forest a little later. Just one alone. He could not see which at first. Then, as she turned into the gateway, he saw the thin girl's face under a pink sunhat. She let the horse amble over the field, scattering the rabbits and lapwings that rested in the long grass.

He groaned, leaned back against the tree and pulled his hat down over his eyes. He did not get up: there was a good chance she would ride straight up the path and go back through the woods. She would never be within fifty yards of him. He continued sketching the yew, staying Pug when he started to move.

The horse's hooves made a flat, soft sound in the dry grass. The girl rode past, no more than ten feet away.

'Good afternoon,' she said.

He raised his hat slowly, peeped out at her one-eyed.

'Afternoon.'

She rode on.

Next day, he found a stack of roof tiles under plastic fertiliser bags in the shed, and decided to do some repair work on the roof before the autumn rains came.

He got up there via the shed, tying himself to the chimney stack for safety. Pug ran about below, barking at him.

He was fitting the second tile when the dark girl rode up to the house. She shaded her eyes.

'Hello there.'

'Hi,' he said.

'Are you moving in for good?'

'No.'

'Well, I thought I'd tell you. I checked with Bernard, and he said you were all right.'

'Thanks very much,' he said. 'Where's your friend?'

'Oh, Caro's gone back to America. Her parents live in California now. They pretend to be natives and write diet and lifestyle books. They don't like having her around because she spoils their illusion of youth.'

He clambered up to the ridge and sat astride it.

'Did you hurt your leg?' she asked.

'Old accident.'

'You should be careful. It's a long drop if there's no one around to help.'

'Pug looks after me,' he said.

The dog trotted over and nuzzled the horse. The girl leaned

down and petted him.

'He's not pedigree, is he?'

'Only on his mother's side.'

'Do you use him as a gundog?'

'When he feels like it.'

'He looks intelligent.'

'He plays a lousy game of chess.'

She straightened. Her pointed face was pale under the sunhat. 'How long d'you think you'll be staying?'

'Why? Are you afraid I'll take another shot at you?'

She blinked. 'I was just wondering.'

'I don't know how long. It's nobody's business, anyway.'

'I only asked—'

'What is it you want?' he said.

She took a deep breath. 'For your information, Mr bloody Sayers, I came up here to apologise for the other day. I'd begun to think I was a bit hasty, but now I don't think so. Where did you get your lovely manners? Charmless school?'

He said nothing, resumed working on the roof.

Pug nosed up to her foot in the stirrup.

'Oh, get out of it, mutt,' she yelled at him, and spurred the horse out of the clearing. When she was gone, he looked up. After a moment, he saw her galloping over the meadow. A gust snatched the sunhat off her head. She did not stop to fetch it.

Next day, he picked up the hat on his way back from shooting. He perched it on the edge of the well and went fishing for the afternoon. He stayed out until dark, when the silence began to get on his nerves. Hungry, he ate unripe blackberries. Pug began to whine for food after that, so they made their way home. He built a fire and fried the fish. He felt sick eating it.

The hat was still there.

In the morning, he went to the village again. He asked at the post office if there were any letters for him, found there were not. He wandered into the churchyard, watched people passing in the road. He bought half a bottle of whiskey in the village stores, also another sketchpad, since the first one was full. As he was leaving, he saw a box of children's watercolours. He bought them too.

131

He did not sleep much that night. He was snappy with Pug and irritable over stupid things. At two o'clock, he was pacing round the top floor of the house with the hurricane lamp. The steady flame of the lamp threw swaying shadows before him. Everything took on a strange perspective. He sat down and forced his mind to concentrate, took out the chess set and began to play a problem. His head was so disturbed that he kept thinking: If only I had one more bishop, I could thrash this guy all over the board. The guy was Bobby Fischer, and you can have only two bishops in any game. This made no odds with Michael; he kept working out how he could have crushed Fischer if only he had a third bishop.

29

'I think he's a lunatic, if you ask me.' Jo threw herself on the settee and lounged there for a moment.

Grandpa John put down his *Shooting Times* and looked at her over his glasses. He had a fat, weathered face that disappeared into the folds of his neck when he sat down.

'Then I should avoid him, sweetheart. Lunatics can be dodgy characters.' He sucked on his empty pipe. His doctor had told him to stop smoking, but he couldn't break the habit. So he clenched the empty bowl between his teeth all day: it did not improve his temper.

'But it's annoying,' Jo said. 'He's sitting there in the middle of my land—'

'Yours?'

'Nobody's lived there as long as I can remember. It was always my riding country before. Now I come home and find him sitting there. I know Ralph said he's been through some rotten things, but that's no reason why I should put up with a madman taking pot shots at me.'

'Once,' he said. 'And that was before he knew you were there. And what size gun did you say?'

'A .22,' she admitted.

'Do you a lot of harm with that, I'm sure.'

'He thinks he's the wild man of the woods or something,

running into cover every time someone goes by. It's so shitty.'

Grandpa John frowned.

'Sorry, pathetic.'

'Don't know why your father spent all that money on your education. You could've gone to the local comprehensive to pick up vocabulary like that.'

'Watch it, Grandpa, your class consciousness is showing.'

He drew hard on the unlit pipe and went back to an interesting article on fly fishing. His granddaughter was a constant problem to him. He did not understand the way she thought or the things she did. She was nearly twenty, with just about every advantage one person could have in life: looks, intelligence and a great deal of money. Yet she had no apparent idea what she wanted to do with herself. She had all her mother's beauty – the look of a dancer – and an unpleasant streak of her father's coolness and calculation, but none of his drive and ambition.

He liked her, of course, but that was probably just an old man's failing judgement and the fact that she was the only child of his eldest son. He wished her mother was still alive to take charge of her, since neither he nor her father had ever exercised much discipline over her. That was probably the trouble; they both saw the mother in the daughter, but she, who suffered badly when her mother died, could not.

'Do you think there's a by-law to get him off the land?' she asked, rapping the magazine in his hands.

'Not if Bernard has given permission. I'm afraid you'll just have to put up with him until such time as he decides to leave. After all, there's only the whole estate and rest of the forest to play in.'

'But the meadow's good galloping ground.'

'Good God, Joanne. He hasn't fenced the place off with barbed wire.'

'I don't think you understand the problem at all.'

'I'll tell you what I think. On the one hand, you say he's not well, on the other, you want to run him out of the county. You're making mountains out of molehills because you're bored. Perhaps you should've gone to America with your friend for a while. Would've given you something to do.'

'You don't know what it's like to spend time with her parents.

133

Caro's mother wears a pink leotard *all* the time, and they feel it's their duty to show affection for each other, so Caro knows her parents still have a loving relationship.' She grimaced. 'All that wrinkled skin and dyed hair.'

'Enough about wrinkled flesh,' he said. 'Why not have some of your abominable friends down, then?'

'Like who? Everyone's on the tail end of their summer holidays. Besides, they're all going to university or joining daddy's company.'

'Bitter,' he remarked.

'Well, I'm not doing either, am I? I've got to think about earning myself a living before Dad decides to chuck me out.'

Grandpa John smiled to himself. That'll be the day, he thought.

'Anyway,' she said, getting up. 'I'm going to do something. You're obviously not in a sympathetic mood this afternoon.'

'At last,' he said. 'Peace and quiet.'

She kissed the top of his bald, pink head and went downstairs. He heard her talking to the housekeeper, Mrs Walker, then the big front door slammed.

She took the Range Rover and went into Thaxton in search of things to buy. Nothing took her fancy but a bag of vanilla fudge, which she ate as she drove the long way home, through the villages scattered around the battle area's perimeter. Reaching Middlecott, she turned down the cart track which led eventually to the Hall.

Two miles along, she saw Michael limping towards Oak Farm with Pug. She started to accelerate round them, but suddenly put her foot on the brake. She had time to wonder why she was doing it, as she pulled up beside them.

He looked up and saw her through the passenger window.

'Hello, again,' she said. 'Can I give you a lift?'

He frowned. 'Well, I've got the dog . . .'

'He can jump in the back. That's what it's for.'

Michael shifted uneasily. Then he said: 'Thanks,' and opened the tail gate for Pug to get in. He climbed in beside her. She started off again, going slower as the track grew rougher.

He sat awkwardly silent for a time, staring out through the

windscreen. She saw the small white scars on the backs of his hands. He coughed, then said:

'Look, I think I owe you an apology.'

She was surprised.

'I was rude the other day,' he said. 'No call for it at all. But, uh, I wasn't feeling too good at the time.' He lapsed into silence again.

'Everyone has bad days,' she said. 'Probably the weather.'

'Weather?'

'Yes, aren't you weather-sensitive?'

'I don't—'

'Well, headaches before a thunderstorm, that sort of thing. I am. When I was a little girl, I could tell when rain was on the way because I'd get a headache. And if there was a storm brewing, I'd get twinges in my bones.'

'What about snow?'

'Pardon?'

'What happened when it snowed?'

'I made snowmen and went sledging like everyone else. What did you do?'

'The same,' he said.

She floundered for something else to talk about, saw the sketchpad sticking out of his pocket.

'What've you been drawing?'

'Flowers, leaves, birds. Anything interesting.'

'My mother was good at drawing. We've got all her sketchbooks at home. She was drawing right up to the time she died.'

'I'm sorry.'

'Oh, it happened when I was ten. Three days after my birthday . . . I haven't got any of her talent, unfortunately. It always amazes me how you actually make things look real on paper. I've never been able to get it.'

He shrugged. 'It's something you either can or can't do. Nobody's come up with a decent explanation.'

'Do you think it's something you learn, or it's born in you?'

'I don't know.'

She tapped the steering wheel.

'Do you know the Wodehouses well?'

'I used to work with their son.'

'Really? What did you do?'

'Graphics. Stuff for commercials.'

'That sounds exciting.'

'Yes.' He shifted uncomfortably. 'What do you do?'

'For a living, you mean? Oh, not a lot, just now. I've been off getting an education which I'll probably never use.'

'That sounds gloomy.'

'Not really. After all, there must be three of four million things I'd rather do than work. What's the point in working yourself to death when there's so much to do?'

'Most people discover one thing they want to do more than anything else,' he said, 'and they shoot for that.'

'That explains it,' she said. 'I've never found anything worth slaving for. Grandpa John says the only thing I'm good for is marriage, and then he can't think of anyone who'd have me.'

He glanced across at her. Close to, he realised she was not so much thin as slim. Her face was lovely.

'I'm just hanging around at the moment,' she said.

'Where's that?'

'Fairstone Hall. About three miles south of you. Haven't you seen it?'

'Haven't been out that way much,' he said.

'It's my father's place. Grandpa John lives with us. It used to belong to some local squire until Dad struck it rich and bought him out. The old family arms still hang in the dining room.'

'Sounds expensive.'

'Well, I could tell you I'm just a simple country girl, up at five every morning to muck out the pigs, but it wouldn't be true. Besides, it's not my fault Dad's an internationally successful whatever-it-is.'

'What is it?'

'Oh, bits of everything these days. Originally he was a turkey farmer – humble beginnings, and all that – took it over from Grandpa John. But you know how it is. The bigger you get, the more you have to diversify, as Dad says. He's in Holland at the moment, doing some deal.'

They came over the rise and Jo speeded up a little where the track was smoother. She stopped at the gate.

'I could take you up to the house,' she said.

136

'No, this is fine, thank you.' He got out, let Pug out of the back, then came back to the window. 'I'm sorry,' he said, face pained. 'I'm not much of a talker.'

She looked at his cool grey eyes. 'Well, I promise not to come bothering you any more.'

'That doesn't matter. You have to come by anyway, pick up that hat of yours.'

'I will,' she said. 'See you.'

He watched her take the Range Rover into the forest until he could not hear the engine. Pug ran into the meadow, picked up a loose stick. He stood, anticipating exercise while Michael ambled along.

'Nicer than we thought, yes?' He took the stick and threw it far off. He suddenly realised he was hungry.

30

Temple watched the place all morning. It was an old house in Belsize Park which had been converted into flats. One of the flats had Sayers's telephone number. He had tried calling the day before and got no answer, and watched the house to see if Sayers went in or out, but got no results.

So just before one o'clock, he went in. The letter boxes on the ground floor were neatly labelled, except the one where Sayers lived. Temple climbed the stairs to the second floor, carrying a silenced .38 Smith & Wesson under his coat. He knocked on a red-painted door and heard scuffling inside. He fingered the gun, stroking the cool metal. No one answered.

He knocked again. This time there were footsteps – bare feet on wooden flooring – coming closer. He looked quickly round the landing and knocked once more.

A voice said: 'What is it?'

'Mr Sayers?' Temple asked.

'Who?'

A bolt was fumbled at the top of the door. He thought: If it's Sayers, I could take him now, through the door. But he did not pull the gun because a woman in a plum-coloured dressing gown walked past just then, carrying a bottle of milk.

The door opened. A chain held it to a four-inch gap. A peaked face stared out. 'What is it?'

'I was wondering if I could speak to Michael Sayers.'

'There's no one here of that name,' the peaked face said.

Temple considered. What was bothering this guy so much? Why was he sweating?

'Are you sure you haven't heard the name? Michael Sayers.'

'Look, I don't know him, right?'

'What is it you're frightened of?'

'Nothing. Fuck off, will you.' Peaked face tried to slam the door, but Temple got this foot in. The face disappeared and Temple flexed his arm, put his power behind the door. The chain snapped like paper. He went in, gun out, stabbing at peaked face.

'Oh shit, don't shoot for Christ's sake.' Peaked face sprawled on a king-size double bed, naked. An equally naked girl, looking about fourteen, lay on the bed. She stared at him with dazed eyes. On the table by the bed lay a hypodermic syringe and a small bottle.

'Christ, I didn't seduce her,' peaked face was saying, still scrabbling to cover himself. 'She's older than she looks, right? I didn't know she was on that stuff until I came back from the bathroom and found her shooting up. Christ's sakes, I swear, I swear it's true.' He could not decide which part of his body he should protect with his hands. 'Don't take me in. They'll crucify me.'

Temple slipped the gun away. He bit his lip, trying not to laugh. The girl on the bed, focusing hard, smiled at him.

'The way things look,' he said, trying to slip into a passable imitation of a Special Branch man, 'they probably will. Now tell me, do you know Michael Sayers?'

'Never heard the name,' peaked face groaned. 'What is he? Her pusher?'

Temple sighed. It was obvious that peaked face knew nothing.

'When did you move in here?'

'What? About two months ago. But I'm no drug fiend, right. I'm an accountant. You've got to understand that. She told me she was eighteen. She—'

'Shut up,' Temple said. He turned to the door, then glanced

back at peaked face. 'An officer'll be here in a minute to deal with you. Don't try to get out—' He savoured the next phrase. 'We've got the place surrounded.'

Peaked face buried his head in the bedclothes. His groans of 'Oh shit! Oh shit!' followed Temple all the way down to the street.

31

The air was crisp and stark so early in the morning. Jo was wearing a thick pullover with a giant ocean liner on the front, there was sleep in her eyes, and she had not been up at half-past six in the morning for years. She sat shivering on Arab while he nibbled the dying grass at the edge of the meadow. It was barely light.

She had no idea why she was awake and riding around at such an hour. She had not slept well, and at half-four she had decided to get up and do something with herself. Grandpa John was snoring when she passed his room. She went down to the kitchen and had a bacon and egg sandwich and a cup of coffee. That took her headache away. Then she washed, dressed, went down to the stable and saddled Arab.

Now she paused at the edge of the meadow, watching a fox come out in the growing light. She yawned.

A moment later, he came out of the woods. He carried his gun and a rolled towel. The dog was at his heels. They were some distance away, but she turned Arab into cover before he could spot her, and watched him as he went down to the gate. His limp was worse in the morning – probably because of the cold. He climbed the verge, went into the trees. She spurred Arab on to follow him at walking pace.

Because she had lost sleep, everything was bright and solid, as if it made a sound even when still. The hanging branches of the firs stroked her head, wetting her hair. Dawn light did not penetrate far into the dense cover, but shreds of it spread out on the damp earth below. She could not see him now, but guessed he was heading for the river.

Arab shook his head suddenly, showering her with drops. She pushed a half-broken branch out of her way and saw him crossing the path between two plantings. He was further up, pausing for a moment to look at the sky to the east. It was a sheet of fire colours. She realised that, lately, she saw daybreak only when she stayed up all night.

He went on, she followed; down to the long field above the river. She stopped at the edge, tethered Arab to a low branch, and skirted the field.

He stopped at the river bank, put the gun and towel down and took off his clothes, folding them neatly on the ground. Then he went into the water. She watched his pale, hard body, saw the long scar down his back. He ducked below the surface. She shivered. The river was a flood of smooth black. He came up, shaking his head. His face was unreadable.

Pug trotted over the field to her. He began to growl deep in his throat, until she bent down and stroked his ears, calming him. He saw a rabbit springing for cover and left her to chase it.

She watched Michael washing himself, swimming back and forth. A water rat appeared from the grass and dived sleekly, slicing the deep. He went under at the same time. She rose, watching the flattened shape of his body glide. He surfaced suddenly, close to her. She stepped back into the shadows. He turned, swam back to his clothes and stood drying himself thoroughly. She kept thinking how cold the water must be.

He dressed. She went back to Arab and started for Oak Farm. She rode fast, criss-crossing the forest via the paths.

When he arrived a while later, she was sitting by the banked fire. Coffee boiled over the flames. She wore the pink hat again.

After pulling up short, he walked in across the clearing. He hung his gun in the porch, came back to the fire and warmed his hands.

She smiled up at him. 'I thought,' she said, 'I'd invite myself for breakfast.'

He scratched his beard and squatted before the fire. She took the coffee off the heat.

He said: 'I've only got one cup.'

'I'll share yours,' she said. 'You haven't got any disgustingly

140

contagious diseases, have you?'

He passed her the powdered milk.

'Do you take sugar?'

He shook his head.

'Neither do I. That's handy. Pity there's no real milk.'

'Maybe I'll kidnap a cow.'

'Is that enough?'

'Fine.'

She passed the mug. He drank a little, then gave it back. Her eyes were bright; she looked around.

'It's lovely here this time of day.'

'What time of day is it?'

'Nearly eight o'clock.' She passed the mug. He drank.

'I woke up early, and I thought I'd see how our truce is going.'

He raised his hand. 'Peace.'

'That's what I thought.' She took the mug and drank. 'Have you been shooting yet?'

'Not yet. It looks like rain.'

'Probably not. They didn't mention it on the weather forecast last night. And I haven't got a headache.'

'Wind's blowing north-east,' he said. 'There's rain on the air.'

She shrugged. 'Then I'll get wet . . . I suppose you think I'm pretty cheeky, invading your castle at this time of the day?'

'I was wondering what your father would say.'

'Dad's away, remember.'

'Grandfather, then.'

'I've been doing what I please for a long time now. Besides, you must be respectable—'

'Hell's bells.'

'Safe, then. Bernard Wodehouse said so.'

'Is he a good judge of character?'

'I'm not sure. I don't see much of him these days.'

He took the cup, topped it up a little.

'Isn't it cold for swimming?' she asked.

'What?'

'Well, the towel, and your hair's wet. You've been swimming.'

'It'd be easy to get dirty out here. It's not too cold yet.'

She wanted to ask about the scars. 'What will you do today?'

'Pick off some food for the evening, maybe rig up some shutters

141

for the windows. The nights are getting colder.'

'I'm at a loose end today.' She drained the mug, threw the dregs on the fire. It spat between them. 'Grandpa John's right, I don't have enough to do. Maybe I should catch my own food too.'

He stood up, checked his pocket for slugs for the gun, and fetched it from the porch.

'Are you going now?' she said.

'Before it rains.'

'Would you mind some company?'

He called Pug. 'Come along if you like.'

She mounted Arab, turned to follow him. He was already gone.

It took most of the morning, but rain did not come. They wandered near to Minton, crossing a minor road that ran straight from one horizon to the other. She noticed how restless he was, how he got off the road as fast as he could. And she saw how, when silence fell and they were just walking, his face changed. It happened only briefly, but she saw the cool, uninterested look leave his eyes. There was a sadness, as if he were thinking of something that hurt him.

He always snapped out of it in a second, and she did not mention it. She made him talk instead about the plants they passed, about the birds. He knew all the names. Sometimes she got the feeling that he was tired of her, but when she mentioned going home, he did not answer.

Just before noon, they came to a fence that stretched out through the forest. He paused, touching the wire.

'Private land?'

She dismounted, peering into the gloom. 'It's probably the battle area.'

'I didn't realise it was so close.'

'Oh, it's pretty big. Starts beyond Minton, goes all the way across to Thaxton and up to Badney.'

He raised his head. 'Look.'

She saw the red deer buck going slowly parallel to them beyond the wire. It was twenty feet away.

'You should pot him. Enough venison there for a month.'

'I'd have to have the barrel of this thing in his eye to kill him,' he said. 'It's illegal anyway.'

'Pity. Venison's nice.'

142

The deer stopped, listening, then tracked away from them.

'Let's follow it,' she whispered.

'Through the wire?'

'Oh, come on. I used to run around here when I was a kid. Never saw a single soldier.' She tethered Arab to a low branch and vaulted the fence, then beckoned Michael to follow. He went reluctantly.

The ground was the same for a hundred yards or more, then they were out of the firs and into woods again.

'What do they use this place for?' he asked, staring at a white sign that said:

DANGER
HM FORCES
NO ADMITTANCE

'Everything. They've got firing ranges and battlefields, and the villages.'

'Villages?'

'Yes. Stanton and Tollington and all those.' She kept the deer in sight as they climbed over a fallen tree. 'How much do you know about this?'

'Nothing.'

'It was because of the war, you see. The Second World War. The army wanted a place to practise manoeuvres and stuff like that, so they evacuated the little villages in this part of the heath. The forest only started being planted back in the twenties, and this part was still the Breckland. The army told everyone to move out at a month's notice and said they could all come back when the war was over.

'Trouble was, when that war finished, they started on the Cold War, and so they never got round to letting the villagers back in.'

'Like that place on Salisbury Plain?' he said, as the deer ducked out of sight behind a blackberry tangle.

'Yes, except that round here, not many people were worried. The villages were small, out in the middle of nowhere, and the residents were all re-housed on silly rents. Nobody made much fuss about it.

'Since then, they've been using it for NATO exercises and God

143

knows what else. Haven't you seen the flashes in the sky?'

The deer reached the edge of the woods. Michael crouched low beneath some clumps of elder.

'The villages are still there,' she said. 'What's left of them, anyway. They shell them for target practice.'

'Wonderful,' he said. He gazed across a wide field gone to grass. It was a matted tangle of bracken and scrub grass. Beyond were some twisted Scots pines, and further off, a round Norman church tower, gleaming pale and still against the grey sky.

'Except they never touch the churches,' she said. 'They shelled the villages to the ground, then rebuilt them for practising street warfare, for Northern Ireland and that sort of thing. But they never hit the churches. They're surrounded by fences, and no one's allowed in them. They're looked over now and then by people from the Church authorities. That's Stanton, I think.'

He blinked, eyes gone far away to the lonely church tower among the elms.

'They keep them in good order?' he said quietly. 'Even though no one worships in them?'

'That's it. Grandpa John told me all about it. He can remember it before the war. The river runs through the middle of it and all the roads are still there, but if you drive along them you come to barriers and dead ends. If the army's doing something there, they have sentries.' She remembered more. 'It frightened me when I was small – all those villages, and no one living in them, just empty houses and empty roads and miles of empty countryside.'

He could not take his eyes off the church tower in the deserted village. The country was wide open as far as he could see.

She put a hand down and touched his shoulder, felt him stiffen suddenly. He stood up, shrugging her hand away.

'We'd better get out.'

'Don't you want to see it close up?'

He parted the branches again. 'No. You're right, there's something creepy about it.' He wheeled round. In a moment, she was hurrying to keep up with him.

The final count was two pigeons and a grey squirrel that she caught as it rested halfway down the trunk of a spruce.

She handed him the gun. 'I'm a pretty good wing shot too.'

'Squirrels don't have wings,' he said. 'But they have one advantage over pigeons.'

'What's that?'

'Everyone gets a leg.'

'Is that the kind of thing you'd have made up when you were in advertising?'

'Wouldn't have lasted long if I had.'

They passed the letter box by the gate. It had fallen over. He lifted it, resting it against the gate.

'You expecting a letter?'

He walked on without answering.

'Well,' she said, 'it's been interesting.'

He stopped. Without looking at her, he said: 'What is this all about?'

'Pardon?'

'Why have you spent most of the day following me around? You can't have enjoyed it.'

She gripped Arab's reins tight in her hand. 'I thought – I thought you could use the company.'

'Have you been talking to Ralph? You do know him, don't you?'

She sighed. 'Yes, I know him. He's a friend of the family. He used to bully me when we were kids.'

'What did he tell you?'

'Nothing.'

He stared at her. She felt cold all over. There was no way she could lie.

'All right. He wrote me a letter after I asked Bernard about you. He said you'd been through a bad time, that you were all alone up here. He said if I had some time, I might get to know you. He's worried about you.'

His eyes lost a touch of frost.

'That's all,' she said. 'He just told me you were a nice bloke, and you could do with cheering up.'

Michael looked away from her to the forest. He did not speak.

'Oh, go on,' she cried suddenly. 'Say something proud and offended, why don't you? Ask me what other charity work I'm involved with at the moment, or do I take in waifs and strays as well.'

He raised his eyebrows.

'It's the sort of thing you'd say,' she went on, too far in to reverse. 'You're so full of snotty pride, aren't you? If you think I'd spend all day doing something that bored me to death, then you're a lousy judge of character. I don't do anything I don't want to.'

He opened his mouth to speak.

'And now you'll say I have to be bored to follow you about. Well, don't bloody bother.'

He closed his mouth.

She glared at him, face flushed, breathing hard. His expression now was bemused, and the defences were down.

She thought: Well, that's you told.

'How old are you?' he said.

'Twenty, near as damn it. Not that it's got anything to do with this. Unless, of course, you're going to say, "Go home, child," which is just about your mark.'

He touched the side of his head, as if there were a slight ache. 'Amazing,' he said.

'What's that supposed to mean?'

He turned and started up the path to the house.

She stood there, holding Arab's reins, shouting:

'What's that supposed to mean?'

32

The call came in and was transferred to Ralph's desk. He was struggling to put together a set of sketches on the Nelson Cigarettes account, and tired of drawing cigarettes. He snatched the phone.

'If it's not very urgent, I'm out.'

'I beg your pardon,' the voice said. 'I was trying to speak to Mr Sayers.'

'You're half a year too late, I'm afraid.' He fumbled round his board for the 0.4 mm Rotring.

'How's that?'

'He's left, Sir.'

'Oh dear,' the voice said. 'That's a pity.'

146

'That's what I thought, but there you are – the world of advertising's loss is the world at large's gain.' He found the 0.4 mm and began searching for the french curves.

'This is a great inconvenience.'

'Yes, it is,' he said. 'What exactly is it about? Maybe I can help. I'm a dear and trusted friend of Mr Sayers.'

'A friend?'

'Bosom.'

'Ah, in that case, it's about Mr Sayers's insurance policy with us.'

'Really? What company is that?'

'Eagle Alliance.'

'And your name?'

'Anderson,' the voice said, without hesitation.

'Okay, Mr Anderson, shoot.'

'Mr Sayers has an accident and illness policy with us. After his unfortunate . . . experience early this year, and the subsequent hospitalisation, there are a good many matters to deal with. I'm sure you know how it is.'

Ralph cadged a swig of coffee from Linda as she passed. 'Oh yes, certainly do.'

'Well, the point is, we're having some difficulty locating Mr Sayers. He seems to have moved from the last address we have without notifying us. That's a bit awkward. You'll appreciate we can't deal with certain matters without his help.'

'Little late to be clearing things up, isn't it?'

Anderson coughed. 'Mr Sayers only recently finished his last course of treatment.'

'True, true.'

'You'll pardon me, Sir, but these matters are confidential. Do you have any authority to deal with them?'

'Sort of.' Ralph doodled a face in the corner of a sketch. 'Anyway, I'm about the closest you'll get to him.'

'You know where he is, then?'

'Surely do. But I can't divulge my information – sounds like a spy movie, doesn't it?'

Anderson did not sound amused. 'You say you can't let me have his present address?'

''Fraid not, old son. Mike – Mr Sayers – expressly asked

everyone to keep *stumm* about it.'

'That's really a pity.'

'Look, I'll tell you what I'll do. I'll be in contact with him pretty soon. How about you give any paperwork to me, and I'll pass it on to him, get it signed, and post it back?'

'Well, it is fairly urgent.'

'You could give it to me today. Are you in town?'

'Yes, Sir.'

'Okay. Do you know the Last Gasp?'

'Beg your pardon?'

'It's a pub off Leicester Square. I usually have lunch there. You could meet me there, I'll take your paperwork, and buy you a drink to relieve your troubled mind.'

'Well, that's very good of you.'

'I know. I'm brimming with Human kindness. At least, I will be when I finish these damn cigarettes.'

Anderson did not ask what cigarettes. He said: 'Would twelve-thirty suit you?'

'Make it one o'clock,' Ralph said.

'And how will I know you?'

'I'll be the devilishly handsome young man. Blond hair, light blue suit, dark blue shoes. Let me see . . . ' He reached over to Linda's desk, grabbed her paperback book. 'I'll be carrying the new Salman Rushdie. Name's Wodehouse, by the way.'

'Okay then, Sir. See you at one o'clock.'

Ralph put down the phone. 'Salman Rushdie? Sounds like the fish course in an Indian restaurant.' He rubbed his forehead. 'I don't remember Michael being with the Eagle Alliance.'

'Does he know your insurance company?' Linda asked.

'You're right.' He checked his watch. 'An hour and ten minutes to finish this.' He picked up a 0.5 mm and grimaced at the Nelson cigarette. 'Be all right if I smoked the bloody things.'

Temple stepped out of the telephone booth and walked along Victoria Street. He was thinking all the time as he went back to the multi-storey car park. Thinking that this Wodehouse guy knew Sayers, was a personal friend, was going to see him soon. Luck, he thought, was on the side of the professional.

Back at the car, he unlocked the boot and put his handgun in the concealed compartment there. This was not a gun job, that was certain, not in Leicester Square. He locked the boot, checked his wallet, and hurried back down the steps to street level. He made his way to Victoria rail station to catch the tube.

He considered possibilities. Wodehouse was going to see Sayers soon – he had said that. But Temple did not like tail jobs. You had to be half-blind or stupid not to know when someone was following you, particularly over a distance. He preferred to deal with Wodehouse straight away – but not the way Wodehouse had said.

He flexed his hands as he went down into the tube station. His hands were weapon enough. They were all he would need.

He scouted the territory around Wodehouse's place of work. It was in one of the side streets between Shaftesbury Avenue and Charing Cross Road, a modernised Victorian building with brass plates by the door. He stood in the shadow of a doorway across the street, reading a copy of the *Daily Mirror*.

At quarter to one, a blond man in a powder blue suit came out of the building. The copy of Rushdie's novel stuck awkwardly out of his pocket. He was a little above average height, but built on the light side. Temple followed him, keeping to the opposite pavement. Wodehouse stopped to buy a paper from the stall nearby, went into Lisle Street, and cut down an alley by the Warner Cinema.

That was when Temple moved in.

It was near-perfect. The alley was momentarily empty, except for an oriental woman who began to backtrack the moment she saw what was happening. No one else was close when Temple did it.

He made it look like a mugging. In practice, it was exactly that. It was easy enough: one swift blow to the side of the neck, enough to paralyse and stun, and Wodehouse went down with hardly a murmur. He never saw it coming. Temple caught him as he fell, kept his body turned away, face on the pavement. Then he went through the pockets, found what he wanted immediately: a pocket diary and an address book. He glanced up, saw that there was no one around yet. He took the wallet and some folding money to give the mugging authenticity. The Salman

Rushdie he left.

It took nineteen seconds from start to finish. Ralph did not see his attacker's face. He lay crumpled against a wall, breathing the stink of urine. He heard the attacker's footsteps as he backed off, then the sound of running away. He tried to get up and found that his whole body was still numb. Someone knelt beside him and a voice said: 'Don't worry, mate. Everything's all right.' And Ralph gasped: 'No it bloody isn't, fool.'

Temple slowed to walking pace as he came into Leicester Square. He strolled past the Empire and the Ritz. Some kids dressed in clown costumes were giving a show for the tourists. He threw one of Wodehouse's pound coins in their hat.

33

Michael came back from the village with the rucksack slung over his good shoulder. The weather had cleared after overnight rain and the sunlight was bright and clean. He had a slight headache from lack of sleep; the dreams had been at him again, although he remembered very little but the occasional whiff of smoke.

He breathed deep, trying to clear his mind. The track fell away and Pug ran yelping after a pheasant that came strutting out on the verge.

After the girl's visit, he had been uneasy. He spent the evening drawing faces that did not exist and playing chess. Pug came close to beating him. He was aware of a flatness about everything when she was gone, and being aware of it, he did not like it. He tried to forget it.

He saw Oak Farm through the trees as he walked down to the gateway. There were rooks on the roof, he saw their crouched black figures. It was a good thing, like having guards on the place.

Pug ran through the gateway. Michael stopped, staring at the letter box. An envelope was pinned to the wood. He moved closer, pulled the drawing pin out and took the envelope. It was pale blue, a heavy paper. Written on the front in big, looping letters was:

Mr Michael Sayers,
    Oak Farm,
        Near Middlecott, Norfolk.

In the top right-hand corner she had drawn a sketchy stamp. It had a crowned head on it, profile of a girl with big eyes and a turned-up nose; a caricature self-portrait. Underneath, in little capitals, the words 'ROYAL FEMAIL'. He bit his lip and turned the envelope to open it. Inside was a single matching sheet of deckled notepaper. The printed heading said it came from Fairstone Hall, and below, the message read:

Dear Mr Sayers,
Thought you would like a letter for your letter box.
    Yours sincerely,
        Joanne Palmer.

It was still a pleasant day. Temple strolled down Charing Cross Road to Trafalgar Square and bought a couple of salad rolls and a can of beer from a shop opposite the Whitehall Theatre. He walked on along the Mall and found himself a lone seat by the water in St James's Park.

There were still plenty of tourists about. Office workers were out having their lunch. Temple watched the lake as he ate one of the rolls; pigeons battered about for a share of the crumbs. He wiped his fingers on the paper napkin that came with the rolls, took out the address book and went through it page by page.

Wodehouse was not an organised thinker. There was no Sayers under 'S', and under 'M', Temple found only 'Mike and Laura', with the Belsize Park address and number. It was crossed out. Below that, in different coloured ink, 'Mike's Folks' – that was the place in Guildford. He checked under 'L' for the girl's name on its own, but it did not appear.

A pigeon rattled down, perching on the back of the bench. He tore a shred off the second roll and threw it on the grass. Ten pigeons went for it.

He pocketed the book and started on the diary. It was a thin Bowmaker thing: Wodehouse was no Samuel Pepys. It contained business appointments, birthdays, lunch dates, parties – nothing more. There was no mention of Sayers at all. Temple checked the notes section, scoured the inside covers, but there was nothing that looked useful. He took a pull of his beer and threw the diary in a litter bin.

That left the wallet.

He opened it as if he were searching for a lost photograph or credit card. No one gave him a second glance.

Inside, there were cards. American Express, Eurocard, Hertz, Diners Club, a number of others. Wodehouse obviously didn't rely on his job for finance. In one of the transparent flaps was a photograph of a girl. He shook out the pockets, and a number of things fell on his lap: a razor blade, two more photographs – of different girls – three cards for his firm, a newspaper clipping with a picture of Wodehouse holding some cricket trophy over his head, and a heavy Greek ten-drachma piece.

Temple frowned. He struck at a pigeon that was trying to hustle him. The pigeon rose, flapping its wings in his face. Temple hit it quickly with the edge of his hand. It spun and fell dead on the grass by the water. An old woman stared at him.

He chewed slowly on a piece of the roll. He was thinking he would have to follow Wodehouse after all. And it could be more difficult now, after the mugging.

Without much hope, he prised the wallet pockets open one by one. He squinted into them, and saw a scrap of dirty paper creased into the last one. He fingered it out. It was blotter pad paper: in pencil, Wodehouse had scrawled:

MIKE (EMERGENCY) – 0465 724871

He smiled. Things were looking up again.

Another short stroll took him back to Victoria rail station. He found a telephone that worked, pressed up the number and waited. It rang for almost half a minute. He thought: The bastard's not even answering the phone.

The ringing stopped. He heard the distant background roar of a tractor passing. A woman's voice said:

'Good afternoon. Middlecott post office.'

Temple replaced the receiver.

'Hello again,' Michael said.

'Don't worry,' Jo said, kneeling as Pug ran up to investigate her. 'You'll get over being irritated by me soon.'

Michael lifted the rucksack off his shoulder, laid it by the dead fire. 'Thank you for the letter. I've just been reading it.'

'Well, you're so attached to that letter box . . . Sorry there wasn't more to it, but I'm rotten at letters. Have trouble filling up a postcard.'

He went into the house, brought down the dixie set. She had already raked out the old ashes and brought a pile of wood from the shed.

'How d'you start your fires?' she asked.

'Rubbing two boy scouts together.' He took out the little box full of charred linen which he used as tinder.

'Wouldn't matches be easier?'

'Ruin the image of man in the wild.'

She watched, fascinated. He took his knife and a stubby twig with a lighter flint embedded in one end of it. He struck sparks off the flint with his knife until the tinder caught. He blew on it, nursing the smoulder into a flame, and added some twigs from the grease pit. They sputtered unevenly as he heaped more twigs on. Soon the fire was burning well. She broke branches over her knee, handed them to him.

'Are you here for lunch?'

'Do you mind?' she asked. She sat down. A slim girl with close-cut black hair and beautiful eyes. She wore Dunlop Blue Flash shoes, jeans, a pale brown blouse and a white windcheater. She looked younger than nineteen.

'There's only this stuff to eat off.' He gestured to the dixie set.

'Wrong,' she said. She heaved a fat holdall from under a tree. 'I thought since I wasn't even invited, I'd bring some contributions.' She took out a plate and cup, knife and fork. Then she handed over a can of spaghetti, half a pound of sausages, four Granny Smith apples, and a pint of milk. 'That's for the coffee. And the apples came off our own trees, so you can bet they're not mass-produced. Picked them myself this morning. Nearly fell off the ladder doing it.'

He spread a cloth on the grass and added his bread, cheese and onions to the pile.

'Now we're cooking,' she said. 'At least, we will be when you get cracking. I'm not much of a cook.'

'Can you use a can opener?'

153

'Only if it has a stop/start button.'

He threw her his jackknife. She hacked the lid off the spaghetti, and watched as he set the wire frame over the fire. He took out a jar and scooped a spoonful of fat into the pan. He set the pan over the fire and let the fat melt. She pushed the knob of fat around until it disappeared. He put the sausages in the pan. They sizzled and began to cook.

'I came up,' she said, 'because I was thinking about what you told me yesterday.'

'Which?'

'About advertising agencies. Working for them. You know I said I was trying to decide what to do with myself? Well, I was thinking about advertising.'

'You were? What angle?'

'I don't know. That's what I was hoping you'd tell me. I've asked Ralph about it, but all he ever says about it is "It's a business for geniuses." '

He smiled at her impression of Ralph's dramatic touch.

'Certainly not the work for women, he says. I mean, what's the use of that?'

'He's just trying to protect his position,' Michael said. 'Some of the best people in the business are women.'

'Well, how did you get into it?'

He turned the sausages. The air was heavy with their rich smell. 'Drifted in via college and art school,' he said. 'When I went in for my "O" Level Art, the teacher said I should go into graphics. I suppose the advice always stuck.'

'You mean there're people who just draw adverts and other people who write the words? And someone else who thinks of the idea in the first place?'

'It depends,' he said. He told her how in large companies this was usually so. But his company had been middle-sized, and there was more overlap from one field to another these days. All the time he talked, he knew she was watching him and not listening to a word he said. He felt that if he shut up completely, she would still go on watching him. His head twinged sickeningly. The smoke from the fire filled his mouth for a moment.

'So you've been responsible for whole concepts?' she asked, looking impressed.

154

'It's a team thing,' he said. 'Except when it comes to who takes the credit.'

'I know. Backstabbing every way you turn.'

'Certainly. Nobody believes a word they write, and they all spend their time selling things they know nobody really wants. They're just in it for the megabucks.' He raised an eyebrow at her.

She was thinking about the way he wrinkled his nose up after he had made a joke or said something to send her up. She had come to Oak Farm not knowing why she persisted, certainly not as a favour to Ralph. It was all very strange. His eyes were not cool grey now. They were almost friendly.

He used his knife to cut the bread in thick slices. She gave him her plate. 'Lovely afternoon, isn't it?'

He looked away. She watched him butter the bread. His hands were flat and strong and clean. They did not look like artist's hands to her.

'That'll stick if you don't keep stirring,' he warned.

She tended to the stirring. 'Is it interesting work?'

'More interesting than canning peas.'

'I suppose you've done that?'

'Summer job at college. Hot summer too. Haven't eaten a canned pea since.'

She picked up the coffee pot. 'I'll get the water for this now.'

'In the porch,' he said, 'behind the door.'

He raised his eyes, watching her walk away from him to the house. She reminded him of a girl he had known at art school; same long legs and easy sway as she walked. He remembered how he had felt about that girl, and how he never did get a chance with her.

The pain went through his head. He turned from her as she came back. She sat down opposite him. Pug stretched and flopped a paw on her leg. She giggled and whispered to the dog.

'Right. Have we got everything?' She clapped her hands together. He cut the cheese and one of the onions in half, put them on the plates. She spooned coffee into the pot. He prodded the sausages and spaghetti, bubbling in the pan.

'Done to a turn,' she said. She filled his plate, then hers. He put the pan aside. They began to eat.

The conversation went on in the same way as before: she made the running, he followed. Sometimes a spark seemed to jump in him, he gained an extra light behind the eyes, became more relaxed. Then he would stop short, as if realising a mistake, and revert again. They talked about their childhood – or he did. She was less easy to draw on the subject. She was quite ready to describe how her mother died, but it sounded like an old, rehearsed piece of recitation.

As for her, she could not recall much of what was said afterwards, but she remembered the afternoon as a good time. She watched him as much as she could: the way he ate; simple pleasure in the food and coffee. He was uneasy sometimes, she knew that, and he always seemed to be looking elsewhere than at her, but she was convinced that the man who showed himself only occasionally was the real one.

She emptied her cup, felt coffee grounds on her tongue.

'Would you like another one?'

He raised a hand. 'Fine with this, thanks.'

She polished an apple, lobbed it over the fire.

'Oh, I forgot until now . . . ' She rummaged in the bottom of her bag and brought out a radio. 'I even brought music.'

'Don't turn it on,' he said. His voice turned cold. 'Please.'

She did not say anything. She put the radio away.

After the food, he went and lay down under an oak, made himself comfortable against the sloping trunk. She considered for a second, then she moved to the tree. She lay down. They were at an angle to each other; ninety degrees. They stayed like this for an hour, dozing and talking. Eventually, she yawned and said:

'Is this how you spend your days?'

'Don't usually eat that well,' he said. 'Thank you. As for the afternoons, I usually do something useful. Build a hang-glider from fertiliser sacks. That kind of thing.'

She found a fallen green acorn in the grass. 'You can make coffee with these, can't you?'

'Roasted and ground, if you like it bitter.' He clambered up. She gave him her hand and he helped her to her feet. They stood close: he was looking down at her, his eyes showing confusion. She was not confused: she finally had a reaction from him. A hot flower opened in her belly. She tilted her head, lips parting.

156

He broke away, releasing her hand.

'Are you going home now?'

She stood still, getting over the surprise. She had never felt the heat like that before. 'I don't have to . . . ' She realised her voice was rough and calmed it down. 'But you must have plenty to do.'

He was already in the porch, gathering together his fishing tackle.

'I'll push off, then.' She stuck her hands in her pockets.

Without turning, he said: ''Bye.'

She stared at the ground. 'Is it Michael or Mike?'

He finally looked up. 'Whichever you want.'

'Michael,' she said.

He tried a smile. It got lost in the confusion. 'Jo or Joanne?'

She shrugged.

'Jo,' he said.

She nodded.

That afternoon, although he did not feel like it, he walked down to the river and did some fishing. But he could not sit still, and soon he returned to put away the fishing gear. Then he walked out to the battle area again. He left Pug tethered in the forest and went over the fence, into the village. It was ghostly even in daylight. Most of the houses that remained were white-roofed breeze-block shells for soldiers to practise Northern Ireland-style street warfare. But the ground plan was the same as when it was Stanton, a real village. In the centre, surrounded by old elms and ash trees, was the little church. It was knapped flint with a round Norman tower, perfectly preserved, except that on the north side a shell had fallen too close. The earth by the fence was ripped up and the wire flapped loose from one post. He crawled under it and walked round the church. The doors were solidly padlocked, the windows covered with corrugated iron. He thought it was secure until he noticed that there was one tiny window in the vestry which had begun to come away. He thought about the inside of the church, what it must be like after forty years, and prised the rest of the iron from the frame. It took some effort, but eventually he managed to open the gap and slither through into the vestry.

Inside it was cool and damp. Very quiet, very calm. Spots of light fell into the thick gloom from chinks in the corrugated iron on the windows. He walked up to the altar, gazing at the plaques on the wall. One said:

In Proud and Loving Memory of
NICHOLAS MELVILLE GAPP
CAPTAIN KO YORKS LI
(Attached Essex Regt)

Who Fell While Gallantly Leading His Men
At Achi Baba in Gallipoli
6 August 1915

Faithful Unto Death

He knelt down for a moment at the altar rail, the way he used to at school harvest festival services. A sparrow, small and perfect like a model, lay recently dead on the stone floor beside him. It had got into the church and had been unable to get out. He stared at it for a long while, then got up. Feeling dizzy, he picked the sparrow off the floor and carried it outside with him.

It was almost dark when he started for home, and his progress was slower than before. Pug sensed there was something wrong even though he was hardly aware of it. Twice, he tripped in the dense mass of fern and thorn.

He reached Oak Farm when the moon was up, stumbled across the clearing and pushed open the front door. He was dizzy and the smell of smoke was in his head. He climbed the stairs in darkness, dumped his gear in the spare room, and fell on his sleeping bag. Pug circled the room, claws scratching the floorboards. Michael crawled across to the cupboard and gave the dog a handful of cereal, lurched back and climbed inside the sleeping bag. Now he was shivering. His mouth was dry. He reached under the bag and found the half-bottle of Haig.

Then he was asleep or unconscious, fading out in a sick, swirling daze. Before he stopped thinking, he was certain he could smell smoke.

34

'So what brings you to my sick bed?' Ralph asked, lying down again.

'You're not in bed,' Jo said. 'You're on a couch.'

'Couch, then. What are you doing here, child?'

She frowned. 'I came down to do some shopping. You know Mary's getting married next month, don't you?'

'I didn't actually. Lost my diary.' He eased his head down on a cushion.

'I was in town, and I thought you'd probably jump at the chance to take me to lunch. When I rang, they said you were taking some days off.'

'Sick leave,' he corrected.

'I noticed you're casually dressed. What's wrong?'

'Touch of the inner-city blight,' he said. 'I was mugged.'

'Brought down by footpads, egad!'

'I'm serious. In broad daylight, no less. Very professional job, too. Doctor who looked me over was of the opinion that the man must have been ex-army or martial arts. The swine.' He rubbed his neck tenderly.

'Did you see him?'

'All I saw was the pavement.' He poured himself a brandy. 'Lost everything. American Express won't forget it . . . Anyway, enough of my little troubles.'

'I don't suppose you feel up to lunch, then?'

'Not paying for it. Tell you what, there's a bloody great pizza in the freezer and a bottle of some kind of wine on the cold shelf. You slap the pizza in the oven – can you handle that? – and we'll dine in style.'

She set the oven and slipped the pizza out of its plastic film. 'You sure you're up to entertaining?'

'For my father's god-daughter? . . . What does that make you? You must be my god-sister. Always got time for a god-sister.'

She opened the wine. They talked: mutual friends, events of the summer. She mentioned her time in Europe.

'You look pretty good on it,' he said. 'You get prettier every time I see you.'

She took the compliment with a nod.

'But to what do I really owe the unexpected pleasure of your company? You didn't have to come to London just for a wedding suit.'

'No, there're plenty of reasons.'

'Name them.'

She rolled her glass slowly between her hands. 'I came down to get away. I think I'm getting a bit stupid sitting up there in the country. Not doing anything with myself. So I came down for the day. Thought I'd liven myself up a bit, see a few people, go dancing maybe. Stop over a couple of days and have some fun.'

'You're not making a good start coming to me. What's wrong with home, anyway? You usually enjoy it, playing lady of the manor.'

'I know. It's just—'

'And you've got all the added excitement of a wild man in the woods.'

'I'll just check the pizza.'

He followed her out. She was searching in drawers for a spatula.

'How is he, by the way?'

'Who?'

Ralph handed her the oven glove. 'Old Mike.'

'Michael,' she corrected softly.

He sat down at the kitchen table, picked up the salt pot and poured a small heap of salt on the table. 'My child, I hate to deal in clichés, but is there anything you want to tell me?'

She gazed at him straight on. 'I'll have some more wine, please.'

He went back to his settee and waited. She came in.

'Can you tell me about him?'

'What do you want to know?'

She spread her hands. 'Everything.'

So they had lunch together. And he told her everything.

The journey home seemed short. She detoured through Middlecott and went down the cart track. She drove up to the woods, then walked to the house. It was dark, the fire was out, there was no sign of Michael. She went to the door and tried it. It was locked. She stepped back, looking up at the top floor windows for signs of life, saw nothing. The clearing was quiet. Then an owl hooted in the trees, and she spun round. It was a spooky place if you were on your own.

She went home with her new knowledge bottled up inside. Her father's car was in the drive. As she pulled up, he came to the front door, looking the same as always. She leapt out of the car and hugged him.

Next day, Dad took her up in the Cessna. He wanted to see how his sites were looking without the bother of driving round them. They buzzed up off the field behind the house early on the fine morning. They flew high out over the country. The forest dwindled, and Thaxton passed beneath like a toy train layout.

Dad said: 'When are you going to learn to fly?'

She shook her head, content to watch. Flying in jets was nothing compared to this. Small plane, big sky. She saw cars threading along ribbon roads and rivers glimmer suddenly under the sun.

On the way home, she asked him to make a pass over Oak Farm. She grabbed a Tempo and a scrap of paper from the map compartment and scrawled, 'Hello there, from a higher intelligence,' on it. She wrapped it round a broken cigarette lighter and opened her window.

'What's that for?' Dad asked.

'I'll tell you later,' she said.

He took the Cessna down to two hundred feet. They went skimming in over the forest, then the soft explosion of the woods. She saw Oak Farm among the trees.

'Remember your angle of trajectory,' he said.

'I'm not trying to bomb the place.'

They were over it and past in a second. She let the bundle go,

161

saw the roof and chimney stack flash by, the little burnt patch of ground where the fire was. She saw no one moving.

'Can we go home now?' Dad said.

The meadow rolled underneath. She looked back on it as they rose and banked to the left. Worry twinged in her like toothache.

Dad took Jo and Grandpa John to dinner that evening, so she did not get to Oak Farm again until next morning. She rode up before eight o'clock and found the fire still dead, ashes undisturbed. She dismounted, glanced about. On the ground by the well was her note. Dew had unfolded the paper; the lighter lay in the heart of a message which had run into a mess of blotches.

She tried the door again. She called Michael's name and heard nothing but her own voice among the trees. In one of the high oaks, a crow answered.

She hit the door and turned away, thinking: Bastard, he's gone. She mounted Arab and spurred him to a gallop. She left the house and the woods behind.

The day dragged through. She wandered listlessly round the house, reading magazines and watching snatches of television, until Grandpa John got annoyed and took her to a pub in Minton for a lunchtime drink. It was a big pub, relying on passing trade from the main road. At lunchtime, half the county seemed to gather there.

'I'm doing a bit of business,' Grandpa John said. 'So keep quiet, look demure, and maybe I'll put something over on the beggar while he's ogling you.'

She was introduced to Hector Potter, an old crony of her grandfather's. Hector was about eighty and had just been banned from driving his vintage cars, which were his passion. He had a 1935 Hirondelle he wanted to get rid of.

'Used to drive one,' Grandpa John said. 'You remember, Hector?'

'I do,' Hector said. He kept saying 'I do,' nodding and smiling toothlessly. He had a glass eye that seemed more alive than the real one.

The old men talked. Jo went to the bar for another vodka and orange, then took her change and began to play the fruit machine

162

in the corner. The first coin got nothing, the second returned thirty pence. She put the thirty pence in and got a hold on two oranges. She pressed the start button and the machine jangled out more coins. She bent down to rake them from the tray.

A man at the nearest table watched her as she moved. She tried her favourite tactic – stared back at him – but he went on admiring her as if she were a picture in a magazine. She sighed. He was in his thirties, she guessed, a man with brown hair and a moustache, all dressed up in a cheap suit. He looked like some kind of salesman – except for the eyes. She shuddered.

'Won anything?' Grandpa John asked.

'I'm lucky with money,' she said. She nudged the centre wheel two places and brought three bells in line. The machine pumped out her cash.

'You can afford the next round.' Hector grinned.

Jo looked back. The salesman was still watching her. It was getting on her nerves: she liked a certain amount of audacity in a man, but he was plain rude. She crossed her eyes and stuck her tongue out at him. He smiled and finished his drink.

She listened to the two old men talking, wondering where Michael was.

And Temple, sitting quietly with his empty glass, listening to the juke box, thought: There's a pretty girl in this dump after all.

Through the afternoon, she got more and more restless. She was certain that Michael had not just packed up and gone for good: the way he had behaved did not suggest that. So he was either out in the forest somewhere, thinking things over, or he was not answering his door. She knew now why he acted as he did, and wished she could talk to him.

Dad returned in the evening with some business acquaintance, but she did not do her usual job as hostess. She was on the way out as they came in. She saddled Arab and rode out to Oak Farm. Night was closing in, and the moon was on the wax. She saw a sword blade of it in the eastern sky, lighting ragged shreds of cloud.

She went slowly all the way, watching for him. When she was halfway across the meadow, she saw the gleam of a fire. As she

163

went into the woods, Pug came whimpering up to her.

The clearing looked empty at first, but the fire was large and recently lit. She stayed on Arab, uncertain.

'Michael?'

Something stirred by the fire.

He lay on his side, curled up facing the flames. Even by firelight, he was pale. She knelt behind him.

'What's wrong?' She touched his shoulder, felt him shivering. He coughed and struggled round. He breathed shallowly, his face was thin and drawn.

'My God, what've you been doing?'

He coughed again, mouth dry. 'Hello.'

She went to the porch, found the water container and put some on to boil.

'Where've you been?' she said, taking off her jacket and rolling it for a pillow.

'Right here,' he whispered. 'Upstairs, anyway. I think I've been ill.'

'You might say that.' She wet her neck scarf and mopped his hot face with it. 'Didn't you hear me call earlier?'

'When was that? What day is it?'

'You're impossible.'

'Don't yell. My head feels like a bag of nails.'

'Well for God's sake. If you're going to play at being Robinson Crusoe, you've got to be healthy. What would've happened if it had been serious? Nobody would've found you for months.'

Pug crept up, licking at her hand.

'And as for this dumb animal . . . Why didn't you bark when I called? Lassie would've brought me a signed SOS.'

'Don't be hard on him.'

'Shut up. I haven't finished being hard on you. Have you got any aspirin? Any medical stuff?'

'I took some of my pain-killers. They didn't do any good.'

'Surprise.' She added coffee to the water.

'I think it was a touch of flu.'

'Food poisoning, you mean. Here, have some coffee. I'm going home to get you some proper food. You look half-starved.'

'Look, I'm okay.'

'Of course you are.' She stroked his hair back off his forehead.

164

His skin was burning. 'I'm behaving like Florence Nightingale. I should just leave you to sweat.'

'I'm already doing that.'

'You fool,' she said, not harshly. She buttoned up his jacket to keep out the cold.

She rode home fast, stabled Arab and crept in through the back door. Mrs Walker was cleaning the kitchen. Jo asked her to put together a bag of essentials.

Father and his friend were roaring away in the billiard room: she crept by the door and tip-toed upstairs to get another coat and some blankets. She took her Walkman and a couple of tapes.

As she closed the door, Grandpa John stepped out of the bathroom. He was fresh from a hot bath, red-faced and robed in his huge dressing gown. His hair stuck up like candy floss from his pink scalp.

'Where're you off to?' he said.

'Going out,' she said. 'To see a friend.'

'Be gone for the night?'

'I don't know.'

He puffed out his cheeks. 'I'm not going to say anything old fashioned.' He took out his pipe. 'You're not my daughter.'

'Okay then—'

'You can go to degradation and sin whichever way you please.'

'It's Michael,' she said. 'He's sick.'

'Michael now? What's brought about the change of heart?'

She paused, kissed him on the cheek. 'I'll tell you later.'

'Not very likely. Somebody in this house has to be in his own bed at a reasonable hour.' He watched her go, sucking at his pipe, wishing more than ever that he was allowed to smoke it.

She skipped downstairs and collected the food from Mrs Walker. In a minute, she was swinging out of the drive in the Range Rover. The windows were rolled down and she was smiling. She felt as if someone had given her a puff on some really good grass – or better than that. Everything had an edge to it – for once, she knew what she wanted to do.

Back at the house, she fed him soup and bread. He said he could not stomach more. She put the rest of the food in the cupboard upstairs, then helped him to his sleeping bag. 'How on earth did you get down in the first place?' she asked, as they slowly climbed the stairs.

'On my backside,' he said. 'It's easy when you can't stand up. Mind that step.'

She zipped him into the bag and went back for firewood. She made a fire in the old grate and lit it with her own matches.

'The chimney could be blocked,' he said.

'We'll soon find out.'

The fire caught and held. A little soot fell but that was all. She moved back to him.

'You don't have to do all this,' he said. 'Please, you've done enough already.'

'Quiet, you. I'm getting very self-righteous. Doing good turns is a new thing for me. You must bring out the saint in my soul.'

He winced.

'What's wrong?'

'Nothing. Headache's bad.'

She dosed him with aspirin. He still looked terrible, but his breathing was easier and his temperature was down. She guessed she had missed the worst part of it. She spread a blanket over him and sat cross-legged on the floor at his side.

'You should get a chair for your guests.'

'I never expected to have any.'

'How's your throat?'

'Dry.'

She tipped the mug to his lips, holding his head up. When he sank back again, she kept her hand there.

'You're a mess.'

'Thanks. You'll be going soon I hope?'

'Oh no.' She smoothed his hair back again. 'I'll stick around until you fall asleep.' She glanced at the bare room with its gaping window frames. 'It's a rotten place to be ill. Don't you ever feel lonely here?'

He said nothing.

She took her hand away. 'Try to get some sleep. I'll be here if you need me.'

'There's no reason . . .' he began, then lapsed into silence.

She shuffled backwards to the fire and leaned against the wall.

She stretched her legs out and wrapped the other blanket round her shoulders. The wind blew cold and sharp through the window. A few hazy stars showed beyond the trees. Pug trotted over and lay down at her feet.

She could not believe this was her.

She put the Human League on the Walkman and tried to relax. Michael turned a few times, then settled.

When the tape finished she got up and added more wood to the fire. She turned out the hurricane lamp – fireshadows started dancing on the walls.

She lost track of the time, thinking or dozing. Michael began to groan, and she moved to his side. He was asleep but dreaming. She touched his chest, felt the heart tripping hard. She had an idea what he was dreaming about now.

She took his hand, held it until he was calmer. He lay on his side, huddled up with his face half-hidden in the blanket. He looked younger now. He was helpless, not like all the other times, when he was strong.

She leaned down and kissed him.

Temple relaxed in his bed in the Middlecott Arms. The curtains were drawn apart, a faint glow of sky lined the flat country to the east. He put down his copy of *The Man Without Qualities* and took a drink from his bottle. Some of his gear was stashed in a corner of the room; the fishing tackle, cameras and walking shoes that made sure his landlord, and everyone else, thought he was taking a holiday. Other gear, the guns and equipment which would have caused awkward questions, was hidden in the Renault's secret compartments.

He switched out the light, still tasting the whiskey. It was all right at the moment, the booze. He was not really working until he found Sayers. So he relaxed and took a drink now and then. He was good at being patient – and he enjoyed the hunt almost as much as the kill.

35

Michael sat up. He clasped his head in both hands and kept his eyes closed. He pushed back with his feet so he could rest against the wall. The pounding in his head was not so bad now. It was still bad, but he could think straight about it. Before, he knew there were times when he was hazy about what was real. He screwed his eyes shut, then carefully opened them. The daylight filtered through. He lifted his head and saw the girl fast asleep by the fireplace. Her head was on her knees, she had wrapped herself tight in the blanket. She looked exhausted. Pug snored quietly next to her.

He climbed unsteadily out of the sleeping bag and crept downstairs. His stomach was hollow and his head felt light, but he was okay. He took a pee, then kicked out the remains of the fire and built a new one. He sniffed the air, realised he smelt pretty bad.

He used the grease twigs to light the fire. It did not take long. He sat close as it flared up and consumed the wood. He warmed himself at the flames.

Jo came out. She yawned and ran fingers through her hair.

'I wish I'd brought a comb,' she said, walking slowly round the fire. 'I feel like a zombie. Must've fallen asleep . . . How are you?'

'I'm fine,' he said. 'You're the one who had to sleep on the floor.'

'Didn't mean to,' she said. She had spent most of the night by his side, only moving when she woke towards dawn. 'I was going to make sure you were all right, then go home.' She pulled her coat straight. 'I've got neck ache.' She glanced up, realising that he was staring at her. 'I'll get breakfast,' she said, quickly.

She cooked the bacon and eggs she had brought, while he took a full container of water into the trees and washed himself from head to foot. He had not gone far enough, though: she saw him through a screen of leaves, his body shining under the water and sunlight. Her insides lurched and she wanted to touch him.

He came back to her in clean clothes, his hair still wet. They ate the food nervously, drinking several cups of coffee. She kept yawning and saying: 'I bet I look awful,' which she did not.

When he had washed the breakfast things, he found her fallen sound asleep again by the fire. He swallowed hard, then knelt beside her. He watched her the way he watched a deer in the forest; barely breathing. She was beautiful, and he had spent so long trying to ignore the fact. Trembling, he touched the curve of her throat.

She stirred. Eyes still closed, she grasped his hand and kissed it.

He tried to pull back. She spoke his name, opened her eyes slightly, and saw the confusion in his face.

He yanked his hand away, stumbled up and ran towards the house. She remained for a second, stunned, then it turned to anger. She leapt up and followed, caught him at the top of the stairs.

'Wait a minute,' she hissed. She pushed him into the room. 'Who the hell do you think you are?'

He was shuddering, trying hard to resurrect the old distance between them. 'Thanks very much for everything, but . . . please, go away, will you.'

She shook her head furiously. 'You can't . . . You can't just cut things dead like this.'

'There's nothing,' he said. 'I don't want—'

'You know what you want, as well as I do. These last few days, you've been looking at me as if . . . but it doesn't suit your idea of grief, does it?'

His eyes turned to glass. 'Wait a minute.'

'No, I bloody won't.' She forced him back against the wall. 'All you've done is lose someone you love. Everyone's lost somebody, but it doesn't make them storm around like the hero of a Russian novel. I know you were hurt, I know, but you've gone on too long with it. It's just self-pity.'

He clenched his fists. 'If you've finished now—'

She almost screamed it at him: 'I thought I was getting close to you.'

169

'Well, thanks so fucking much.'

She lashed out at him. 'Don't you swear at me.' The blow swept across his cheek. A diamond in her ring cut the skin.

'You bitch.'

'Shut up!' She was right in front of him, standing close. She could hear him breathing, see the sweat on his face, smell him.

She opened her mouth, staring at him. The flower opened in her belly again. Her hands went out, touched his chest.

He did not move, but she saw his excitement. She felt as if something were choking her. She reached down and started to unzip him. Her fingers had gone numb and useless, but she did it, and pulled him out, held him for a moment with both hands. She wanted it so badly. She fumbled with her jeans, pushing them down over her thighs. She touched herself, soaking wet already.

'Come on,' she whispered, unable to breathe. He did not move. She shoved her panties down, caught the smell of her own juices as the jeans and panties fell around her feet. She kicked them off. A part of her mind could not understand what was happening, another was saying that, Yes, this was what it was about.

She curled her arm around his neck, pulling herself against him. He still did nothing to help, and it was awkward, impossible. She felt his penis slither between her legs, used both hands to haul herself onto him.

Red sparks flashed in her eyes and she thought she was blacking out. The smooth tip of him nudged her thighs this time, and she lifted her body, then she was on him. He speared up inside her. She felt every millimetre of it with her flesh, heard the wet, slopping sounds as she settled on him. She was already coming; it burst over her in a wave, and her head jerked back in the spasm.

She kept moving, face on his shoulder, eyes full of tears. She came again, biting at the material of his shirt, pulling herself back and forth on him to make the feelings better. She drooled on him like a baby.

She felt it coming again. She panted in his ear: 'Oh, Michael, please . . . '

His hands came round. She felt them cup her backside and take the weight off her arms. She swung her legs up, crossed them

170

in the small of his back as he took her. He carried her, then the wall was against her back and he was beginning to move, going into her slowly at first. She felt his heart beating faster than it had last night, and the fluttering of his muscles as he held her.

She closed her eyes, gasped as he speeded up. She started to cry again, and clasped him tighter, vaginal muscles sucking at him. He pumped against her, sweat pouring off him.

She stopped thinking, body intent on coming, on making him come. Then his thrusts became harder, lost rhythm. He cried out as his semen spurted. She felt it inside her, then the hot, sticky crawl of it down her thighs. She came again, crying like a child.

36

He left her sleeping and went to Middlecott. He bought envelopes and paper, then he sat in the churchyard and wrote his parents a short letter. His body ached, but it was a good ache. He felt everything was sharp and lovely. A strong wind blew out of the west, bringing masses of high, white cloud, the sun sparked on the church and houses across the road.

He wrote:

I'm getting better, I think. The days are shorter now and the leaves are turning, but it's still warm enough to sleep out.

There was more, about the house and how he lived. He did not mention Jo. He could not think of anything to say about her yet.

He went to the post office to buy a stamp, and found there was a letter for him. He took it back to the churchyard to read it. It was from Ralph. In his usual, semi-literate scrawl, he said he would be down soon. There was also a mention of his mugging. A picture at the bottom, of him with his entire head bandaged and a red cross nurse giving a blood transfusion to his wallet.

171

Michael folded the letter and put it in his pocket. He smiled and thought about the fishing they would do when Ralph came down. He left the churchyard and crossed the road. He was anxious to get back to Jo.

Later, when they had been lying together for hours, she said:

'You're very nice when you relax.'

He turned over and pulled her blouse up, kissing her back. 'You've got smooth skin,' he said. 'But you're bony.'

'Not voluptuous enough for you?' She grinned. 'Well, you're all scars, but I don't complain, do I?' She began to comb her hair.

He blinked. Touching the ugly puckering on his back for the first time, she had not snatched her hand away or flinched in revulsion. Neither did she do what someone with a more melodramatic turn of mind might have; she did not kiss the scar. She ignored it, as if the skin were normal and whole. He remembered the feel of her ribs against his chest when he was coming in her, her small breasts crushed flat under his weight. It reminded him at the time of how Laura's body used to feel. He had come inside Jo thinking of Laura. Now he felt guilty for Jo's sake and a little sick with himself.

She got up and let Pug back into the room. She leaned out of the window and sunned her face.

'Do you want me to go now?'

He covered his head with a blanket. 'No, stay if you like. I'm not doing anything, though.'

'In that case, how about taking me to lunch somewhere?'

He groaned. 'After last night?'

'All right. I'll take you to lunch.' She sat down with him again. 'No people, I promise. I'll announce it to the entire county that they have to stay indoors while you're around.'

'I need to do some shooting.'

'You don't. I saw all those birds you've got hanging in the room downstairs.' She kissed his forehead, then realised how awkward it felt to be intimate with him when they were not aroused. 'There's a little market in Minton today. They sell all kinds of old junk. You might find an oil lamp so we can have romantic dinners here – come to think of it, you'll need a table and chairs too. And if we get hungry, you can buy a pig there. It's

172

an old-fashioned village market. We can have lunch at the pub and browse around.'

'All right, then. If you want to go.'

'What else? All these years of hobnobbing with the jet set, all those wild nights in the capitals of the world, all I really wanted was to go to Minton Market.'

He watched her get up and walk across the room. He felt peaceful.

They went to the market in her Range Rover. It was sited in a large, walled-off field in the middle of the village. There were sheds in one corner where livestock was sold at auction, and in other places people were selling junk, antiques, cheeses and meat. There was a bookstall where Michael picked up a copy of *The Chess Reader* for a few pence, and a man selling wood carvings, who sold Jo a strange horse's head which looked like a knight from a chessboard.

After half an hour, they went into the King Edmund pub and ordered a couple of salads for lunch. Jo was nodded to and greeted by several customers and the landlord. She introduced Michael as a businessman from London. They ate in the pub garden.

He glanced at problems in the chess book and smiled to himself. 'Do you play?'

'Piano, yes. Chess, no. I mean, I know where the bits go, but it's not worth bothering with me. I treat it like draughts with prettier pieces.'

Just then, a man came into the garden and sat down at a table near them.

'Oh God,' Jo whispered. 'It's that creepy guy again.'

Michael glanced round. He saw Temple sitting there, but had no flicker of recall. Parker's was the only face he knew from nine months ago. 'What's wrong with him?' he asked.

'Oh, nothing, I suppose. I just hate men who stare, and he's a real, unashamed ogler. He was here the last time I came in. Horrible little creep.'

Michael waited for a second, then saw the man look up. It seemed to him that the man stared at him more than her.

'You're paranoid,' he said, as a girl came out of the pub calling their ticket number for the salads.

173

Temple sat quietly, drinking his beer and watching the faces around him. He was thrumming like a guitar string, but nothing showed on the surface. He finished his drink, then left the pub.

Jo dropped Michael off at the gateway. Pug jumped out and ran off after a couple of rabbits.

'Michael,' she said.

He paused and leaned back inside the car.

'I've really enjoyed today,' she said. 'I mean, apart from this morning. It's been . . . fun.'

'I know,' he said.

She took his hand, rubbing her thumb across the back where the tiny scars were.

'I don't want to run off, but Dad's arranged for me to meet some people at a dinner in Bury tonight. He thinks he'll set me on the road to a career if I meet the right people.'

'Aren't you going into advertising, then?'

She kissed his hand and let it go. 'If you'll take me on as a partner.'

'I'll be flat on my back before they get me into that again,' he said.

'Don't you want to teach a young apprentice?'

'Go away before the bears come and eat you.'

'Oh, aren't we confident now?' she jeered.

He leaned closer, uncertain of his own role in the situation. He wanted to show her some sign. He kissed her cheek. She turned her face for another.

'This do, whatever it is,' she said. 'It should all be over by eleven. Do you want me to come over tonight?'

'If you like,' he said. 'Put your seat belt on, will you?'

She put the Rover in gear and drove away. He tasted her on his tongue. It was strange: everything seemed distant from before he was ill.

He called to Pug and strode across the field. The air was warm and moist, he was sweating from the ride, so he decided to take a swim later. Pug turned, looking for him. Michael picked up a stick and threw it far out, back towards the gate. As Pug ran for it, Michael saw a Renault Nine pass the gate.

He must be lost, he thought, watching the car as it trundled out of sight into the trees.

He took his gun and a towel and walked down to the river. It was early evening, the sun was scarlet and red. He wandered through the forest, out over the fields, and reached the water's edge. Pug seemed nervous and frisky. He went barking at shadows under the trees and sniffing under bushes as if the fields were alive with vermin. Michael took a handful of cereal and fed it to the dog. Then he said: 'Go on,' and let him run free.

He stripped off, laid his clothes neatly on the bank and dived into a deep place at the bend. He went into the water, gasping at the sudden cold, but it was a good shock. He felt the day's dirt running off him. His head cleared, he gained a kind of control over his thoughts. It was the first day he could remember for a long time that did not seem to have happened to someone else.

Meanwhile, Pug skirted the edge of the field. He had an unfamiliar scent on the light breeze. Searching carefully, he drew closer to it. He stopped at the edge of the forest, head raised, eyes wide. A snarl began to curl his lip. He shot into the gloom under the branches.

Michael ducked under, turning a somersault in the water. Surfacing, he saw a short branch floating past. He grabbed it and called Pug, because it was funny to watch the mutt paddling along after a stick in the slow current.

Pug did not come at his call. He yelled again, but Pug did not appear. Shrugging, he flicked the branch downstream and turned on his back to gaze at the sky. He whistled quietly.

The forest was silent, and the field was empty.

When his limbs began to ache with the exercise, he climbed onto the bank and picked up his towel. The air was growing colder, and he wrapped himself tight in the towel, covering his head with it. He sat cross-legged in the grass and called to the dog again. Pug did not come. He muttered something in annoyance and pulled on his jeans, then walked barefoot to the centre of the field, shouting louder. He turned a circle and told Pug to leave the rabbits alone and come on back.

He put on the rest of his clothes and, shivering with cold, wandered over the field, peering into the trees for a sign of the

175

dog. He stopped, and wondered why he felt afraid. His leg began to ache.

The sun dipped behind the forest. Everything became blood-stained.

Michael rolled his towel and headed back to the house. Perhaps Pug had gone there by himself. It was possible, since he was hungry. He went slowly, looking out for movement, but the forest was quiet. When he crossed the meadow, he called out several times.

The only one who heard was Temple.

Michael approached the house with a hollow sensation in his stomach. When he was a kid, they had a dog who ran away one afternoon while they were playing. They searched and called for hours, put adverts in the local newspaper, but the dog was never found.

He leaned against the well. It was stupid to worry, since Pug would probably come panting home in half an hour, but he could not stop it. The dog had been with him all through the bad time. To lose him now would be like some kind of jinx taking effect.

He built a fire and made some coffee, sat drinking it as the darkness fell. Autumn was beginning to take hold now, and he knew the damp weather was affecting his wounds. He wished Pug would come back, and that Jo would turn up, because he needed to talk. He went to the room where the birds were hung and took down a pheasant for the pot. He made a stew of it, which took up a couple of hours, and in the meantime played problems out of the chess book he had bought. Every time a branch cracked in the woods, he looked up for Pug. Then, still restless, he went to bed, and was asleep when Jo arrived.

'I never wanted to sleep with anyone before,' she said, lying with her head on his chest. 'I don't mean sex. I mean actually sleeping. You're the first man I ever wanted to . . . cuddle up to, I suppose.'

He lay wakeful and watching. 'I'm glad you came.'

She stroked his belly gently, going over the muscles. 'Where's that damn dog? He usually tries to join in.'

'I don't know. He wandered off this afternoon, hasn't come back.'

'Are you sure? I thought I heard him snouting around in the trees when I arrived.'

He got up and went to the window. He called down into the woods. The garden was empty, the smudge of the fire and deeper patches of shadow under the trees.

'If he's out there,' he said, 'he's playing hide and seek.'

'Come back here,' she said. 'I'm getting cold.'

He went to her, and when she touched him he was trembling.

'What's wrong? You're not worried about Pug, are you? He'll be scratching at the door in the morning. Probably thought it was his turn for a little bit of screwing.'

He sank down beside her, taking a kiss from her upraised lips.

'It's all right,' she murmured. 'It's all right.'

Down in the trees, Temple watched the house for another five minutes, then withdrew. He walked a mile through the forest to his car, got in, and drove back to the Middlecott Arms.

In the morning, he would continue.

37

There was no sign of Pug, so they ate a frugal breakfast indoors.

'You won't be able to stay here much longer,' Jo said, putting on her jacket as he brought the coffee up.

'That depends,' he said.

'What about the weather? It's been a mild autumn so far, but you wait till October. It can get pretty cold out here, not to mention damp. You'll go down with pneumonia before the month's out.'

'Maybe I'll just insulate the place a little better.'

'But you don't mean to carry on like this for ever, do you?'

'Probably not.' He swallowed the good hot coffee, leaning on the windowsill. 'Just as long as I feel like it.'

'There must be people who want you to go back.'

'There are. But it doesn't change things. This is no one else's business.'

She scowled, thinking that it was hers as much as anyone's. 'What're you going to do today?'

'The usual,' he said. 'And chop some firewood in case it gets colder.'

'I'll be bored to death,' she said.

'I'm not asking you to stay, am I?'

'Thanks.'

He became conciliatory. 'I didn't mean it that way.' He took her hand. 'I'm just wound up about Pug. I've got to look for him.'

'He can't have got caught in a poacher's trap. They're not allowed.'

'Don't be naïve. I've seen them.'

'So you want me to go home?'

'Do whatever you want. Aren't there things you have to do?'

She shrugged. 'Not really. Grandpa John's probably wondering where I've got to. I told him I'd explain everything about you – but I can't think where to start.'

'Well, why not go home for a while, and I'll see you later?'

She stood up. 'When?'

'Come whenever you like.'

She shook her head. 'I really love the way you make me feel so wanted.'

He gave no reply, but she could not leave on those words, so she bent down, kissed him on the top of his head. 'I'll keep a look out for Pug,' she said, and went downstairs.

Michael lay on the bed for a while after the sound of the Range Rover had faded into the morning. He thought of the places where Pug might have got stuck, and made a route in his head that would take him past all of them. Then he picked up his gun, rolled a towel, and made his way down to the river. At one point, halfway there, he thought he saw Pug in the shade of some small pines, but there was no answer when he called. He blamed it on a deer and carried on. By the river, he searched up and down the bank for a clue, just in case the dog had gone into the water. He stripped and dived in, still wondering. Pug was a well-trained animal; he had been taught not to run far, or to go chasing after anything without his master's consent. As a tracker, he was only fair, but it seemed unlikely that he could wander off, get lost, and not find his way back again.

There were two alternatives: one was that he had had an accident – in which case, where was he? The other was that somebody had seen him, thought what a good-looking dog he was and decided to 'adopt' him. But Pug was trained not to trust other people that way.

It was confusing, and he wished the damned animal would suddenly appear on the bank, yapping his head off and begging for food.

He dried himself on the bank, noticing more than before how summer was over. Leaves not yet turned were dull and dry, the grass was coarse and old. The river, once choked with weed, was clearing. He dressed, combed his hair, and wandered into the forest.

Jo reached home just after her father and Grandpa John got up. She ate breakfast with them, and noticed that both men were watching her more carefully than usual. Afterwards, she went out to the tennis court and smashed some balls around for a while, wondering how she came to be in such a situation. Caro would be surprised, that was for sure. If she was lucky, it would all fizzle out in a few days; this year's silly season fling. After all, what could you expect from a relationship based on – admittedly terrific – sex? She knew that Michael was some kind of walking wounded, and she was probably no more than sexual relief to him. She only wished she knew what the other girl, Laura, looked like. It would make her feel less like successor to a ghost.

But while she did her best to take a realistic view of the whole affair, she also knew it wasn't ordinary for her. Nor did she want it to fizzle out. She slammed one ball after another against the court's wire fence, then strolled across to pick them up.

'Working off some frustrations?' Grandpa John asked.

'Haven't got any,' she said, scooping up a ball in her racquet and lobbing it over the fence to him. He caught it easily and threw it back, where she, standing ready, hit it into the opposite court.

'I was talking to your father before he went out,' he said.

'Where to this time?'

'Norwich. Seems he's wining and dining some chap there. He was asking what you're doing with yourself.'

'He could've asked me,' she said, swatting balls at the net while she talked to him.

'You weren't in a talkative mood at breakfast. Besides, he's not getting anxious. He doesn't know all the facts about our young friend in the woods. He just wonders if you're coming to any conclusions about your future.'

She ran to get the balls, shouting back: 'It's early yet, isn't it?'

'Perhaps so. But you don't want to spend your time playing hostess here and keeping an old man company.'

'Grandpa, don't be stupid.'

He tapped his walking stick against the fence. 'If I were him, I'd take a practical line. Put you out on your ear if you don't come up with a plan by Christmas.'

'Big deal.' She grinned. 'I'll go and live in the forest.'

He sighed. 'He's hardly a suitable target for your affections. I don't think there's much profit to be made, living in the forest.'

'He's an advertising man,' she said. 'Was, anyway. And what if he goes back to it? Suitable enough for you?'

He took out his pipe. 'Look, unusual romances won't save you from decision-making. You have to make some decisions about what you want.'

Jo lobbed her last ball over the fence.

'I know what I want,' she said.

Lapwings were twanging high in the sky over the fields, and Michael walked out of the forest. He had shot nothing to eat, because he was distracted by searching for Pug and his aim was off. When he realised he would end up wounding something rather than making a clean kill, he gave it up and headed for home. There was no evidence of Pug to be found. There were some tracks through the trees by the river, but only human ones.

He looked in the letter box for a note from Jo, found nothing, went on to the house and built a fire. Dew had begun to settle and the house loomed over him in the gathering dusk. He felt the oppressiveness of it tonight: the house decaying in its lonely place, surrounded by the emptiness of the woods and the forest.

Shivering, he went to the house and took out his key for the room where the birds were hung.

But the door was open. The lock hung to the frame by splinters.

'Oh no,' he said wearily. Who said vandalism was a city

disease? How far did you have to go before people would leave you alone?

He pushed the door wide, listening for any movement. The room, shuttered and on the dark side of the house, was difficult to make out. For a moment he saw nothing but the shapes of the birds on the walls. Nothing, apparently, had been disturbed.

Then the thick, gagging smell hit him, and he drew his head back for air.

The birds which he had hung, four of them, had been slashed to pieces. Their putrifying guts hung down, smearing the wall, dirtying the floor. One was so badly cut that the head hung on a hook and what remained of the body was spread all over the dusty floorboards. Feathers and shreds of skin lay everywhere.

He ran upstairs, not knowing what to expect, but nothing was touched. He lay down on the bed and closed his eyes.

When Jo came later, he had cleaned up the mess. He sat by the fire, concentrating on a chess problem.

'What's wrong?' she asked.

'Some bastard broke in and played Jack the Ripper with all my birds.'

He told her what it had been like and asked if she had seen any strangers around.

'No, but it could've been kids from the village.'

'Weird kids.'

'They can be.'

He threw a twig on the fire and watched it blaze. She stood on the edge of the light, not yet sure if he wanted her there. She said: 'Pug hasn't come back?'

He shook his head. Then she saw the tears in his eyes. She went to him.

'Oh, Michael, I'm sorry.'

He controlled the tears and spat in the fire. 'It just gets me down. First of all, Pug disappears, then some bastard comes and shits all over where I live. I mean, this was the one thing I had that no one had touched or fucked up. Now some lunatic – probably just a loony old tramp – makes it like everything else.'

She touched his face. 'It's not so bad, is it?'

'It's like watching everything go down the drain. I figured I could get far enough away to shake the muck off.'

She said nothing, but wondered at how naïve he was, to believe it was possible.

'Ralph rang me,' she said, after a time. 'You know he's coming down?'

'Yes. When?'

'Probably the day after tomorrow, he said. He wants to go fishing. I told him no chance. Fishing's the one thing I won't do.'

'He means me, not you.' Michael smiled. 'It'll be good to see him. He helped me a lot.'

'I know. He's good at that.'

She shuddered, although the fire was high.

'This old dump,' she said.

'Did you come by car?'

She nodded.

'Let's go to Middlecott, then. Fancy a drink in the pub?'

'If you're buying,' she said.

When the pub closed, they drove back to Fairstone Hall. She stopped by a small red-brick bridge. He saw the Hall, several windows lit, shining between long rows of London plane trees. He got out, but she followed.

'Please,' she said. 'Come in.'

He shrugged reluctantly.

'No one'll be up. Dad's away, and Grandpa John's in bed at this hour.'

'Who says he is?' Grandpa John hailed them from the other side of the bridge. He came over, leaning on his walking stick. 'Just out taking the evening air, and I hear my nearest and dearest talking about me.'

They stood in the yellow glow of the sidelights. Grandpa John sucked at his pipe, looked at Michael.

'Mr Sayers, I presume?' He stuck a hand out.

Michael was frozen for a second, as if he had forgotten how to greet other people. Then he turned on something like a smile and took the outstretched hand.

'Good evening, Sir.'

'Formal for a young chap, aren't you?'

'I—'

'Never mind, nothing wrong with manners.' He grinned. 'So you're the lad who's been using my granddaughter for target practice?'

'It wasn't—'

'Don't mind me, old chap. Just ribbing.'

Michael bit his lip, fidgeting from one foot to the other. There was an embarrassed pause.

'Well, I must be off indoors,' Grandpa John said. 'Why don't you do what the girl says? Come on in, have a drink, stay the night. Better than a damn sleeping bag.'

'Thank you, Sir, but – well, I ought to get back.'

'Fair enough.' He glanced at Jo, and she thought she saw some unease in his expression. 'You can pick me up on your way down the drive, if you like. G'night.'

They waited until he was out of earshot, then Jo turned to Michael. 'Why don't you come with me? You could sleep in a proper bed for once – mine, if you're lucky.'

He laughed quietly, though the discomfort of meeting Grandpa John was still in his face.

She continued: 'I mean, I don't want you to go away. I hate thinking about you all alone in that place.'

'I've got to go back,' he said. 'If I'm not there, who knows what might happen?'

She kissed him, holding on. 'Well, be careful. Don't get lost or anything. And if there *is* a mad axeman in the forest, don't be brave. Scream, and I'll get the shotgun out.'

He watched her drive down between the plane trees and pick up Grandpa John. He took a couple of deep breaths to clear his lungs of the pub's smoky air, and set off for Oak Farm.

The night was misty again. It was warm enough to take off his jacket. She was right, of course; he did not want to go back to the house. He would have preferred to spend the night with her, to have the sound of her relaxed breathing and her warmth. Laura used to say that he was hopeless about sleeping alone and he knew now that she was right.

A branch cracked in the forest to his right. He glanced into the dark. Nothing there. Probably a deer taking fright. He went on, getting off the lane and following one of the paths between the trees. The air grew colder, and he put his jacket on again.

There was another movement in the trees. He heard it, and paused long enough to feel a cool shaft of nerves go through him. It seemed as if something was out there in the gloom, keeping pace with him.

He said softly: 'Pug? Here boy.' And heard the floor of ferns and twigs rustle some distance off.

His eyes strained for something to see, finding nothing at all. Everything was hidden in the moonless black. Again, there was movement – a step forward, no more. He started walking again, and his ears caught the sound of something moving parallel to him, a little distance behind. His heart rate began to rise, and the new skin on his back and leg ached deeply, like hot embers under the flesh. He kept going, trying not to worry, but his imagination was working. He thought of the sick mess in the downstairs room that afternoon, the pheasant's head hanging from a hook.

He stopped, fighting back a sudden attack of panic. He had forgotten to turn. He was walking deeper into the forest instead of towards home. He swung round, but each row of trees looked identical. He stuck shaking hands in his pockets. He had no gun, no knife – only the trailing leather strap of the dog's lead sticking through the hole in his pocket. He set off back along the path, trying to remember the turning. The movement in the trees followed, he was sure of it. He did not stop this time – he couldn't – but shouted into the forest:

'Whoever you are out there, bugger off.' No reply came, no sign that it was more than an echo. 'You hear?' he said. 'Bugger off.'

Still it went on, until he was sure it was footsteps. He broke into a run, slow at first, but picking up speed after he dodged into the path home. The injured leg made him clumsy, and he could not go very far. Soon he dragged to a halt, lungs burning. He tried not to breathe so hard, to hear the sounds around him. There was nothing now; he thought he must be all right. He straightened up.

Then a stone dropped through the branches and struck the soft earth at his feet. He ran again until he saw the house, and stumbled across the clearing, cursing the pain in his back and leg, stuck the key in the front door and slammed it open, hobbled up the stairs to his room. He lay on his bed, locked in, safe.

The woods were very large, very dark beyond the windows.

38

Morning sun glittered on silver coffee pot and milk jug. The dining room was bright and airy, also empty except for Ralph and his mother. The rest of the family could be heard bustling out of the hall, going out for the day *en masse*.

Ralph yawned his way through toast, marmalade, bacon and eggs, orange juice and coffee. He read his father's *Times*, checked his shares in the *FT* index, and shook his head at his mother.

'The old man must be losing his touch. I bought those Wallrite shares at twelve pence because he was sure they were on the way up. Now they're at threepence, and I'm staring bankruptcy in the face.'

Ralph's mother was a thin, graceful woman in her middle fifties. She looked like an older model for the heroine of *Brief Encounter*. Ralph was her youngest son, and she tended to watch everything he did with a vaguely amused concern.

'Nonsense, dear,' she said. 'They're a long-term investment.'

'He can afford them.' Ralph snorted. 'I can't. I don't have his financial back-up. Any more of this bear market, and I'll be forced into desperate measures – like working for promotion.'

'You're obviously working yourself to death.' She eyed the remains of his breakfast. 'What are your plans for today?'

He slurped more coffee. 'Going over to Joanne's place.'

'To see Michael?'

'I dropped him a line the other day. We're going fishing. I'll probably stay over tonight.'

She leaned towards him. She knew Michael well, and liked him because he had been more down to earth than some of Ralph's friends. She had sent him a card in hospital last Christmas.

'How is he now?'

'I don't know, to tell you the truth. Haven't seen him since he

185

went away. I hope he's coming round.'

'From what?'

'From that bloody depression. All that talk about giving up work for good, and this daft idea about backing out of the world in general.'

'I can sympathise with that,' she said. 'After all, look what it's done to him.'

'Oh, I know. He got badly hurt, inside as well as out. I understand him wanting to run away and crawl into a hole – everybody does sometime. But he's got to get out of it before it gets to be a habit.'

'Perhaps he's the best judge of that,' she said.

'No . . . No, I don't think he is. The last time I saw him, he was just as closed-up as at the beginning. No fuss if you tried to talk to him about Laura or his sister; he just turned you off the subject. I never saw him shed a tear. Don and Audrey said the same thing. They wanted him to see a psychiatrist or some such, but he wasn't having any.'

'Grief's a very private thing. Some people bounce back, others take a long time to get over it.'

'I suppose you're right. But what really gets me down is that he doesn't seem to have any fight left in him. He didn't care who did it, he didn't want to know when they got caught. I call that strange.' His face changed from concern to a grin. 'Still, you never know. If Jo's been working on him, he may be all right by now.'

'Working on him?' she said, with exaggerated shock. 'What *do* you mean?'

'She came up to London to ask me about him,' he said. 'I was grilled over lunch.'

'You surprise me,' she said. She had always disapproved slightly of Jo. 'Perhaps she's finally growing up.'

'Well, I'll find out today. I'll see her if she's in. If they're not sharing a sleeping bag in the forest already, that is.'

'Ralph!' she said.

He went upstairs and had a bath, lounged in it for an hour, adding hot water whenever it got cool. Then he rose, dried himself, shaved and dressed. He stood in front of the bedroom mirror in his new suit of flannels, and thought what a wonderful sight he was. Like something from the thirties, which was the

186

intention. He even had the straw hat.

'Today will be a good day,' he said to himself. He picked up his father's second set of keys to Oak Farm, and went downstairs to check his fishing gear.

Temple sat on his haunches in the trees, watching the house. Sayers came to the window and peered at the garden. He looked tired and nervous, as if he had been awake half the night, worrying over every noise. Good, Temple thought. He was breaking down almost as if to a schedule.

The watch went on through breakfast. Temple noted Sayers's use of tinder to start the fire, the way he favoured one leg, the discomfort every time he strained his back. He recorded every twitch and move. It was his method. He liked to know everything about his target – not the family details or recent history: none of that mattered. He concentrated on the physical things, the instinctual ones, because they would be useful for the job. Was the man slow or fast when he moved? Were his reactions quick? Could he defend himself? How strong was he? How were his nerves? All these things Temple looked for, noticing with satisfaction that Sayers was jumpier than he had been at the beginning. And at the beginning he was not much: more of a boy than a man, who had run all this way to avoid fighting. He would prove less than difficult. In the last couple of days, he had lost his dog, been frightened, and seen the birds cut to shreds. He was edgy, but not close to breaking yet. Temple was taking it one step at a time with George Parker's instructions to make the boy suffer, and he judged how far to push Sayers the way Michael would have considered an advertising campaign. He knew that Sayers was trying to cut out the rest of the world, so only something very bad would make him go to the police, and by the time the bad thing happened, it would be too late.

Judgement, he thought. It's all about judgement.

He watched Sayers sit down beside the fire to consider his next move on the chessboard. Crouching in the bushes, Temple did likewise.

Ralph drove through Borden on the way to Fairstone Hall. He stopped in his favourite pub there, had a pint of bitter, and bought a couple of bottles for Michael. Outside the pub, he walked up the road and watched fish from the bridge. There were some nice fat specimens down there, and he was certain to catch something, even if it was only a chill from sitting about for hours on end.

Whistling loudly, he got back in the car and ambled over to Fairstone Hall, going slowly through the forest because he usually missed the turning.

He noticed that Jo's car was not there when he reached the gates, but carried on down the drive and parked in front of the house. He got out, carrying the wine he had bought as a present for Jo. The sun did not warrant his wearing the hat, but he put it on and strode up to the door.

Grandpa John came round the corner, lugging his shotgun. 'Morning, chum. No use knocking. She's gone to Norwich to do some shopping. Always buys things when she's fed up.'

Ralph doffed his hat. 'So I've missed her?'

'You have to be pretty fast to catch her these days.' Grandpa John slammed the shotgun together suddenly and took a shot at some sparrows on the lawn. He missed by a mile, churning up the lawn, but the sparrows rose in panic. 'That friend of yours seems to have charms that none of the more suitable suitors have had.'

'That bad?' Ralph said.

'How should I know? I'm not her father, thank God.'

They went inside, and Ralph put the wine on a table while Grandpa John broke the shotgun and emptied out the shells.

'What're you up for, anyway?'

'Going fishing with Michael,' Ralph said.

'That's good, good. Strikes me that skulking around in the forest is the worst way to get over an emotional upset.'

'I'm glad someone else thinks so. You've met him, then?'

Grandpa John said that he certainly had, and they talked of this and that for a few minutes. Ralph realised that the old man was more than a little worried about his granddaughter's relationship with Michael, and he wondered how far things had gone. It would be interesting to pump Michael for the full story later. Grandpa John, who was complaining by now about the price of a 1935 Hirondelle, suggested that he'd offer Ralph a drink if it wasn't a little early, and Ralph said he didn't think it was, so they went to the sitting room.

'But only one,' Ralph said. 'Then I'll be off to visit Jungle Jim.'

Michael reached into the cupboard and got his fishing gear together. He packed the weights and lines into his rucksack, gathered up the rods and went downstairs. He locked the front door, then went into the remains of the garden to dig out some worms for bait. As for him, he had half a loaf of bread and some cheese – what he did not eat would go for ground bait. He put the worms in a plastic container and picked up the rest of the stuff. Then he headed for the river. His nerves were jangled from last night, and he knew he had over-reacted. A day's fishing would settle him down. He turned and took one more look at the house before he left, wanting to be sure no one could get in. If Ralph happened to arrive, he had his own set of keys, so it was no problem.

By an old reflex, he started to call Pug, but the dog was not there. He walked away.

Temple followed Sayers until he went into the forest beyond the cart track, then he returned to Oak Farm. There were several details about the house that he wanted to learn before he put the final stage into operation, and there would be plenty of time while Sayers was fishing.

He went back along the edge of the meadow, keeping out of sight. In the woods it was not so muggy. The shade was cool and green. Underfoot, the earth was loamy, his feet sank into it.

He investigated the outside of the house again, circling it before moving in. He checked the front door, which Sayers had been locking since the birds. It was not much in the way of security, and when the time came it would be easy to smash, but for now he let it be. Today was not for action, only for final preparations.

He moved beneath the bedroom windows, looking for a way up. In the end, he used the same route as Michael, climbing on to the shed roof. He straightened up on the sagging tiles, then leaned to reach an upper window. He tested the partially rotted wood, checked for any stray shards of glass, then grasped the sill and swung out. He hauled himself up and through, dropping

189

silently to the floor of the spare room. He breathed the damp air, and began to look around.

Ralph put down his glass and shook Grandpa John's hand.

'I'd better be moving on,' he said, 'before you get me too wobbly to stand.'

'Sure you won't have another?' Grandpa John grinned.

'You can drink me under the table at dinner some time. Jo owes me a meal.'

'All right, then. Tomorrow evening, perhaps? And try to get that chap to come along.'

'You want a disturbance?'

'He'll be all right with people he knows.'

'I'll see what I can do.'

They went to the door. Ralph picked up his hat.

'Don't go into the villages like that, will you.'

'Why not?' he asked, adjusting the brim.

'They're not used to sights like you, not since the 'twenties, I should think.'

Ralph smiled at his image in the mirror. He left the bottle of wine, and climbed into the car. The last he saw of Fairstone Hall was Grandpa John reloading to pot a couple of blackbirds.

The bed looked comfortable, Temple thought. He smiled, thinking of Sayers and the girl fucking on the blankets. He looked through the chess book by the bed. The travelling set lay open on the floor with a problem set up. He tried to work it out, but it was beyond his skill in the game. He picked up Sayers's sketchbook and flicked through the finely detailed watercolours of leaves and flowers, pieces of wood bark and, on one page, a study of a mouse's skull. At the back of the book were the notes Jo had left him, and Ralph's recent letter. He read them, replaced the book and opened the cupboard door, sorting through the clothing and other items inside. He picked up the tobacco tin which contained tinder, and sloshed the remains of the half-bottle of whiskey around. He saw the ammunition for Sayers's rifle stuck behind a shirt.

The separate parts came together suddenly in his head, like the winning moves in one of the boy's chess games. He had all the ingredients for a plan. He knew how he would run the final day of Sayers's life.

Ralph stopped at the gate and looked inside the letter box. The Beach Boys were singing hymns of praise to summer on the cassette player, and the warmth made him feel as if the best of the year was yet to come. It would be good to have old Mike back in circulation. He got back in the car and drove across the meadow, stopping at the edge of the woods. There was no way you could get a car into the woods, he had decided. Not his car, anyway. He grabbed the bottles of beer and got out, then set off through the trees, wondering why Michael could not be a recluse in Hyde Park or somewhere. All this way to go fishing.

Temple turned over a pile of old newspapers in a corner of the spare room, reading the headlines of ten, twenty years ago. One of them was a front page on the Israeli athletes at the Munich Olympics in 'seventy-two. He put the papers back in order and sorted through the rest of Sayers's fishing tackle. He was looking for anything that might be used as a weapon, just in case Sayers happened to turn nasty at the end. He went back to the bedroom.

Ralph held the two beer bottles by the necks, thinking that the first thing he and Michael would do was sink these to take the edge off their thirst. He saw the house through the trees, looking tall and gloomy and a little more decayed than he remembered. There were no signs of life. The old bastard would probably be out in the forest, playing Tarzan. He swiped at flies with his hat and stepped over a fallen branch. The undergrowth was alive with insects and the clearing rang with birdsong. Last days of summer trying to assert themselves, giving up the ghost for autumn.

He reached the door and tried the knob.

Temple lifted his head, eyes flickering back towards the stairway. He heard the handle turning.

Ralph cursed quietly, because it was locked. Michael was, therefore, out. He fumbled in his jacket pocket.

Temple did not move. It was not possible to reach a window at the front of the house without crossing the sagging floor of the

191

master bedroom. It would cause so much noise, he would be heard. He waited, listening for another sound. The door was locked, so if it was the girl she would soon go away. Only Sayers had a key. He rested, poised on the balls of his feet, waiting. Perfectly calm.

Ralph dug the keys out of his pocket. He fiddled two into the lock before finding the right one. It took a little effort, but finally moved. He gave the door a shove and walked in.

Temple heard it open. He realised there was no way to get out. It was too high to jump safely, and the way to the spare room was now in the intruder's view. He moved quickly to the corner of the room by the door and flexed his left hand into a fist, flexed it out until the fingers splayed, re-flexed it to a fist. The skin over his knuckles tightened, he breathed evenly, thinking that Parker would not like it this way. The end was meant to be slow. He prepared to injure and immobilise, but not to kill. Not yet.

Ralph stood in the porch, gazing up the stairs. He was sweating into his flannels, and the house was not clean. His suit would be ruined if he was not careful. He thought: Maybe I'll wait outside. Then he thought: No, let's give him a surprise. He climbed the stairs.

Temple listened to the footsteps, the cautious tread on the rotting steps. Flexed.

Wonder which room old Mike's living in? Ralph thought. He wondered about the spare room on the right, then recalled that it was small and had bad light. A step creaked under him, and he grabbed the banister rail to get to the top of the stairs. Only when he got there did he realise there was a black streak across the elbow of his jacket. The bottles of beer clinked together as he dusted off the worst of it. Michael, my boy, he thought, you owe me a cleaning bill. He looked down just before he moved and saw, for less than a second, the toe of a shoe projecting beyond the doorway. He had long enough to begin thinking that Michael was playing silly buggers with him, hiding round the corner, and he began to raise his head to yell 'Boo!'

Then Temple hit him.

It was a crushing blow. Temple, his shoulders against the wall, swung the clenched fist backwards at the level of the jawline. It struck like a hammer, smashing the windpipe, rupturing the thyroid cartilage of the larynx. Ralph's head snapped back – a little harder, and the impact would have broken his neck. He fell heavily across the spare-room doorway. The beer bottles shattered on the floor. The hat spun off and bounced down the stairs.

In the moment of striking, Temple knew it was the wrong man. He recognised the face from London, and knew he had made a mistake.

'Shit,' he said, and stood thinking.

The man lay on the floor, semi-conscious. The choking gargle of his desperate attempt at breathing was loud in the room. There was blood on his mouth, and every time he writhed, his suit became dirtier.

Temple shook his head. It was inconvenient but not fatal. The only certainty was that the man could not be left as he was. Of course, he could always become part of the plan. Temple liked that idea.

He straddled the body. He finished the job.

Afterwards, he took the body's car keys, leaving everything else, and disposed of the body. He pushed it downstairs and watched it tumble awkwardly into the narrow passage. Picking up the hat, he got a grip under the body's arms and heaved it outside. He dragged it round to the well, turned it over and lifted it, with difficulty, until head and shoulders were over the wall. Then he tipped the feet up and listened as it hit the water below. By morning, it would be floating.

He returned to the house and cleaned up the broken bottles, soaking up the spilled beer with one of the old newspapers. When it was done, the floor looked too clean, but there was no way to make it right again. He left it and went downstairs. He found Ralph's bunch of keys still in the door. He locked it behind him, and covered over the drag marks which the body's heels had made in the earth. Lastly, he drove the victim's car down to the cart track and hid it in the forest two miles away from Oak Farm. There was very little chance Sayers would go that way before morning. Then he made his way back to his own car and drove to Middlecott. He prepared himself for tomorrow.

Tomorrow, at twelve o'clock, he would kill Michael Sayers.

39

That evening, Jo came home from Norwich and found the bottle of wine on the hall table. When Grandpa John told her that Ralph had called, she smiled and opened the bottle. If anyone could help her bring Michael fully out of his shell again, it was Ralph. She drank two glasses of the wine while she ran a bath, then she soaked for a while, reading a book she had bought in Jarrolds, *The Roots of Depression*.

She arrived at Oak Farm with some cheeses, cold meat and another bottle of wine, expecting to find them chatting over the fire, probably a little drunk. But though the fire was lit, no one was there.

She called Michael's name, then Ralph's, and heard Michael answer from the house.

He was at the stop of the stairs, on his knees examining the floor. The stairway smelled of stale beer.

'Hello, you been dropping your glass in a drunken frenzy?'

He hardly looked up. 'You smell it too?'

'You'd have to be suffering from a bad cold not to,' she said.

He wiped his finger across the floorboards. 'Some bastard's been in here again.'

She shuddered. 'They haven't—'

'Not this time. Nothing's been touched. But someone's spilled beer all over the place.' He got up and they went outside again. His face was pinched.

'I don't understand it,' he said. 'The door was locked tight. It hasn't been messed with.'

'Oh, wait a minute,' she said. 'It must have been Ralph.'

'What?'

'He came by today when I was out, left me a bottle of wine. He was on his way out to you. He'd have a key, wouldn't he?'

194

'Then why isn't he here?'

They sat down, and Michael stirred the fish around in a pan.

'He probably got tired of waiting, drank some beer, dropped some more, and decided to go home.'

He thought about it. 'He would've left a note.'

'Not if he's coming back soon.'

He frowned. 'I don't like it. He would've left a note. He always does.' A small bird moved suddenly in the trees and he glanced up sharply.

'What else is wrong?' she asked.

'Nothing,' he said, wiping his eyes. 'Just I got spooked last night coming back here.'

'And now you think someone's broken in again? Or climbed in through a window, by the look of it?' She put down her bag. 'Why don't you go to the police, then?'

He turned the fish. It sputtered and sizzled. 'What's the point? There's nothing to tell them about.'

'Only a room full of dead birds.'

He was reluctant. 'There's nothing they'd waste time on. Besides, I don't want coppers running all over the place.'

'I'll come round one morning and find you with an axe in your skull. You're getting paranoid. First of all, you're worried because someone's out to get you, then you don't want to tell anyone because you don't trust them either.'

He stared coolly at her. 'Shut up, will you?'

'Well, what's wrong with you? You'll end up like chickens in a shed when they think there's a fox around. They go running around until they find a hole, and they kill themselves trying to squeeze in. And often as not, there's no fox.'

'I'm hungry,' he snapped. 'Now leave it alone.'

'Are you going to do something, instead of just sitting here worrying yourself to death?'

'There's nothing to do.'

'The police could tell you if there's a suspicious character around, couldn't they? Or will you wait until this supposed lunatic's got his hands around your throat?'

'It's probably kids, like you said.'

She stood up. 'When are you going to do something?'

He threw the skillet in the pan. 'Leave it, will you?' He was

195

angry now. 'I've told you before, it's none of your business, but you won't let it alone any more than they will. Now for Christ's sake shut up about it or go away.'

She froze, glaring at him. Then she said: 'I seem to spend ninety per cent of my time arguing with you . . . It's not worth all the agony.' She turned and walked out, the wine turning sour in her belly.

Michael watched her until she was out of sight. Then he knelt beside the fire and put his face in his hands. He stayed that way for a minute, then picked up the skillet and turned the fish again.

Temple listened to her car droning away into the dark. Fine, he thought. Fine, fine, fine.

When she got home, Jo felt lousy. She wished she had kept her temper with him, especially after reading that book and making a solemn vow to treat him gently. She wanted to go back to him. But he had let her go without a word.

She rang Ralph's home number, found the line engaged. She avoided Grandpa John and her father, grabbed a sandwich and ran upstairs. She spent the evening watching television. Not watching it at all.

40

Overnight, the warm sticky spell of weather ended. It grew colder, and thunder vibrated far off, like the sound of jets over the battle area. Towards dawn, a shower of rain fell. Michael woke once to hear the heavy drops splattering in the trees. Half-drowned in a dream, he turned over and went back to sleep, semi-consciously wishing Jo were there to keep him warm.

In her bed, Jo sat up and realised her television was still on. She switched it off and settled back with a groan.

At the Middlecott Arms, Temple was already awake, writing on the loose pages of a cheap notebook. Beside him in an open case was his gun, the Lee Enfield. In a few minutes, he would clean it ready for the day.

The rain ceased. A light mist rose as the sun came up. The woods were ghostly.

And in the well, the body surfaced slowly. It parted the water, disturbing the scum of algae, until the face was nearly exposed. The eyes were open. They seemed to watch the daylight growing in the circle of the well.

Michael got up at eight o'clock. He dressed blearily, rolling his head and trying to clear his thoughts. He was cold, and wanted exercise to gain some heat. He stooped and took a handful of slugs out of the box in the cupboard. He cleaned the rifle, using the fine oil for the metal and linseed for the stock, and trudged downstairs. He locked the door and went out to the meadow to see what was available.

The trouble was that hunting made him uncomfortable now that Pug was gone. He had never been sentimental about the dog, but the whole thing of going out to shoot had been fun when Pug was running ahead of him. Now, the meadow was haunted. He walked about, missed a couple of rabbits and went on towards the forest. The air was crisp and electric, every sound magnified. The blaring fart of a tractor starting up three miles away sounded as if it were just over a rise. He listened for the movement of birds in the branches, waiting to pick them off, then shot quickly, efficiently, and brought down a pigeon. He ducked into the forest and walked south for five minutes until he came to a fire watchtower. He slipped the gun over his shoulder and climbed up the wide-spaced rungs, then stood on the platform, gazing over the treetops in the direction of Jo's home. He could see nothing of the Hall, but to the east he recognised a stand of firs on the horizon, black against a grey-blue sky. He looked for more landmarks, perhaps the tower of Stanton church in the battle area, but it was too far away and hidden. He turned again and plugged a squirrel in a tree nearby, watched it fall. That was enough for the day. He went down, dropped carefully into the long grass, and cut off for Oak Farm again. He did not go into the forest any more. He kept to the path and watched the vapour trails of jets high in the sky. His breath misted the air slightly, and he thought about a time when he would have to go. The land

197

was not his, and he could not hang around for ever. He would discuss it with Ralph later.

He reached the house, unlocked the door and put his catches in the side room. Warm now, he lit the fire and made coffee, ate the last of a loaf of bread with jam smeared over it. After washing up, he decided to go to the river. He took his gun along, locked the house up and headed off over the meadow.

It was 10:02.

Temple waited until he was out of sight, then picked up a bulging carrier bag and hurried across to the well. He looked down, saw that it was good, and went on to unlock the front door. He was in the house for three minutes, arranging things. When he left, the bag was empty and his pockets were heavy. He set off after Sayers, moving at a gentle trot to catch up.

Jo had breakfast and went back to bed. She lay under a single sheet, alternately staring out of the window and reading the newspaper. Her mind was on neither, because she was thinking about Michael, and how they always ended up arguing. One minute she wished she had not left him last night, the next she damned his lack of decisiveness. Then, she would think of what he had gone through, and she would feel angry with herself for leaving him. How long, after all, could it take to get over so much hurt? How long did she take to recover from her mother's death? Then she thought that you had to hit back eventually, or else get trodden into the ground, and her insides were churning all over again. She glanced at the clock, wondering where he was, and promised herself that this time he would have to come to her.

10:38.

The grass snagged Michael's feet as he went down the river bank. Away in the distance smoke was rising from the fields; farmers were burning stubble. He made sure he was alone, then laid the gun down, took off his clothes and sat down on the bank. He pushed off and sank in up to the waist, walked slowly to the middle, weed and mud oozing under his feet. He fell forward easily against the current, breaststroked upriver for a dozen

198

yards, turned on his back and drifted down again. Brown leaves floated with him. He clutched at them as they passed, feeling the sodden tissues go to pulp between his fingers.

Temple went to a mound of branches and ferns in the forest. He pulled the camouflage aside and reached in. Flies swarmed up and the smell was overpowering. He picked up the heavy bundle and carried it to the riverside, holding his face away from it.

He swam for ten minutes, then let himself glide a good distance, until he was almost into the trees. He kept thinking: What if I keep going? But it was getting cold. He put his feet on the bottom and wiped the streaming hair out of his face.

Right up past the spot where his clothes lay, he noticed something big in the water. It came gently round the bend, spinning slowly in the current.

Weed, he thought, or a log. Or somebody's bag of rubbish. People chucked all kinds of junk in the river. He splashed forward again, starting a steady crawl that would take him back to his clothes. He swam thirty yards or so, then paused for breath. The patch of weed or whatever was out of his sight now, light on the smooth water helping to conceal it. He saw it as he dived, and thought he would surface a little in front of it. He went under, feet kicking strongly off the riverbed, hands outstretched. Water rushed past his ears; he swam in darkness, eyes closed, holding his breath. It's good, he thought . . .

Until his fingers touched the object. It had been closer than he thought. His fingers brushed it, and it should have slid away from his touch, or swallowed his hands if it were weed. It didn't. It was heavy, bulky under the water. It bobbed against his hands, rolled over them lazily.

He could not read the sensations for a second. It was smooth and cold, slick. Then he felt patches of hair. He began to open his eyes, to kick back in revulsion, scrabbling at the thing to keep it off. Pieces of it shredded under his fingernails. He opened his eyes and saw a blur under the water, found the riverbed and pushed up to get his head out.

Then he could see it.

And although it was several days dead, although the warm

199

weather had swelled it up and let purplish skin show through the fur, although the head had been severed from the body and was gone, he knew.

Knew it was Pug.

Temple saw it happen, heard Sayers's cry. It was a strange sound, like an animal. He checked the time – 10:58 – and watched Sayers slip back into the water; watched him come up, vomiting violently. He waited, saw the dog's body bump against the river bank and drift again.

He stayed until Sayers's fit of sickness passed, until the boy looked up in fury to see who had done it. Then he backed off quickly, knowing what would happen next.

He tried to stand, but his legs were shaky and he fell. The sour trail of vomit washed away from his chest and chin like scum. He spat out what remained in his mouth, tried to hawk up the rest, and began to retch again.

He struck out for the bank, knowing someone was out there in the trees. He reached the shallows and clambered out, using clumps of grass for handholds. He was too angry for a moment to be scared. He ran up the bank to his clothes. The gun was still there. He snatched it up and fumbled for ammunition. Eyes widened suddenly. His fingers dug into all the pockets of his jacket. There should have been a handful of slugs. He had put them there this morning.

They were not there any more.

He spun round as if he expected someone to be behind him, about to crush his skull in with a brick. No one was there. He put on his clothes and ran towards the trees. The forest was silent, but he stopped for a moment and saw the footprints in the needle-covered floor. He saw where the body had been heaved off the bank into the water. He tracked back and found the pile of branches where it had been hidden. Flies and maggots flocked to the dried blood on the ground.

'Why?' he said. 'Why?'

Then he was off and running again, making for the house. He wanted ammunition for the gun, he wanted to shut himself in the house and sit there, safe.

He ran towards Oak Farm.

Jo threw the paper aside and got out of bed. She knew she was wasting the morning, letting herself get bogged down by indecision. She trotted along the hall in her dressing gown and used the telephone in Grandpa John's room. She rang Ralph's home number and got Ralph's mother.

'Oh, he's not come back, dear,' Mrs Wodehouse said.

'Really? He can't have arrived till quite late.'

'Presumably, he's there now. Either that, or lost in the forest.'

'I suppose so,' she said.

She had a bath and dressed. No wonder Michael had not come to her. If Ralph was there, they had probably spent the night boozing: likely as not they were still snoring in their sleeping bags now.

Well, she thought, that's just fine. I'm going to buy myself a dress, an expensive one. Bugger both of them.

It was 11:23 when Michael came through the gate and across the meadow. He was limping, but he hardly noticed the pain any more. He had not paused since leaving the river, and the strain was telling on his injuries, but as if in compensation, the rest of his system was harder and stronger than it had been. Besides which, he was running on adrenalin.

He plunged through the trees. Birds scattered from his path. In a moment, he was through and he pounded up to the house. He reached for his key, realised that the door was open.

I locked it, he thought. I'm sure I locked it.

He slipped on the tile floor of the porch, cracked his head against the door jamb. It slowed him a little. He climbed the stairs carefully, afraid of falling through, passed the beer stain on the landing, went into his room and knelt down at the cupboard to get some more ammunition.

He should have noticed the smell. It was the same smell that clotted the air where Pug's body had been. But he was moving too fast to notice. He yanked the cupboard door open and stuck his hand under the spare clothes for the box.

201

He touched the putrid thing under the clothes. His face changed, although he did not let the thing go. He reached in with the other hand and drew the clothes away, knowing what he would find.

A fly buzzed up and smacked in his face, then careered away towards the window.

He stared at Pug's head, lying there on his clothes. He saw his forefinger poking into the socket where one eye had been eaten away. He clenched his teeth, muttering: 'Christ,' as if he would be sick again. And he tried, heaving his empty belly almost inside out. Nothing came but spittle.

'Christ.' He dropped the head, searched to the back of the cupboard, found no slugs. His eyes were streaming tears but he hardly knew it. He sagged down and rested his forehead against the wall, fingers frantic in the cupboard. Finally, they discovered a piece of paper. He looked down and saw, written in biro on a notebook page:

LOOK IN THE WELL.

He got up, screwing the paper into a ball. He fell down three of the stairs, caught himself on the banister and reached the door. Swung it open, ran around the house, drooling and gibbering like an old man. Collided with the well before he saw it, and ripped the last rotten planks off to see down the dark tunnel.

Ralph looked up at him.

The cry came out of his chest: horror, disbelief, fear. He lurched back, five drunken steps into the centre of the garden. His hand went to his mouth.

Temple steadied his aim and squeezed off the first shot.

41

'Grandpa, have you got the keys to the Rover?'

'Possibly,' he said, 'possibly. Why?'

'Well, believe it or not, I'd like to drive it around, and you can't get the engine to work without the—'

'Don't annoy your granddad,' he said, scowling at her. He rose from his chair, put down his newspaper and took the keys from his back pocket. 'Where're you off to, may I ask?'

She took the keys, shrugged. 'I was going into town, but I don't know now.'

'If it's only into town, use your own car.'

'I said I don't know now.' She crossed to the mirror over the mantel and looked at her hair. 'God, rat's tails.'

'Something bothering you again, my dear?'

'No,' she said. ' . . . Yes, of course there is. And you know what.'

'That young friend of yours again.' He nodded. 'What is it now?'

'We had another row last night. We're always rowing.'

'Perhaps it's not worth the trouble.'

She looked as if the suggestion had not occurred to her. 'It is . . . I think it is.'

'In that case, why not pop over and put yourself out of your misery?' He stared disconsolately at the charred bowl of his pipe. 'I don't know why I'm encouraging you.'

She turned away from him to the mirror again. 'What d'you think of him, really?'

'Shell-shocked,' he said. The phrase surprised her. 'Go over and see if he's all right. You won't stop fidgeting until you have.'

The carriage clock on the mantel chimed the half-hour. She jingled the keys indecisively, tossed them in the air and caught them. 'I'll go and see him. Ralph's probably there too.'

'Invite 'em over for lunch then. Your friend'll be all right with us, won't he?'

'I'll see,' she said, kissing him on the cheek.

She went outside and climbed into the Range Rover. She noticed the weather was uncertain, so she went back inside to pick up her kagoul. Then, waving at Grandpa John, whose concerned face was at the window, she turned the ignition and started up.

Michael heard the shot in the same moment that it hit him. It felt like someone had clubbed his right leg with a cricket bat. He started to look down to see who was doing it, but his leg jerked back suddenly and his balance was gone. He spun round, arms raised, and sprawled on the ground. His face smacked the coarse

203

grass and he smelt the green smell of it mixed with the coppery sensation of impact.

Then the pain started, and instinct said he had to get out of the way.

Temple stood up now from his place in the bushes and watched Michael begin to crawl. He moved fast for someone in shock like that, pushing himself along with the good leg while the injured one left spots of blood on the grass.

He raised the gun again, but let Michael get round to the porch and slam the door. He was not worried about that. It was his situation now, and there were a couple more formalities to be dealt with.

Michael pulled himself up the stairs. Every movement added to the initial deadweight of pain in his leg. His heart rate was near double the normal, his breathing was ragged. He knew what it was about now: not in his head, not intellectually – his body was telling him. As he gained the landing, he rolled over on his back and struggled to a sitting position. One look was enough to confirm it: the blood was all down his leg, and the fire was beginning to eat its way in.

The bastard had got him in the same leg, the same fucking leg. Months of work to get it back in shape, make it good, and now someone had plugged him again. He was lucky in one way though: the bone was undamaged. Flesh hung through the wound like mince bursting out of a plastic bag, but it was not broken.

He heard breath coming out between his teeth as a sob. He closed his eyes, wanting to clasp the leg in both hands to stop it hurting.

'Mr Sayers?' the voice called.

He flinched against the landing wall.

'Mr Sayers,' the polite voice said. 'Come into your room, please.'

Michael could see the room. The sleeping bag and the chess book and the board laid out with a problem from Szabo-Hort's game of 1973. It looked safe, but he did not move.

'I'm going to throw something in,' Temple said. 'You

understand?"

He opened his mouth, wondering if it was going to be a bomb this time as well.

A small object entered through the side window. It bounced off the wall and struck the floor a couple of feet away. He knew immediately that it was not a bomb. When he dragged himself over to it, he saw that it was a red Silvine exercise book, the pages held together with a rubber band. The note in the cupboard had been torn from it.

'Read it, Mr Sayers,' Temple said.

He eased the rubber band off.

Temple sat down on the edge of the well and waited. It was 11:42, and he was on schedule.

On the first page of the notebook was the heading:

JUDGEMENT

Then it said:

> In January of this year, you identified Daniel William Parker to the police as one of the 'Waterloo Bombers'.
> On August the seventeenth this year, Daniel Parker died in a prison hospital.
> You are responsible for his death.

Michael gazed at the words. 'What does it mean?' he whispered. Then louder, to the man outside: 'What does it mean?'

Temple considered for a moment. He disliked talking to his targets, and he had already gone a long way with this one. He said: 'You murdered Danny Parker. You've been found guilty. You understand?'

Michael moved closer to the window. He slumped against the wall. He wanted to say No, but he was trembling too much to speak.

'You understand?' Temple said. 'You're guilty of murder. I'm your executioner.'

* * *

Jo left the Range Rover in the meadow and walked along the path to the house. She had heard the shot as she drew up. She thought Michael and Ralph must be target shooting.

With autumn advancing, the trees did not conceal everything. When she was still some distance away, she saw a figure through the leaves. Probably Ralph. She heard talking, a raised voice, and as she closed in, she realised it was not Michael or Ralph.

She slowed, still approaching, but suspicious.

The voice came clearer. She picked up some words:

'. . . Never done this before . . . unusual for me . . . explaining . . .'

She saw him almost in profile, recognised his face – the man from the pub in Minton. She saw the rifle he was holding, and she remembered the break-ins at the house, Pug disappearing, the dead birds. She crouched.

'You have to know, you see?' the man was saying. 'It's part of my orders. To show you what crime you're being punished for.'

Michael's voice suddenly came from the house. 'What about my girlfriend? What about my sister? What about all the people you helped to kill?'

'I don't know about any of that,' Temple said. 'I'm not into the rights and wrongs of the situation. It's not religion or politics with me, just the job I do. I'm not concerned with you personally . . . It's ten to twelve.' He raised the rifle and sighted it on the window. 'Will you come down, or shall I come in to you?'

Jo got away quickly. She dodged through the trees and ran to the Range Rover. She had to get help. But the man was talking as if Michael would be dead in ten minutes. There was no time; she had to do it. She bit her lip, trying to think. Then she looked at the Rover and at the path through the woods, and she thanked Grandpa John for having the keys to the thing. It was not a quiet vehicle, but it was powerful and it was heavy. She got in, forgetting to fasten her seatbelt, and started the engine. She reversed until she had a good thirty-yard run-up to the path.

The time on the dashboard clock was 11:55.

She stamped on the accelerator.

'I'm coming in soon,' Temple said. 'Not long now.'

Michael shook his head. The nausea passed, leaving him

hollow inside. He reached for the Lynx knife in his pocket, but it was gone too. All he had left was that bloody dog chain stuck down in the jacket lining. The man had a rifle, and he could hardly think straight. The war was one-sided; he was on the losing side.

Temple was still talking. 'I hope your leg doesn't hurt too much. I wanted to incapacitate you, but I missed the bone, didn't I? Sorry about that . . . '

He stopped, heard an engine start up with a roar. At first he thought it was a tractor somewhere. Then he heard the sound of branches snapping and the noise getting louder. He rose, confused, lifted his rifle.

The Range Rover exploded from the trees, its bonnet scattered with loose branches and twigs. He vaguely saw the girl's face behind the windscreen, but could do nothing; the vehicle was bearing down on him too fast.

He dived to one side, and the Range Rover ploughed through the well like a tank. The old masonry gave way, stones sprayed across the grass, one shard taking a flap of skin and hair the size of a tennis ball off Temple's head. The front wheel passed over his right leg just above the ankle. He screamed and lost his grip on the rifle. It clattered against the wall.

Jo saw his body under the Rover. She jammed into reverse and tried to back up for another run. The remains of the well caught at the chassis for a second, losing her time. Temple was beginning to scramble up. He was after his rifle. She spun the wheel and put a few yards between her and him. If she could get him by the wall, she could squash him flat.

On all fours, Temple scuttled across the grass and picked up the rifle. He slapped it into his hands and began to rise on one knee, swivelling to take a shot at the car. Turning, he saw it was already upon him. He dropped the gun, threw himself forward, and the vehicle rammed into the wall.

Jo's head hit the steering wheel so hard that she blacked out. Tiles fell from the roof of the house and smashed on the bonnet. The car's radiator began to hiss steam.

Temple got up. His leg hurt like hell. Probably not fractured, but it would bruise badly. He touched the bleeding mess on the back of his skull and began to lose control. The girl was dead for

207

sure. The rifle lay in pieces under the Range Rover, but he had his .38 Smith & Wesson, and he had his hands.

He approached the car.

Michael thought the house would come down when the Range Rover hit. He grasped the windowsill and pulled himself up to a standing position. He saw Jo's head slumped against the steering wheel, her face hidden. He thought maybe she was dead until he saw her breathing.

Temple was on the ground below him. He was getting up, he was going to hurt her.

Jo and Laura and Jilly and Ralph. And him.

He lifted the bad leg over the sill, then the good one. He levered himself into a sitting position. Temple was moving towards the passenger door, stooping slightly.

This is going to hurt, Michael thought. Like sacrificing a knight to save the queen.

He launched himself into the air.

Temple should have remembered about Michael. It was the first rule: keep the eyes in the back of your head working all the time. But he had never been badly hurt during a job before, and had not been angry for years. He forgot for the amount of time it took, and remembered only when he felt the rush of air behind him.

Michael struck him like a coal sack, both arms smashing down on his shoulders. He went down, and his head struck the side of the car, so that for a minute he could not see.

Michael heaved himself up. He was not thinking now of finishing Temple. Ordinary people do not know these things. He got on his feet, biting back the pain, and began to run. He wanted to get Temple away from Jo. Running was the only way he knew. His leg was stiffening fast, but he was moving.

Temple clenched his fists, stopped himself from fading out. He saw Michael disappear into the trees. Everything was going wrong all of a sudden, like a nightmare. At the very least, he had to bring the boy down before anyone else got involved. It was spreading too far.

He took the pistol out of its shoulder holster, flicked off the safety catch, and, almost as crippled as his target, set off in pursuit.

42

The running was not so hard once he was going. Of course, his leg hurt and he limped badly, but he had been limping for so long now that it was hardly worse than usual. He cut away from the house to the south-east, then turned east and kept running, trying to think where he could find help. Middlecott was across open fields, and if Temple had another gun, he would pot him like a rabbit. Jo's house was several miles off, and he didn't know how much distance he could go. The only thing was to head for the Minton road. There would be traffic there, and Temple would not try anything in public.

He ran quite fast considering how bad he felt. The wonderful thing about the forest was all the cover it provided. He needed to be only thirty or forty feet ahead of Temple to be out of his sight. He did not know yet how close the killer was, since he could hear nothing but his own breathing, the thud of his heart, and the heavy drum of his footsteps. He thought: If I can run far enough, I can lose him.

Temple was familiar with the forest. He had studied maps, reconnoitred the countryside for miles in every direction. He knew there were no houses, no major roads. The only danger was coming across some Forestry Commission workers, but he figured he could plug the boy before that. He had to finish the job properly, in any case: his reputation had taken something of a dive after the business with Danny and Barlow. If he messed up this job, he would be very cold. Very cold. Not that he foresaw failure. He knew the boy's limitations: still scampering for his life, running out of energy soon. He had taken several violent shocks this morning. It would not be much longer.

If only he could get a decent shot.

* * *

Two men running in the dark shade of the forest, covering ground slowly. Temple with his gun out, but intending to fire only when the aim was sure. Now and then he saw a flash of Michael's back between the trunks and the undergrowth, but it was not enough.

They both fell occasionally. The thorny blackberry vines were the worst. Michael went down as if felled by a trap, and the thorns ripped at his legs. Temple sprawled in a patch of nettles, sprang up cursing.

Michael found the road and paused for a second, fighting for breath. There were no signs of traffic. He jogged along the road towards Thaxton for half a minute, praying for someone to appear. Then Temple came out of the trees a hundred yards away and loosed off a shot at him. Michael lunged into cover on the other side. His lungs burned and blood ran warmly down his leg. He wished he could stop for a second to tie it up.

He heard Temple break in somewhere to his left, smashing branches out of the way as he came. Michael picked up speed and turned north. He remembered that the battle area was ahead. If he could get there, maybe there would be soldiers. Someone, at any rate, had to notice when guns started going off.

But how far was it?

He stumbled on with Temple close behind now. Once, they crossed a space where the trees had been felled. Temple tried to take a shot, but he was shaking so badly that it never stood a chance. With a .38, you have to be close. He fired anyway, and wood splintered above Michael's head.

The hazy sun was behind cloud now. Everything was flat and grey like a photograph. They frightened a deer by the wire and Michael saw it bounding away into the battle area. He went over the fence and headed for the edge of the forest.

Temple did not know what it meant at first. Not private land. He recalled the maps then, and knew this was the edge of the battle area. He slipped over and felt the increasing stiffness in his leg. He knew he could not do much more, and he was aware that this was unknown terrain; modern maps were vague about it.

Michael pushed on. He was wheezing like a chronic bronchitic but still moving, though his rhythm was going; he thought that when he stopped next time, it could be for good. He burst out of the forest, saw the deer springing across the flat scrubland. Ahead and to the right was the row of Scots pines that marked an old field boundary. One hundred yards, he said to himself, then another bunch of plane trees beyond that, then the village. Maybe they're repairing that fence. Maybe they're on exercises.

Please let someone be there.

He had been running all the time, had covered half the distance to the pines. Any minute now, Temple would come out of the trees too. Any minute. Any minute. He kept at it, thinking about the gun, working on fear and pain.

He was almost at the trees when the shot came. He heard it, sounding small and childish in the great expanse of open country. It was like a pop-gun going off. He thought: Shit, missed me.

It smacked him hard in the left shoulder and spun him off his feet.

Face in the dirt, he raised up and saw through one eye that Temple was coming. He thought: I'll wait until he's up close then throw a handful of dirt in his face, just like the movies.

It was a stupid idea. It only ever worked in the movies.

Come on, you reached the trees. You can do the rest easy.

He pushed himself up using the good arm. His shoulder felt numb, but for some reason he supposed it wasn't so bad. He saw Temple skidding to a halt, taking up the stance for another shot. He feinted left, then swung right and plunged behind the trees. There was no point hiding there, so he staggered off across the next field. Another hundred yards to the village, zig-zagging all the way. He kept his eyes on the glittering tower of the church, thinking: Where the fuck's the army when you need them? and beginning to form the idea of barricading himself in the church. The thick old doors were locked, windows boarded up. If he could block the vestry window, he would be safe until someone arrived to investigate.

Temple did not try to shoot again. He was wasting ammunition, and every time he fired, there was more chance they would be discovered. Sayers was going for the village, and once they were in an enclosed space, the boy would not last sixty seconds.

Michael found himself on the black strip of road that led into the village, what was once the high road to Minton. He passed a fifty-year-old sign that spelled out STANTON in letters of rust. To right and left, smothered in the long grass, were the jagged remains of shelled houses. Every time his feet struck tarmac, pain ripped through his shoulder and leg. The ruins of a garden wall

211

gave him some cover, and he slowed a little. He glanced back: Temple was reaching the road.

He passed a row of rebuilt cottages. Doors were locked, windows shuttered; no sanctuary there, but there was the village hall, where people once held bazaars and dances. He felt his strength going fast.

If I can reach the church, he thought, labouring past the overgrown village green. He broke away into a narrow lane between two ruined cottages, hoping to confuse Temple enough to give him some time. Jumped through the garden of one, past an old well, and emerged behind the church. He scrabbled under the still-gaping fence and climbed through the vestry window. It hurt very much, particularly when he fell heavily on the stone floor, but his energy was gone and he lay without moving, crying for breath. His cheek was on the cold floor. He knew he should block the window, but he could not move yet.

Temple collapsed against a wall and drew air into his lungs. Red dots flashed in front of his eyes. The gun hung limp in his hand. He reached down and touched his leg. It was swelling up, going useless. The wound on his head had crusted up. He was getting dizzier all the while.

He looked at the grass and saw spots of blood on it. He thought it must be his, then realised that it stretched ahead of him.

Despite everything, he still felt calm. He had not lost the boy. It was just a matter of resting a minute before going on. He rested, got his head clear, and followed the trail.

Jo fumbled the door catch, shouldered the door open and fell out of the Range Rover. Her head and neck felt as if they had been stepped on, and bruises were rising on her cheek and forehead, but she was alive and able to wonder what had happened.

She saw the stranger's gun broken in pieces under the front wheel, the evidence of a scuffle in the grass. But there was no sign of either man. Groaning with the pain, she got up and ran into the house, found nothing more than some smeared patches of blood.

Think, think, you idiot. She tried to push the confusion out of her mind. It was like a cloud behind her eyes. She went down the stairs, and it came to her as she saw the trail of blood leading into the trees: if she had killed the stranger, Michael would have been there when she woke; if the stranger had killed Michael, she would never have woken at all. They were out in the forest somewhere, and there was no way she could follow their trail fast enough to be any use.

She got back in the Range Rover, tried to start the engine. It would not turn over, and she beat furiously at the steering wheel as a heavy smell of petrol filled the car. She had to get home, find help for Michael.

She gritted her teeth against the raging ache in her head and started running. Home was three miles away, but at least she knew where it was.

Michael probed his shoulder wound awkwardly. It drained slowly, but it was not serious; his shoulder was still in one piece and the arm moved a little. He rose and went out to the chancel and the nave, searching for something to block the window. Since the day was dull, the interior of the church was much darker. He tripped over a step and fell in the chancel.

He was out of luck: the pews were fixed, nothing else was big enough to reach the window, except for the altar table, which was so heavy that he could not budge it.

Temple wormed under the fence and saw the broken window. He smiled.

Michael heard the fence jangle. He raised his head, looking at the sanctuary that was about to become a grave. He thought: He'll kill me, and that'll be all. After all this. Jilly and Laura and Ralph. Then back to the house to finish Jo. He'll get the full set. After all this running. Christ.

He listened to Temple climbing through the window, struggling to get his body through the frame. He limped past the choir, pulling at the carved heads on the seats, up to the pulpit, dragging at the rail. None of it was rotten enough to come away. He dug back in his pockets and touched the choke chain and lead inside the lining. He ripped through the pocket and yanked it out. But what good was it? Was he going to kill a man who carried a gun with Pug's choke chain?

Temple dropped to the floor of the vestry.

You have maybe thirty seconds to go, Michael thought. Or to do something.

He saw the crumbling stone of the south wall, the masonry falling away from the plaque commemorating Nicholas Melville Gapp.

Not me, he thought, digging his fingers into the clammy plaster. Not me.

The vestry door creaked gently open. Temple was coming.

The wall disintegrated under his fingers. He gouged out a piece of flint bigger than his fist. It came away suddenly, filling his hand with weight. Now he had the stone and the chain and the beginning of an idea, remembering the deep marks the chain had made in a fence post.

Okay, then.

The gun appeared first. He saw it as he crouched in beside the pulpit, struggling to silence his breathing. Temple's face came next. It was sweaty and exhausted. The leg must be hurting badly by now, and the head wound would not help.

Michael waited. His forehead throbbed with blood. He smelt a faint odour of smoke. He thought of Ralph trying to get him back on the track to normality, of Jo and her crusade to help him. He thought about Don and Audrey, who worried for him when they should have been thinking of themselves. And about Laura and Jilly, who were dead.

That and the stone and the length of chain were plenty to work with.

Temple moved silently from the vestry to the altar. He gazed into the long darkness and did not speak. There were several places the boy could hide: between the pews or the narrow choir stalls, up in the pulpit perhaps.

He walked over the memorial stones of dignitaries long dead, leaning to left and right to check the choir stalls. He reached the pulpit and laid his hand on the rail.

Where are you hiding, you bastard?

The chain flashed up from behind the pulpit. He saw the ring flicker cleanly in its swing. He got his gun up, but there was nothing to aim at. The chain slashed across his face, whipping round his head and biting into the flesh below his left ear. Carrying through the action begun, he squeezed the trigger of the pistol: It sounded like a bomb going off. He stumbled back, hauling at the tangled chain.

Michael rose up in front of him, all shadow and movement in the gloom. He saw the boy's eyes and knew he had made another mistake. Something fundamental in their relationship had changed; it was not so simple as hunter and quarry any more.

All that, he knew in part of a second.

Then the blow fell on the side of his head and everything went out of him suddenly like the power turning off. He felt himself go down, the heavy crunch of his knees on the step. He tried to get up again, struggling to send signals to his arms and hands. The effort failed. Another blow cracked his skull; he heard the sound of it, and wondered dully what the boy was hitting him with. It was so hard, so heavy. His hands fluttered up and the gun dropped to the ground. He toppled sideways.

Michael hit him again. Blood sprayed in his face. He moved as Temple descended, keeping with him, using the jagged stone on the man's head and face. It got a rhythm, a sweet fresh simplicity to it. He sank down astride the man to keep doing it, muttering: 'Fucker, fucker,' at each blow.

It took a long time.

And only when the body stopped twitching, stopped trying to breathe, and there was blood over everything, did he realise that Temple was dead. Still clutching the stone, he pushed himself away and rolled onto his back in the aisle. He lay there. The air was heavy and sick. He became aware again of his shoulder wound, the blood gradually leaking out of him. He closed his eyes and thought about Temple. He did not look, because there was no face left to speak of, but he thought about having killed the man, and he finally began to know what they had been talking about when they said it was good to stop running, to fight back. The stone rested cold and slick in his hand, his muscles still remembering the rhythm while his mind tried to forget it. He did not feel good for having the knowledge, but he knew it now, and would not ever be able to un-know it as sirens began to blare out of the still afternoon.

A bird got into the building through some upper window. He watched it screeching from end to end in the dark.

He lay on the floor, wondering if Jo was all right, wondering if they would find him in time.

215